firefly

COUP DE GRÂCE

firefly

Big Damn Hero by James Lovegrove (original concept by Nancy Holder)
The Magnificent Nine by James Lovegrove
The Ghost Machine by James Lovegrove
Generations by Tim Lebbon
Life Signs by James Lovegrove
Carnival by Una McCormack
What Makes Us Mighty by M. K. England
Aim to Misbehave by Rosiee Thor

firefly

COUP DE GRÂCE

BY UNA McCORMACK

TITAN BOOKS

Firefly: Coup de Grâce
Paperback edition ISBN: 9781789098389
E-book edition ISBN: 9781789098426

Published by Titan Books
A division of Titan Publishing Group Ltd
144 Southwark Street, London SE1 0UP
www.titanbooks.com

This Titan edition: September 2024

10 9 8 7 6 5 4 3 2 1

This is a work of fiction. All of the characters, organizations, and events portrayed in this novel are either products of the author's imagination or are used fictitiously. Any resemblance to actual persons, living or dead (except for satirical purposes), is entirely coincidental.

A CIP catalogue record for this title is available from the British Library.

Printed and bound by CPI (UK) Ltd, Croydon, CR0 4YY

For Amy H. Sturgis

1

From the journal of Anne Imelda Roberts

You may call it unlikely that a girl of my age and size might find herself out in wild country chasing her daddy's killer with a cut-price ragtag band of rebels, and if you won't take my word there's always the sheriff's report, should you care to read that kind of thing. My name is Anne Imelda Roberts—Annie to those who care to call me 'friend'—and I was eighteen years old when the events I describe here occurred. Eighteen years old, suddenly all on my own, unsure who I could count upon. Turns out friends can be found in unexpected places, and don't always look the way you might expect. If there's a lesson to this story, then perhaps that's what I learned.

But that is starting at the end, and perhaps I should start at the beginning. Our family was an old one on Abel. Daddy's granddaddy came here when the world was opening up, and made a tidy fortune, and none of us have squandered it, though my daddy's pockets were deep when he saw folks in need. I have been left more than comfortable, and there are still many on Abel right now who cannot say that.

My daddy, Isaac Roberts, was Abel-born and Abel-bred, which counts. I don't hold those few years away at the Core against him, and nor should you. On the contrary, the Core was where he met Mamma, Alicia, and if he hadn't met Mamma, they wouldn't have had me. I call that a blessing. Other folks have opinions of their own. There are some in Yell City right now who might say that my being born was a good thing, and others might say something to the contrary, but those are the kind of folks always looking to blame another for their bad fortune. I'll say this now, and let me be plain: none of what happened over those few days was my fault, and if people expected me to behave any differently, they didn't know my mamma and they certainly didn't know my daddy.

Daddy was a good man, by which I mean he trusted people who were not worthy of his trust. I will never make that mistake, and I would say that the events of those few days have proven to me the wisdom of this. Mamma, when she was alive, used to say that Daddy was a fool to everyone and himself most of all. She was in no way a mean woman—quite the contrary, in fact, everyone always said she was like summer in the mountains—but I suspect that even she must surely have found Daddy a trial at times. Always taking on cases that wouldn't bring in a penny, because of some sob story or other. A big heart, people said to me after he died, as if that's enough to pay one's way in the world, enough to protect you from those whose hearts have shriveled away to nothing.

Maybe I should start with the last few days of my daddy's life, even if that comes painful to me. And to tell you about those days, I must make clear straight away that Daddy was, above all, a man of the law. He loved the law, by which I mean laws made by men and women, and seeing the right thing done was the centerpiece of his life. Well, the truth of this 'verse is that there ain't no law but God's law, and that truth isn't always clear. In the end, what is clear is my daddy was not wise to put his trust in the law of mortals. In the end, we all stand before Our Heavenly Father, and it is by him that we are held account for all we have said and done in our days. What I will say, however, is that sometimes there's no harm in giving His law a helping hand along the way, as I believe this tale of mine once told will show.

My daddy went to the Core to do his training, and when he came home to Abel (bringing Mamma), he set up in Yell City. At first folks were not sure what to make of him—Abel-born, yes, but sent off to the Core to do his studying, and coming back with a Core-born wife—in the early days, persuading people to let him represent them was a struggle. That changed when he defended a group of folks living in one of them tenements down near the space docks who were under threat of eviction. They didn't have anything to their names, but Daddy took on the case anyway, not only did he stop their landlord from throwing them out on the street, he even got written into their lease that the building should be properly maintained, so the landlord couldn't let the place fall to ruin and say they must leave on account of safety. Daddy won—of course he won—and his victory was a big deal in Yell City: changed how a few things were done round here (although Daddy would be the first to say 'not enough'). The case changed everything for Daddy too. Word went round ordinary folk that this was a decent man who cared for those who found themselves in trouble through no fault of their own. Many's the time that a fellow and his family, in trouble with the bank or the landlord, came to my daddy, and found themselves with a few weeks' grace (and more often than not a good few credits). Daddy had a knack for finding loopholes and letting the light shine through.

So his practice was always busy—if not always profitable— and between his own fortune and the money Mamma brought with her from the Core, I daresay we did more than fine. By the time of Daddy's death, Mamma was long gone. He and I rubbed along together very nicely: him busy with his legal practice, and me doing the books, running the house, and keeping an eye on his diary. So I knew, of course, about the case that was coming up. In the three weeks before my daddy died, it seemed as though every evening, right when Daddy and I settled down for some talk or a game or two of checkers, the bell would ring, and poor Daddy—who didn't have a moment to himself all day—would haul himself up from his armchair and take himself off into his study for yet another late-night meeting. He was busier than ever in recent years, what with the drought happening and so many farms failing and folks in need of his help. And sometimes the folks that came weren't so humble. That night, it was Monseigneur de Cecille (yes, we were honored by a visit by that great man). The Monseigneur came with two or three others—rich fellas, local money—and from what I heard (I would not stoop to listening at the door, although I did happen to pass along the corridor outside the study a coupla times), it was a jovial occasion. I heard Monseigneur's deep booming laugh again and again. It was well after midnight when they left, stumbling out to their fancy hovercars, stinking of whisky, their drivers running out from our kitchen to cart them home. My daddy, looking at me hazily, said, "Oh, Annie, I ain't sure I been wise."

I can't rightly tell you whether he simply meant the liquor or something else, but I knew the case was coming, and I guess knowing what I know now I should have seen that it was going to be big. A smallholder named Jacky Colson—who had lost his farm to the bank—was trying to win his land back. Exactly the kinda case my daddy took on: small chance of success and even smaller chance of remuneration. "I won the lottery when it came to inheritance, Annie," he would say to me. "A fellow's gotta do some good with everything they've been given."

Still, even knowing what I knew, I didn't connect the case at first with what happened, not least because it was more than a month before the hearings were due to start. The day of my daddy's death, so far as I was concerned, was an ordinary day—particularly pleasant for autumn, but not so grueling as that summer had been. I decided I might as well go for a walk that afternoon. Daddy and I had a cheerful breakfast, and I sent him on his way to his office, me telling him not to give away all our money, him telling me not to get into trouble. He kissed the top of my head, and off he went, whistling.

That was my last sight of him.

After he left, I took myself to my desk, where I wrote to Mamma's sister back on Londinium, giving her the news from Abel. After Mamma died, my aunt suggested I should go and live with her, and at first Daddy was of a mind to send me, saying how much he'd learned out there, and how much I might benefit from the experience, but I was having none of that. Leave Abel? Daddy? Never. Plenty to keep me busy. Daddy's practice, for one, not to mention helping more and more around town. Many folks were in a bad way, farms failing, forcing them into the city, but there weren't enough jobs or places to live, and plenty were struggling. Lending a hand there was taking up more and more of my time: writing and asking the great and good of the city for money; helping out some charitable people that were getting clothes and other necessaries out to these people. My days were busier than ever, which speaks to the need on Abel at that time.

Mid-morning, I went for a walk around the park on the corner, which was looking sorry these days. Another hot summer had left the flowerbeds parched dry, and there hadn't been anywhere near enough rain as yet this autumn. Place still dry as a bone, and I saw a couple of tents at one end too. That worried me. Last couple of winters had been particularly hard, snow even here in our part of the county. Those folks didn't want to be outdoors and freezin' when the snows came. Things weren't right on Abel at that time, that was for sure, although I didn't know how wrong they were, nor how close to home everything would soon be. I got home to find the hall full of a dozen sacks of clothes and other essentials from the collection drive I'd organized the previous week. My afternoon would be busy with Maisie (that's the maid), sortin' through what we'd got to pass along to folks in need. I had just finished lunch when I heard the bell ring. Maisie came back from the door and said, "Miss Annie, there's two fellas from the sheriff's office here to see you."

She brought 'em in—them holdin' their hats in front of them, the younger one not quite meeting my eye. I guess I knew then what they was there to tell me. You get a feeling about that kind of thing. I thought at first there must have been an accident, but it was worse than that. Much, much worse. Daddy'd been shot—in broad daylight, on Main Street, on the very steps of his office, and these men weren't here to take me to the hospital. They were there to take me to the morgue.

Over a dozen people saw my daddy's murder, happening as it did in broad daylight on Main Street, and half-a-dozen of them witnesses could name his killer: Young Bill Fincher. Some folks— my daddy was one—would say you shouldn't speak ill of others, but in the case of the young man who murdered Daddy, I believe I'll say whatever I choose, and I say now, and this comes from first-hand experience of the fellow, that he was nothing more than a piece of junk, something you would find on the sole of your shoe and hold your nose while you wiped it away. There are words I could use to describe that boy, but I shall not lower myself to his level by saying them. Even now, I can hear Daddy resting his hand upon my good arm, and saying, "Annie, love, that ain't fair. You must think of where he came from, and you must think of his troubles. Life ain't been easy for that young man." To that I say, I too have had my share of griefs and losses, but none of them have turned me into junk.

Do you see what I mean about Daddy? Bill Fincher was the kind of fellow would come to him with a sob story to which Daddy would listen; indeed he'd saved Bill Fincher from the lock-up three or four times already, spoken for him in court, and all without earning a peck of platinum for his efforts. And this is how that man repaid him. I wouldn't say Young Bill Fincher was born bad, for that's for the Lord to judge and the Lord alone, but I feel no compunction in saying that he was born weak. That in itself doesn't mean a child cannot be saved, for with the right guidance anyone can make something good of themselves. But it's plain to all to see that there was no strong nor firm hand to guide Bill Fincher onto the right path. Quite the contrary, before he'd reached his teens he was known throughout the area as a thief and a rustler, and now he was eighteen with a murder under his belt. That boy was lost before he started.

Young Bill Fincher arrived at my daddy's office a little before noon, most likely already the worse for wear since he had, by several separate accounts, been in Malley's across the street since it opened. From what I understand (since there was no appointment with Fincher booked in Daddy's diary, and Daddy had not mentioned to me that he would be seeing him), he had come to speak to Daddy about a matter concerning his mamma's farm, which, like many such homesteads on Abel those days, was in trouble on account of the drought and those hard frosts we'd been getting. That, at least, was what he told Sadie Ryan, my daddy's secretary, although I quickly had my own suspicions about the truth of this. Poor Sadie, whom I hold in no way responsible for what happened next, saw the state of Fincher and the nasty gleam in his eye (I said he was junk), and knocked on my daddy's door.

"I tried to warn him," she told me later. "But you know your daddy—Mister Roberts, I mean. 'Send him in,' he said. 'I'm here to help.'"

So in the assassin went, by invitation, and we do not know in detail what transpired between them in the room, since the door was closed, and Daddy had thickened the glass on the door to make sure that his clients had privacy. After about ten minutes—certainly not more—the door swung open, and Fincher came stumbling out, his voice all slurred, and shouting, "It ain't good enough! It ain't nowhere near good enough! I have friends, you know! Friends in high places!" Sadie said that Daddy was calm, unruffled, saying to Fincher, "You keep a cool head, son. I know this ain't the news you wanted to hear, but we'll find a way." Fincher, stormed out of the office, Daddy following behind—and the next thing Sadie heard was a pistol being fired. Young Bill Fincher didn't hold back. Daddy must have known for a split second that he was shot, and that he weren't going to make it, but from what I understand (and folks ain't got no reason to be kind to me) he went quick and weren't in much pain. Fincher was off like a bullet. I do not know if anyone tried to apprehend him, and I suspect not. Sadie, running out onto the street, held my daddy while he died. I guess that counts as a blessing.

When those two young men from the sheriff's office came to tell me what had happened, and who had done the deed, I absented myself to visit the bathroom, where I cried and cried and cried. I loved my daddy so much, and I knew that, prickly as I could be, he loved me exactly as I was, because I was his girl, his and Mamma's. I thought how losing him was like losing her all over again, all those memories of her that he had as a young woman. It was like Bill Fincher had stolen them both.

Hate isn't good for you, but I hated that boy, and it was only the fact that we knew who the killer was that brought me any relief. I thought, at least we'll soon have that fellow behind bars, and after that I'll see him hang. If only that had been the case. Those that got in the way of justice have only themselves to blame for everything that came next. Vengeance is mine, saith the Lord, but a little earthly help jogging things along doesn't do any harm.

But Fincher weren't behind bars, not that day, nor the next, nor the one after, nor the one after that, and nor was he by the time it came for my daddy to be buried.

That was a hard day, hardest of my life so far, even counting when Mamma died, because I was small at the time of the accident that killed her, and because Daddy was there.

Now I was on my own.

I have not been much of a one for travelling, but I dare say that there is no place better in the 'verse than this good world of Abel on a clear autumn morning. This morning was glorious, showing proper respect for Daddy. I wouldn't believe that even Earth-That-Was could have put on as pretty a display of color. The trees decked out in their best, like soldiers in dress uniform or ladies in their finery. Old Man Sun himself out, tipping his hat like he does in the children's rhyme, so warm one might even call it unseasonable. I did not see any wildflowers, but we cannot ask for everything. This, then, was the day we buried my daddy—Isaac Roberts, father, husband, and lawman—a bright morning at the start of the fall. A fine day for a fine man—this is what I always tell myself. I must admit it ain't much in the way of consolation, but you have to take what you can in this 'verse. They say that Earth-That-Was turned dry as dust and bare as bone before the end. Each day and night I thank the Lord Almighty I was born on Abel.

Six white horses pulled the carriage carrying my daddy's coffin, all wearing silver harnesses, each animal plumed with two black feathers. I was in the carriage behind, with Monseigneur and Madame de Cecille. Outside our house, the road was quiet, but when we came down onto Main Street, I saw that each side of the street was lined—three deep—with people, ordinary people, from across the divides in Yell City. There had been bad blood between the city folks and the incomers, the farmer folk, in recent months, but all were united that day in wanting to pay their respects to my daddy, Isaac Roberts.

There were faces I recognized, folks whom Daddy had helped, who had next to nothing, and yet had put on their finest. Oh, but how threadbare were some of them suits of clothes, and how thin and pinched were some of their faces. Something was wrong on Abel, something was out of balance, and my daddy being murdered was the latest proof of that. Anyone with their eyes open and half a brain in their head could look down Main Street and see the signs: boarded-up buildings, paint cracking and peeling from the heat of the summer, graffiti everywhere. Folks weren't happy, and they were finding a way to have their say.

I saw too how some people were trying to paper over the cracks. Every single one of them buildings on Main Street, even the ones that had been shuttered and their businesses gone to the wall, was decked out in white flowers. I will say here and now (and I am not simply saying this because of what came after), that I was not particularly happy at the sight of such expense. Seemed a mighty great extravagance to me, but Monseigneur and Madame, whom my father called his good old friends, insisted that a man such as Daddy deserved recognition, and before I knew it, the arrangements were out of my hands and the money spent. Well, it was their money to do with as they saw fit, although I myself might have put more in the way of those poor people lining the streets. It ain't a thing to be proud of, on a world like ours, to see folks struggling. And yet still they came out, to pay respects to Daddy. I saw men take off and hold their hats before them as our cortege went by; I saw women curtsy. And I saw tears, yes, heavens above, I saw plenty of tears that day, and on the faces of hard men, who'd seen bad things done in the war and after, whom I don't think are much in the habit of weeping. I would say there weren't a man in the whole of Yell City as loved as well as my daddy, for all the good it did for him.

Madame de Cecille was right beside me that day, and her grief: good Lord! You mighta thought it was her own father she was burying! I don't know how many lacy white handkerchiefs that woman used that day, but I have never owned so many in my life. I saw tears spot the satin of her dress, and got to thinking how much *that* would cost to clean. I was in plain black; I ain't much of a one for show. When the service was done we went back out to the carriages, and Madame de Cecille took hold of my good arm, refusing to let go, all whilst we committed my poor daddy's mortal remains to the good soil of Abel. The whole time, she was murmuring, "You poor child... Your poor child..."

I know that it was kindly meant, but I was fair sick of the sight of the woman. "Madame," I said. "I'd like a moment alone now with my daddy."

Praise God, she left me in peace. I stood for a little while, thinking. I prayed of course, asking Our Heavenly Father, the last Judge and Redeemer of us all, to stand beside me as I went in search of justice. I asked him to guard me from all ills, and to smite my enemies. And I made a promise too. I said, "Daddy, the fella that did this wicked thing to you—he's walking free right now, and that ain't right. I swear to you, I swear in the sight of the Lord God Himself, who sees all and knows all and weighs the balance of our actions, that Bill Fincher will pay for this."

That might sound to you like a dangerous thing to say, but I don't make a promise lightly, and when I do, I move heaven and earth to keep my word. I wouldn't make myself a liar. You use your own judgement as to whether that promise was kept. Myself, I know I rest easy at night.

There ain't much comfort to be taken at the sight of your daddy's coffin lying there in the ground, and after a while I started to feel lonesome. I said another little prayer—it seemed the right thing to do—and I thought about life without him; my goodness but that did make me feel low. I was giving myself a good hard shake, for what was there to be done about that, when I felt a hand upon my shoulder.

"Annie."

I turned and saw the mayor. Mary McQuinn. I did not know her well. She was new to the job and had not visited the house. I knew that Daddy had met her several times in the course of his daily business, and he spoke kindly of her, but then my daddy spoke kindly of everyone.

"I'm so sorry about your father," she said. If I had a grain of salt for each time someone said that to me during that week, you'd mistake me for Lot's wife. I guess she saw a little of that in my face, as she went on, "But I think you've heard that enough already. I want to make a promise to you."

"A promise?"

"We're going to find who did this, and we're going to bring him to justice."

"Is that so?" I said, and she looked mighty surprised to hear me.

"Why yes, Annie, that is so—"

"Because it's been almost a week now, and you and I and everyone on Abel knows who did this deed, and yet still he's running around free."

She didn't answer straight away. And that was the moment that I thought, they're none of them going to help me. Not one of them has the will to do this.

"I learned a lesson long ago," I said. "That if you want a job doing, you do it yourself."

"Annie," she said. "We don't know each other well. But when I make a promise, I mean it. We'll get that fella Fincher."

"I ain't got any grounds to disbelieve you," says I. "But I ain't got grounds to believe you neither. So where does that leave me?"

"Annie," she said, her voice becoming stern. "I hope you're not getting ideas—"

"Ideas?"

"I'm not going to let this pass."

"Talk's cheap," I told her. "I want action."

"You'll see action," she said. "I know you ain't got reason to listen to my advice, but I'm going to give it anyway. Leave this alone. I said justice will be done, and it will." She looked down at the ground. "Ain't no need to go complicating matters any more than they already are."

I will say here and now that if she had simply stopped talking a mite sooner, I would most likely have been persuaded to leave well alone. But no, she had to go and add that last. Complicating matters indeed. As if I was some child, messing about in the business of her elders and betters. He was *my* daddy!

"I thank you for your advice, Madame Mayor," I said, and I think she caught the chill in my voice because it would have frozen blood, "and I'll take it under consideration."

"I hope you do," she said. "You'll find, you know, that you have friends where don't expect 'em. If you keep an open mind."

"I ain't in need of friends, Madame Mayor," I told her. "I'm in need of justice."

"I understand."

"I think," I said, "I'd like to be alone now."

"Of course." Before she went, she said, "You come to me if you need help."

She left me staring down at the grave.

The diggers were starting to fill it in now. I watched them work. That talk with the mayor had set wheels turning in mind. More and more, I was starting to think that something wasn't right here. Something out of season. After a while, I made a few decisions, and I turned to go. I was expected at the house for the wake, but I didn't head that way. Why would I want to hear everyone saying their piece, making a fuss? I didn't want to hear stories about Daddy. Daddy was dead, and he weren't coming back, and stories about him weren't going to help do that. I'll say now what I said to Mayor McQuinn, that what mattered most to me was finding Daddy's killers and seeing them punished. Justice mattered to Daddy too, of course—although I daresay he was more of a one for mercy. As God is my witness, there ain't much mercy in me.

So I didn't go home. Still in my mourning clothes, I marched back into town, down along Main Street, looking sorrier than ever now the flowers were fading, and straight into the sheriff's office to get some answers to all my questions. In fairness, Sheriff Ned Peters did not keep me waiting. That is about the best that I can say of the man, who was in the habit of treating me like a child. Folks do that sometimes with people like me. But I ain't a child and I ain't been since Mamma died.

"Miss Annie," he said, taking my good arm, "won't you sit?"

It ain't right for a man to touch a woman uninvited, but people seem to think they can take these liberties. I shrugged my shoulder, and he took the hint, moving that paw of his off of me. I sat in the chair he offered, removed my hat, and rested it upon my lap.

"Young Bill Fincher," I said.

"What about him?" said the sheriff.

"He ain't in jail."

"No, Miss Annie, he ain't."

"And I'd like to hear straight from the horse's mouth why not."

I think he could see that the only way I was leaving that room without answers was if he dragged me out by the hair, so he sighed and settled back in his chair. "It ain't simply Fincher," he said.

"What do you mean?"

"Fincher's running with Frankie Collier these days. We move on Fincher means we move on the whole gang."

"Not before time," I said. They'd been making life a misery for folks in some of the small towns, as if life wasn't hard enough at that time. "So when are you doing that?"

"We ain't," he said.

"You *ain't*? Well, sir, I think I'd like to know why—"

"Miss Annie," he said, and I know exasperation when I hear it since I hear it often enough, "you seen the state of this city these days?"

"I ain't a fool. I know there's more trouble than there used to be."

"All these folks coming in from the sticks. Vagrants—" It weren't their fault that the weather was bad. And it didn't help tarring everyone with the same brush. He musta caught my look. "Not that everyone's the same, of course."

"Too much liquor about," I said, eyeing the flask on his desk.

"That certainly don't help. But whatever the cause, it's all I can do at the moment to keep these streets quiet and safe—"

"Daddy was shot dead in broad daylight. You ain't even doing that."

Oh, the look he gave me then. But I ain't scared of men like that. They're weak, and I ain't.

"What I'm tryna tell you, miss, is that I ain't got neither the men nor the money to take on the Collier gang. If Young Bill Fincher is fool enough to come back into the city alone, then I'll make my move on him, I promise you. Until then—I can't go sending men out after Collier and his people. I got enough on my plate here."

I sat for a minute or two and thought about what he'd told me. And I said, "I'll pay."

"You'll what now?"

"I want justice," I said.

"As do we all. Your daddy was a fine man—"

"And I'm willing to pay to see it done."

"Miss Annie," he said, shaking his head, "a sheriff can't take money. That ain't right and you know that."

"I ain't talking about *you*," I said. "I'll pay for someone to find Young Bill Fincher and bring him back. You tell me the name of the man for the job, and I'll pay him to have justice done."

He gaped at me like I'd told him I wanted to buy an elephant or maybe Londinium itself.

"You must know men who could do this job."

"I guess," he said.

"Then tell me their names."

"There's… Oh, Miss Annie, you can't be serious about this—"

"Sheriff Peters," I said. "My daddy was shot in broad daylight and his killer's still strutting around scot-free. There must be consequences, so tell me their names."

After a moment, he gave in. Toldya he was weak. "Well, there's Moody Jones," he said. "He cleared up over on Jacinta after Unification. Took down Cain O'Leary; didn't get the older brother, mind you. Moody's a good man and god-fearing. You would not go wrong with him."

Why, I thought, would I want to hire someone who only got the younger brother?

"Looks like you might prefer someone else," said the sheriff. He thought for a while. "I guess you could look up Tad Rourke. Likes his drink but not on the job. Best shot in these four systems."

Neither of these fellows was exactly firing me up. One missed his man and the other didn't miss a tipple. "Anyone else?"

He sighed. "There's one other fellow. Mal Reynolds. You know, I can't rightly say whether he's fool or hero, but he don't give up 'til the job's done." He thought for a minute. "I'd say that Moody Jones is the man for you. He'll play fair by you."

I said, "Where do I find this Mal Reynolds?"

2

At the precise moment his name was being invoked, Mal Reynolds was being utterly destroyed by a teenage girl. Her brother, looking up smugly from his plate of noodles nodded over at the checkerboard. "Told you not to take her on. I haven't beaten her since she was five years old."

Mal gave Simon the sourest of looks. "And I imagine that you were Mister High-and-Mighty Inter-Core All-Collegiate Checkers Champion," he said bitterly. He watched River's right hand, which had been hovering over the board like a vengeful god getting ready to smite, went and did its smiting, collecting up three more of Mal's pieces.

"Actually," said Simon, in that picky tone that was all but inviting a smitin' in turn, "no, I wasn't—"

River, looking up from the board, gave Mal a scornful look. *Wǒ de mā*, when did this girl get so sassy? She saw off one bounty hunter, she thought she was queen of the whole gorram ship. "Simon wasn't checkers champion," said River. "Checkers is a *child's* game."

"Thank you kindly," said Mal.

"Simon was *chess* champion," she finished, with considerable pride.

Mal moved his hand toward one of his pieces. River's eyes followed the motion like a vulture waiting for a dying man to corpsify. Mal moved his hand back. River smiled. This was what he got for making an effort. For trying to be nice. A quick game of checkers, and it was turning out to be the most gorram stupid idea in a 'verse not short in general on gorram stupid ideas. Mal moved one of the pieces, quickly. River laughed. No, that weren't a laugh. River *cackled*. Sometimes this kid seemed like some kinda gorram witch. At least, thought Mal, she was on their side…

"Checkers is fine," said Jayne, coring an apple with his pocketknife. "It's chess ain't a man's game."

"River beats me at chess too," said Simon, in the mildest of voices. "You're welcome to challenge her to checkers, Jayne. In fact, you're welcome to challenge her to anything."

Mal, listening closely to this exchange, looked over at Jayne. Jayne, catching his eye, scowled back. What you gonna say back, huh, Jayne? You gonna push? You looking for another date with an airlock? 'Cause I'm ready and waiting…

"Huh." Jayne bit deep into his apple. "I ain't interested in kids' stuff."

"That's good," said Simon, turning back to his plate of food. "Because I'm not interested in either."

Mal looked approvingly at Simon. Seemed like he was getting the hang of things. Standing up for himself. Mal couldn't always be there and, besides, he wasn't always minded to help Simon. Simon Tam had caused him a whole 'verse of trouble.

River finished him off, and Mal, against both wisdom and experience, consented to another game. That didn't take long either. Soon Jayne was cackling too, and Simon was smiling, presumably enjoying the sight of someone else losing to his baby sister. The match was heading toward the inevitable, brutal endgame when Zoë walked in.

"Zoë," said Mal, turning to her in relief. "Something to report?"

Zoë, folding her arms, looked down at the board. "That little girl still beating you, sir?"

"Uh-huh," said Mal.

"And yet you keep right on coming back for more?"

"Uh-huh," said Mal.

"It ain't a pretty sight," said Jayne. "But it's gorram funny."

"Well, I ain't never been mistaken for pretty," said Mal. "Something in particular you wanted, Zoë? Something pressing, maybe, requires my immediate and undivided attention?"

"A message for you on the Cortex."

"That'll do fine," said Mal. "It ain't someone offering me money, is it?" He didn't mean that, of course. People didn't get up one morning and decide to offer him money .

"As a matter of fact, yes," said Zoë.

"*Yes?*" said Mal.

"Someone wants us for a job," said Zoë. "Asking for you by name."

"By name?" said Mal. His reputation musta gone before him. He wasn't sure whether to be pleased or troubled.

"What's the catch?" said Jayne. "There's gotta be a catch."

"Isn't asking for Mal by name the catch?" said Simon. Well, that was gratitude for you, thought Mal. He could fight all his own gorram battles in future.

"*Is* there a catch, Zoë?" said Mal.

"Not that I can see," said Zoë. "You want to listen for yourself?"

Mal followed her to the cockpit, the others tagging behind, where she played back the message. A young woman—looked about the same age as River, Mal thought—was addressing him. She was thin, with a rather strained expression that, combined with her hair scraped back from her brow, made her look uncomfortably like one of the schoolmistresses whom Mal had habitually disobeyed as a boy. "*Captain Malcolm Reynolds*," said the young woman. "*My name is Anne Imelda Roberts. I live in Yell City on the world of Abel, and I am looking for someone to bring a killer to justice.*"

"We can do that," said Jayne.

"Depends on what she's offering," said Mal.

"*I'm offering two hundred platinum.*"

"*Gŏu shĭ!*" exclaimed Simon, who didn't, as a rule, swear.

The others stared at him.

"You've been hangin' around with bad company, doc," said Zoë. "Oughta get yourself some better friends."

"Well, it's a lot, isn't it?" said Simon.

"You're not wrong there," Mal said. Cover a few outstanding debts, and there'd likely be enough spare to replace the catalyzer for the starboard compression coil. Kaylee had been fretting about that ever since the port one blew, and since Mal wasn't mighty keen to go through that whole near-death experience again, he'd been planning to give the girl what she wanted soon as the opportunity arose.

"Gotta be a catch," muttered Jayne.

"*Captain Reynolds, sir—my daddy was killed a week ago. Everyone knows who the killer is, but nobody's making a move to arrest him. Sheriff Peters here in Yell City says that in these troubled times he cannot spare the men. And since that is the case, I must find someone myself to get this job done. This is where we are on Abel now, and in the name of the Good Lord it's a sorry state of affairs.*"

Mal glanced at Zoë and Jayne, who both looked unconcerned. Track a man down and bring him to justice? No problem with a job like that. Well within their capabilities. Was there really no catch?

"*Captain Reynolds, sir, I've been told that you are both a fool and a hero—*"

Jayne guffawed; Simon laughed too. Nice to see some amity there at last, Mal supposed; a pity it came at his expense.

"*—and the truth of the matter is that I don't care either way. Because the word is you don't give up 'til the job is done. That's what I want, and I'll pay for that privilege. So I'm hopin' you'll come to Abel, to Yell City, and together we'll see justice done.*"

"There has *got* to be a catch," said Jayne.

"*I have one condition.*"

"Here it comes," said Simon.

"*I want to come along with you. I want to see the moment when you take Bill Fincher. I want to see his face when he knows his crimes have caught up with him. That's my condition, and there ain't no pay without it. I hope to hear from you soon and I pray for your safe journey here.*"

The message ended.

"Fool, eh, Mal?" said Jayne.

"The young lady also said the word 'hero'," Mal pointed out.

"I guess everyone's capable of one really bad error of judgement," said Simon.

"Are we going, sir?" said Zoë.

"For that amount? You're gorram right we are," said Mal. "You, me, Jayne—between us we can bring one man to justice."

"And don't forget Miss Roberts," said Simon. "She was very clear on that point."

"She don't look old, sir," said Zoë, doubtfully.

Mal glanced over at River. She was holding checker pieces in each hand: two white in the left hand, two black in the right, as if weighing them against each other. "Reverse," she said. "Everything is going in reverse."

Jayne shook his head at the sight. "Gorram kids… This girl, this Annie. She'll be more trouble'n she's worth, I bet."

"You're more trouble'n you're worth, Jayne," Mal shot back. "But I keep you 'round nonetheless. Anyways," he went on, "we all of us here have reason to know that youth ain't always a barrier to being able to handle yourself in a tight spot. I say we meet Miss Roberts, see what's she made of, and, if we think she's a liability, we can use some of our famous charm to persuade her to stay home."

"Famous charm?" Simon pulled a face. "Whose charm around here is famous? I mean, not counting Inara."

"Not yours, that's for sure," muttered Jayne.

"Zoë," said Mal. "Give that husband of yours a shake and tell him to get us on route to Abel lickety-split, please. And let Miss Roberts know we're a-comin'."

"On my way, sir," said Zoë, with a nod, turning to head off to the cabins.

"I ain't sure about this, Mal," said Jayne. "Jobs like this, they're not always easy. Some dumb kid'll get in the way—"

"I've made my decision," said Mal, firmly. "We meet Miss Roberts, let her make her case. Find out what she's made of. Abel's a Rim world—young folks often handy with a gun out there, grow up hunting and so on. Besides, you heard what she's offering. Money like that's too good to pass over."

"I guess," said Jayne, but he was still frowning.

Mal looked over at River. "What do you think?"

"Why you asking *her*?" muttered Jayne.

"'Cause she's part of my crew," said Mal.

River smiled at him. Mal had gotten awful fond of that smile in recent weeks. If River was smiling, he reckoned, she wasn't killing, and he didn't want her killing unless there was clear and proximate cause. "I say… best of five?" she replied, hopefully.

And Mal Reynolds, who was both fool and hero, smiled back and said, "Why the hell not?"

"Do we know anything about Abel?" said Shepherd Book, later, as the whole crew of *Serenity* assembled round the kitchen table to hear about their latest job.

"I was there once," said Mal. "During the start of the war. Drumming up recruits."

"Which side were they on?" said Simon.

"Which side were *you* on?" said Jayne.

"Um, I was at *school*—"

"Which side were *you* on, Jayne, huh?" cut in Kaylee.

"Leave it," said Mal, severely. "Way I remember it, they were independent enough for our purposes here on Abel."

"You mean they switched sides?" said Jayne.

"Captain said leave it, Jayne," said Zoë, her voice light but her hand coming to rest on the back of his chair.

"Just sayin'…" mumbled Jayne, somewhat chagrined, although not sufficiently for Mal's taste.

"Nobody was askin'," said Kaylee.

"And what *I* was askin'," said the Shepherd, with that quiet but firm voice that meant he was brookin' no more of this particular nonsense, "was whether we're liable to find ourselves walking into any trouble we'd be best avoiding."

"I recall the place as pleasant, particularly for the Rim," said Mal. "Good farms, temperate weather. Mite too much wealth in the hands of too few people, but not the worst I've seen by any stretch." Mal shrugged. "It was a nice place. Folks were decent."

"Well, it's not looking so good there right now," said Wash, who had been rifling through the Cortex.

"What you learned, honey?" said Zoë, wrapping her arm around his shoulder.

"Dry," said River. "Dry as bones. Ground gone hard and dead."

"She is—as ever—completely and really very disturbingly accurate," said Wash. "There's been a run of bad summers. Crops failing and so on."

Zoë looked at River with something close to awe. "Did you *see* that, honey?"

River looked back unblinkingly, and then nodded down at Wash. "I was reading over his shoulder."

"Ah," said Zoë, much mollified. Wash, however, was not. "I didn't know you were there!"

"No," said River. "You didn't."

"Could you *not* with the creepy?" said Wash. "I'm *nice*, River! Remember? I'm a *very* nice person. Could you do the creepy on someone else? Someone who deserves it? Jayne, maybe?"

"I have," said River. "I do."

"No, you ain't," said Jayne, his voice dripping scorn. "Ain't no way some gorram kid gets past me."

"Big Bertha," said River.

Jayne's face was a picture. Plain as plain he didn't want further discussion, and Mal wasn't minded to hear more either.

"Let's bring ourselves back to the point," said Book.

"Let's do that," agreed Mal. "Anything else up there on the Cortex, Wash?"

"Not much… Some trouble a few months ago in Yell City…"

"Trouble?" said Mal, ever wary.

"Looks like some people got hot under the collar during the summer heat, kicked down a few doors along Main Street. Some commercial buildings got targeted."

"Not our problem," said Mal, briskly. He had no intention of hanging around, finding out what the local grievances were. That was their own business on Abel. In and out, was his plan. "What about traffic?"

"The usual," said Wash. "Merchant ships from the Rim and the Core."

"Anything official?" said Mal.

"Not that I can see."

"What about the authorities on Abel?" asked Book. "Bounty hunters aren't always popular with the local sheriff's office. Showin' them up for not doin' their job. We likely to get any trouble from that quarter?"

"Your guess is as good as mine, Shepherd," said Wash, with a shrug.

"Might also be glad to have one less troublemaker to worry about," said Zoë.

"Something to put to our employer," said Mal. "Once we get there. Any other questions?"

"What do the rest of us do while you're busy?" said Simon.

"Do what you do best," said Mal. "Play checkers."

"It was chess," said Simon.

"I'd keep your head down, son," said Book. "No point you wandrin' round lookin' for trouble when the rest of us have that side of things covered."

"I'll keep you comp'ny, Simon," said Kaylee.

"I'll bet," said Jayne, with a leer.

"Red sky in the morning," said River. "Dead ground. Dry bones."

Which brought the conversation to a natural if not entirely cheerful end.

Mal walked through his ship heavy of heart. In the past, he hadn't much like visiting Inara's shuttle, a mite too close to enemy territory for his taste. But since she'd told him her intention to leave, there was something different about being on her ground. Like he had to take his chances to be there while he still could.

"We'll be landin' soon," he told her. "Got a job on Abel. Good job too, if the pay on offer's to be believed."

"Yes? And what is it this time? Cattle? Beagles?"

"Bounty hunting," he said.

"Rogue beagles," she said. "I'd never have guessed."

"Well, they're the worst," he said, and while she gave him a smile, he could tell her heart wasn't in it. "Thought it would be a courtesy and all, let you know," he said. "But no need for our business to interrupt yours. Can't say for sure yet how long the job will take, but no more'n a coupla days, I'd guess. You're free to come and go as you please in the meantime, of course—"

"I know. Thank you, Mal."

"Thank you?"

"It was kind of you to come and tell me."

"No harm in being kind," he said, uncertainly. These good manners between them. Didn't feel right, somehow. Felt like something unsaid, unfinished, but he didn't know what else to say. Somehow he'd never found the right thing to say to Inara, and now he wouldn't ever get the chance.

"No," she said, turning back to look into the mirror. "There isn't. I'll wait for you."

"Pardon me?"

"Until you're back from town, Mal."

"I see," he said. "Yes. 'Course." Unsettled, he left her shuttle and went to get ready to leave. Zoë was coming with him, of course, and he'd asked Book to come along to meet Miss Roberts. There'd been a mite too much invocation of the Good Lord in her message for Mal's taste, so the Shepherd might make a good impression, as well as preventin' Mal from sayin' something that might be taken amiss. And there was another member of his crew that he needed right now…

He found Kaylee sitting with Simon on the big old sofa near the infirmary. Pair of them lookin' mighty cozy. "Kaylee," said Mal. "You comin'?"

"Comin', cap'n?"

"Comin' out with me and the rest."

Kaylee glanced sideways at Simon. "Cap'n," she said,

meaningfully. "I got *plans...*"

"That's right," said Mal. "You got a date with a catalyzer for a starboard compression coil." Mal, watching her agonized expression, covered his smile. Weren't kind to put the girl on the spot like this, but Mal had to get his fun somewhere.

"Didn't think we had the platinum for that," said Kaylee, her voice suspicious.

"We will, when this job's done, and shouldn't take more'n day or two. I want that catalyzer installed before we leave Abel, so sooner you have it in hand the better."

"Shiny," she said, and turned to Simon. "You wanna tag along? I'll show you the difference between a port-side and a starboard-side catalyzer."

"Imagine the doc would love that," said Mal, "but Wash'll go with you." He gave Simon a genial smile. "You stick around here, doc. Brush up your checkers with Jayne."

Feeling considerably more cheerful now, Mal went on his way, whistling. Kaylee might be put out, but from the sound of things Abel wasn't so quiet as it used to be, and he wouldn't see Kaylee in the middle of trouble without back-up, and Wash was preferable to Simon in that respect. Less of a distraction, for one thing, and Mal didn't want Kaylee distracted. The girl had got shot once already on Mal's watch, and that was more'n enough.

They put down at the docks early in the morning, Abel-time. Mal got Wash to send a message to Miss Roberts to ask when he might conveniently visit and was instructed to come straight over. He, Zoë, Book, Wash and Kaylee all packed into the Mule, and were soon on their way. Kaylee had already located a vendor for the catalyzer on the edge of the space docks, and Mal dropped her and Wash off a short walk from where they needed to be.

"If the part's good, shall I go ahead and buy, cap'n?" Kaylee asked.

Mal gave her the go-ahead. Even if the job for Miss Roberts ran into difficulties (not that he was anticipating any), there was more or less enough in the kitty to cover the catalyzer. When Kaylee and Wash were on their way, Mal pointed the Mule towards the heart of Yell City. Wasn't long before they saw signs of the city's recent travails. Even the early morning sun couldn't put a shine on the place. Buildings in need of a lick of paint; broken fixtures going unmended; an overall air of shabbiness. On Main Street, which should surely be the shining jewel at the heart of the city, every other window seemed boarded up and, at the far end of the street, Mal saw people sleeping in doorways. The city wasn't much like how he recalled from that visit long ago. He knew there'd been a war in the meantime, but he didn't remember seeing beggars out last time, and he didn't see why Abel would have been hit so hard. Like Jayne had hinted, the people on Abel had played their cards carefully throughout the war. Both sides came away thinkin' Abel was with them. Wasn't the war that had caused this. Those bad harvests, he guessed, bringing people from their farms to the city, but there was nothing for them here either. Left nothing and come to nothing.

Beyond Main Street, the plight of the city became more obvious. Narrow streets lined with tenements so rundown you wouldn't shelter animals there—yet Mal saw people leaning out the windows, hanging round the doors, sitting on the steps. Early morning, and nobody on their way to work. Broken glass and trash all around. Sorriest of sights. "Ain't the happiest of places we've visited, sir," remarked Zoë.

"Seems not," said Mal.

"Poverty," said Book, thoughtfully, "is a terrible thing."

"Thought you took a vow on that, Shepherd," said Mal. "Along with obedience and—what's the other one?"

"Chastity," said Book, equably.

"We've all been there, Shepherd."

"Maybe, Mal, but the whole point of takin' a vow is that it's a choice. I don't see much in the way of choice for these poor folks here."

Mal closed himself off from the sights around him. No way they could fix the woes of a whole world. He'd tried saving the 'verse once and it hadn't paid off. There was wealth somewhere on Abel. How else was Miss Anne Imelda Roberts offering them that much platinum to bring her the head of Young Bill Fincher?

They came out of the warren of little streets onto a wider avenue, and suddenly, it was like they were in a different city entirely. The tenements gave way to neat little wooden houses, painted white and nicely kept, although not even this pleasant district was unmarked. Every so often one of the houses was shuttered. Maybe a foreclosure; maybe someone who had left Abel to try their luck elsewhere. Gave the place a precarious air, like nobody was safe from what was going on around them. As the road climbed up into the hills, the signs of trouble disappeared, and the houses became finer. You might even go so far as to call some of them mansions.

"Guess we're finding the money now," remarked Book.

"As long as we find it at our destination," said Mal.

He wasn't disappointed: the Roberts' house might not have been a mansion as such, but stood big and airy in its own grounds. Three storys high, with a little tower on the right-hand side topped by a turret. Pretty as a picture, and well maintained. Mal caught a glimpse of gardens behind the house. The Mule looked somewhat out of place on the neat drive, but if Miss Roberts went about hiring bounty hunters, Mal suspected she wouldn't trouble herself unduly about the appearance of their transport. They parked, and went up to the porch on the left-hand side. There was a big rocking swing there, space for two, some yellowed pot plants that looked like they'd had a tough couple of years. Who hadn't?

The front door was painted black, with a decent security system, customary mixture of the old and the new. A big brass door knocker in the shape of a stallion's head with a horseshoe underneath, which Mal lifted and banged against the door. After a quick security scan, the door was opened by a young woman dressed as a maid.

"Captain Reynolds," she said. "You're expected. Come this way, please."

Mal followed her, Zoë and Book close behind, into a square hallway filled incongruously with sacks. The maid led them through this maze and through a door on the right that led into a tasteful parlor. "Make yourselves comfortable," said the maid. "I'll tell Miss Annie you're here."

"Nice place," said Book, when the maid left. "Poor girl, mind. Losing her father like that." He eyed Mal. "You sure you want her along on this?"

"Like I said," said Mal, "let's be calm, mind our manners, find out whether she'll be help or hindrance. We'll do this our own way—in and out, quick as we can—but an extra pair of hands won't do any harm."

Mal took the opportunity to look around. Pleasant room, decked out in pale greens and yellows, windows looking out towards the street, catching the early morning sunshine. Couple of deep sofas, into one of which the Shepherd was already easing himself, and shelves full of the type of books been read for pleasure and not out of duty. Kind of place you'd like to spend time. Mal went across the mantelpiece, upon which stood a series of framed pictures. Baby pictures. One of a little girl, digging, and the same girl, a mite older, sittin' on a pony lookin' mighty pleased with herself. Man and woman, in wedding clothes, smiling out their happiness for the whole 'verse to see. Couple of other pictures of them, dressed more casual, in different places that looked to be the Core. If that was Isaac Roberts, he looked like a nice fella. Mal, sitting down in the other sofa, wondered where the woman was now.

He heard voices out in the corridor, and stood up again (might as well show their soon-to-be employer some courtesy). The door opened and Miss Anne Imelda Roberts came into the room. She looked much as she had done in her message: stern-faced and serious. Her left arm ended above the elbow.

"*Tian xiao de!*" exclaimed Malcolm Reynolds. "Kid's only got one arm... I knew there was a catch!"

"Mal," murmured Book. "Mind your manners."

Probably good advice, thought Mal. Their employer—potential employer, he should say, and oh *gǒu shǐ* wasn't he supposed to makin' a good impression right now?—was looking at him like he was a complete *yē sū tā mā de* fool.

3

I pride myself on telling the truth, therefore I shall not hold
back. My first impression of Captain Malcolm Reynolds was
that he was exactly the fool Sheriff Peters had warned me about,
indeed I might say somewhat more. You would think that anyone
might assume that I am well aware of my appearance. You might
also assume too that I would have no particular need to be told
that I have lost my arm from a little above the elbow. And yet
even so, out them words came from his fool mouth. A catch. I
lifted my chin, stood up straight, and gave Captain Malcolm
Reynolds a hard look. You can believe I have perfected this over
the years, since there's always someone ready to say somethin'
that does them no credit.

"Somethin' the matter, Captain Reynolds?" I said. "Somethin'
you want to say to me?"

This man recommended by Sheriff Peters to find my daddy's
killer was a tall fellow, and he was wearing that old style of brown
coat that used to be everywhere. You still see such here and there
on Abel, particularly among them folks from the countryside
whose farms have been failin', and have come to Yell City in
search of work. Why they would wear these coats has always been

a puzzle to me. The Independents lost the war. So why would a fellow looking for work and seeking to make a good impression want to advertise that he was on the losing side? Some people put pride before good sense, and it's been my observation that many of them wear brown coats. But we all know what they said about pride and how it comes before a fall. I myself was startin' to think that perhaps I shoulda hired Moody Jones after all.

Captain Malcolm Reynolds' mouth opened and closed and opened again. I was starting to wonder when I might hear anything come out, and I was thinking I'd settle for more of his foolishness if it meant this fellow to whom I was meant to payin' a fine sum of money would start speakin'. At last, he said, "Ain't nothing the matter, miss, but we might have to discuss some of the details of this job more before we, er, commit..."

A quiet voice intervened at that point; quiet, yes, but with authority.

"How 'bout we all sit down? Get to know each other a little better?"

This was from the man dressed like a shepherd. Book, I learned his name was, not long after. Ever hear of a team of bounty hunters travelling about with their own preacher? I've never heard of such, before or since. First impressions count for nothing, so they say, but in the case of Shepherd Book I do not believe I was wrong in my assessment. He struck me as a man of good sense and vast experience. Someone who knew how to smooth troubled waters, if the need arose. Must have been why Captain Reynolds brought him along.

"Shepherd..." said the captain.

"No harm in hearing more, Mal, you said that yourself," replied the preacher. "Besides, think of that starboard catalyzer Kaylee's off purchasin' right now. They don't grow on trees, you know."

That didn't make much sense to me, but seemed enough to

stop Captain Reynolds from shootin' off his mouth any further.

"It's a pleasure to make your acquaintance, Miss Roberts," said the preacher, smiling. "Might we sit? Hear a little more of your story?"

"You might," I said, and nodded towards the sofas. Shepherd Book, who had stood up when I entered the room, took the seat next to me. Nice manners, that fella. The woman that was with them sat on the other sofa. I recall my first impressions of her were of how tall she was, how easily she moved, with great confidence in herself, and an expression that gave little away. My instinct was to like her, and this instinct was borne out. Zoë Washburne, as her name turned out to be, was someone with their head screwed on right, and she had the measure of her captain, that was for sure.

As for Captain Malcolm Reynolds—he stood uneasily for a moment or two more, shifting from foot to foot, until Shepherd Book turned to him and said, in a voice so mild you might not catch the warning, "Take a seat, Mal. Let's hear this young lady out."

Whereupon the captain fell into the seat next to Zoë, shaking his head.

Book turned to me. "Let me say how sorry we are, Miss Roberts, to hear of your loss. Your father's been in my prayers."

"Thank you, preacher," I said.

"It's our understanding that you know who committed this crime—"

"Young Bill Fincher," I said.

"And there's no doubt in your mind about that?" said the Shepherd.

"Ain't only in my mind," said I. "More'n a dozen people saw him shoot my daddy. On the steps of his office. There ain't no doubt."

"I have to ask," said the Shepherd. "Because we can't be going after the wrong man."

"You won't be."

"Do you know why he did it?" said Zoë.

"They say it was a quarrel went suddenly wrong," I said.

"Happens," said Zoë.

"Fincher ain't the smartest," said I. "Shoots before he thinks, and doesn't always get round to thinking even so. That's what they're saying."

"That young man may be regretting a split-second's bad mistake," observed the Shepherd. "This is a sad story, Miss Roberts."

"If that were the case, then perhaps so, though I'd still want justice done. But I don't believe this was spur of the moment. On the contrary. I believe he was sent to kill my daddy, by other men, and that's what he done."

I saw the three of them share a look. Shepherd Book sighed, and leaned back against the cushions. "Carry on, child," he said. "Let's hear this tale in full."

"Fincher runs with a gang," I explained. "The Collier gang. Causing a whole lot of trouble out in country. Times are hard out there right now, and folks can't afford to be held to ransom."

"We've taken out gangs like that before," said Zoë. She turned to Mal. "You, me, Jayne—reckon we can send those boys packing."

"We certainly can," said Captain Reynolds. "But looking at Miss Roberts' face there, I think we still ain't had the full story."

At least the fella was listening now. "Folks are saying this was all a misunderstanding," I said. "That Daddy had the misfortune to say something to Bill Fincher that made him mad, and Fincher, being the worse for drink, shot him without forethought. But I know that ain't true—it can't be true! Someone *paid* Bill Fincher to go to Daddy's office and shoot him dead. I don't only want him hanged, I want the Collier gang hanged, and I want whoever paid those boys to murder my daddy to hang too. That's the job, that's why I'm payin' so well, and I'll be there to see it when you take Fincher."

Well, I'd made my terms clear, and it was up to them to say yes or no.

"That's a whole 'nother job from the one you laid out in your message," said Reynolds. "That sounds more like you're in need of an investigator, not a…"

"A bounty hunter?" I said.

"As good a name for what we'd do as any," said the Shepherd, calmly.

"Miss Roberts," said Zoë. "May I ask you a question?"

"Call me Annie," I said. Yes, I liked her. "And please do."

"Annie," she said with a smile. "How're you so sure there's more behind this?"

"Daddy was a lawyer," I said. "He had a big case coming and I think he got on the wrong side of some powerful folks. He… liked to take care of the underdog, you see."

"Your daddy sounds like he was a good man," said the Shepherd, softly.

"He was a gosh-darned fool," I said, and maybe it was the Shepherd's gentleness, or maybe simply that for the first time since my daddy died I felt like someone was listening to what I had to say, but the next thing I knew I was cryin' away, like a babe in arms. And that good preacher man—a good shepherd if ever there was—laid one of his hands upon mine, and said, "That's it, Annie. Let it all come out."

Oh, but I cried on and on. The whole works, messy old tears they were. I heard the woman, Zoë, go to the door and call for Maisie. Soon enough there was tea, and we was all drinkin' it (even Reynolds) and feelin' a mite better. After a while, the Shepherd glanced round at his friends, and nodded.

"Well," he said, "Miss Annie. We have taken up a great deal of your time this morning."

"I don't mind," I said. "I'm glad you came, Shepherd Book."

"I'm glad too. Now, I'm looking at Captain Reynolds and I'm thinking that we have a number of things we need to discuss—by which I mean our whole crew—before we can give you an answer to as to whether or not we can take on this job. You do see, don't you," he said, and he looked me straight in the eye, "there's quite a lot more involved than we understood would be when we set out for Abel."

I knew my story sounded wild; sounded wild even to my ears. But I don't mind when folks are straight with me—I prefer it—and I could see now that perhaps I could well have been clearer in my message. Ain't right to want straight talk and not give it in return. "Yes, I see," I said. "Sounds fair to me. I'm sorry, Captain Reynolds," I said, looking at him direct, "if my message to you was misleading. But this is the job. I want justice for my daddy—and I want to be there to see justice done."

I stood up—so did Reynolds—and I offered him my hand, which he shook.

"I hope you'll take this job. Otherwise I don't think there'll be justice for Daddy 'til Judgement Day. And that ain't right."

The Shepherd, when it was his turn to say goodbye, laid his hand upon my head. "God bless you, child," he said. "You'll be hearing from us soon."

I followed 'em to the front door and watched 'em go. I believed the Shepherd meant every word he said, and I would hear from them soon—but I'd caught the expression on Captain Reynolds' face as he got into their transport. I knew in my heart that the news wouldn't be good. Maybe I could go back to Sheriff Peters and tell him I wanted to speak to Moody Jones or the other fella, the one who liked his drink, but it struck me, watching the three of them head off down the road, that a bounty hunter in the hand was worth two in the black. Captain Reynolds was here, now, on Abel, and I didn't see why Bill Fincher should be walking round free for a single day more. Reynolds was the one for me, whether he liked it or not. All I had to do was make him see things my way.

So I went back inside, got on the Cortex, and sent a message to the port authorities to check on a ship called *Serenity*, lately arrived on Abel, that might not be safe for travel, given the problems with the starboard catalyzer. They weren't minded to help me 'til I mentioned my daddy's name. That always did the trick.

Sheriff Ned Peters was a man who wanted nothing more than to retire to his tiny cabin up the coast with his sweet wife, Nell, and live out his life in peace fishing in the river and chopping wood. Problem was that people—quite fairly—kept on expecting him to perform his duties as sheriff, and, being a conscientious fellow, and one who didn't quite know how to say 'no', he did indeed keep on performing them. He performed them as best he could, given how tired he was these days, but he couldn't shake the feelin' that he wasn't as on top of things as he used to be. Never enough people to hand to be doin' what needed to be doin', and all kinds of trouble in parts of the city that used to be quiet, and too many folks comin' in from the country, lookin' for work and places to stay when these things were in short supply, and then what happened to that fine young fella Isaac Roberts...

When his daughter, Miss Annie, came to see him, all sharp eyes and sharp words, Ned Peters felt ashamed, and put a few names her way that might help. It was only later, talking to Nell, that he fell to wonderin' whether he'd not been wise, makin' those suggestions.

"So she came and asked you to do something?"

"Yup."

"And you said you couldn't."

Ned, from long experience, was starting to see the hole opening up in front of him.

"Um… yup?"

"And you said, 'How about instead you go and hire some vigilantes?'"

One hell of a hole. "Weren't quite what I said, Nell—"

"And have you heard from Mayor McQuinn yet?"

He hadn't, but she waved first thing in the morning that Malcolm Reynolds arrived on Abel, and she was not a happy woman. Ned didn't like to see women unhappy. Partly because he was, in his own ham-fisted way, a gentleman, and partly because Mary McQuinn struck him as a tough player in a city getting tougher by the day.

"*Might have preferred, Sheriff,*" said McQuinn, "*if you'd asked me first before outsourcin' some of your responsibilities to some fella might be more of a villain than Frankie Collier himself.*"

"Ain't how it is, ma'am—"

"*That remains to be seen. But in general, Ned, I'd prefer we kept our own house rather than hirin' in help.*"

"Now that ain't fair, Mary. You know how I'm fixed right now. Stretched thin as ice and close to crackin'. You know what it's like on the ground. All them new folks streamin' into town, rubbin' the locals up the wrong way."

Moment that was out of his mouth he knew he'd made a misstep. Them folks from the country—they were the ones who'd voted her in. Come as a surprise to many in the city, rich and poor alike, both of whom had their own candidates in mind, and yet here she was, in charge of running Yell City, and everyone here used to having things their own way, or used to complainin' about how things was always done, was suddenly left lookin' round and thinkin', *What the hell's going on 'round here these days?*

"*Those troubles cut both ways,*" said McQuinn. "*Maybe we could say something about the folks already here, taking out their grievances on those poor folks come down from the country to put food in the*

mouths of their kids. I hear some locals been struttin' 'round places like
Westerly and Keyside and so on with pistols on their hips like they're
some kind of deputies of yours. And you hirin' in some offworlder to
pull in Bill Fincher—that'll make 'em bolder. You're stirrin' up trouble,
Ned—and not only for yourself. Me too, and City Hall."

Well, she was making some good points, and he knew he'd
misspoke, but he'd told her the truth, too, about not havin'
enough people, and she was the gorram mayor these days. What
was she doing? Ned Peters wasn't roused to anger easily, but he
did stir himself, sometimes. "Way I hear it, you're doin' your own
part there, ma'am."

There was a pause. Then: "*Excuse me?*"

"Them fellas from the Core. Blue Sun, or Blue Moon, or
whatever they call themselves. I hear they been sniffin' 'round
City Hall, offerin' their services."

Oh, now, that had struck home.

"*If you can't see the difference between contractin' a professional*
company to do some tidyin' up round here, and hirin' a gorram
bounty hunter to go after someone shot a fella dead in Main Street,
then you're more of a fool than folks say you are, Ned Peters,"
McQuinn snapped back.

"Ma'am," said Peters. "That ain't well said. We're all of us
trying to do a difficult job here, as best we can. This week been
the worst I've known it and it's only hard work by me and my
fellas been keepin' the place from goin' pop." He wasn't sure how
much longer that would last either. Every day, by the time the
sun went down, you saw folks out on more or less every street
corner, hopin' for trouble. "We're stretched thin, doin' more than
our share That ain't well said."

McQuinn did not reply straight away. "*You're right,*" she said.
"*My apologies, Ned. You hit a sore spot there. I don't like havin' to ask*
these folks from the Core for help, but there's money back there set

aside for helpin' worlds like ours. Abel was loyal during the war, and we earned our share. Want to make sure it comes our way, that's all."

"Well, I don't know much about the Core, ma'am, but I reckon those fellas are hopin' to make more'n a slip or two of platinum for themselves."

"I'm sure they are, Ned, but they ain't doin' anythin' that ain't legal. So maybe we can hold back a while on turning Abel into a paradise for vigilantes, eh? I know we've all got a soft spot for Miss Roberts, particularly on account of her father, but from what I knew about Isaac Roberts, he wouldn't like to see his daughter takin' up with bounty hunters either."

And that, Ned Peters, had to admit, was a fair point. "You want me to get rid of this fella?"

"If you could see your way to doin' that, Ned, it would surely be a help. Maybe have a word with Annie Roberts? Ask her to reconsider?"

Peters snorted. "No use there. Girl's a law to herself. Might as well ask the world to stop spinnin' as ask her to back down when she's got a notion in her head."

"Then somethin' else? I don't know, Ned! Something to persuade this fella to be on his way!"

"You leave it with me, ma'am. And I'm sorry if I spoke out of turn. No good comes from us two fightin', eh?"

"From your mouth to God's ear, Ned." She sighed. *"Some mornings I wake up thinkin' this whole city'll be ablaze by nightfall."*

She wasn't wrong. Bad times in Yell City, worst he'd ever seen. That little retirement home seemed more attractive by the day. "We'll find a way," he said, comfortingly. "We always do. You leave this Reynolds fella to me. I'll find a way to send him packin'."

He put a call through to the port authorities. Five minutes later, he was trying to track down McQuinn to break the bad news. Captain Malcolm Reynolds wasn't going anywhere.

* * *

"I say we help her," said Book, as they drove back along Main Street. The city was starting to wake up for the day; shutters going up on some of the buildings; the beggars packing up from doorways and settling to their sleeping spots. "What about you, Zoë?"

"I'm minded that way too."

Mal could hardly believe his ears. These two were the sensible ones on his crew. "No," he said, flatly.

"No?" said Book, a twinkle in his eye. "You sure 'bout that? Money's good—"

"There ain't enough platinum in the 'verse for me to take a one-armed girl out into the back of beyond to chase down a gang of killers. *Dǒng ma?*"

"She was pretty clear that takin' her was the main condition of the job, sir—"

"That's right, Zoë, and the reason we ain't doin' that because we ain't takin' this job. We're going back to *Serenity*, and we're leavin'. This ain't no simple task, trackin' down some fool boy and bringin' him back to face a judge. This might be stirrin' up the whole city against us—"

"Done it before, sir—"

"Yes, well, and that's one reason why I ain't doin' it again. This is someone else's problem and I ain't makin' it mine."

"Sir—"

"Enough! That's my decision, Zoë, and it's final!"

There was silence in the Mule after that. They were halfway back to the docks before Mal, slamming his hand down, cried out, "*Wǒ de mā*, will you both say your piece and have done!"

"You said your decision was final, Mal," Book pointed out, in his calmest voice.

Tā mā de, thought Mal, but that tone of the Shepherd's was enough to drive the meekest of men to violence. "When has that ever made a gorram difference?" Mal said. "Everyone usually willin' to chip in, say what they have to say, 'til a man can't hear his own thoughts any longer—"

"The girl needs our help," said Zoë.

"Lots of folk in need of a helpin' hand, Zoë," said Mal. "Look out in the street there. We could walk into any house in this city and find folk in dire need of help."

"Money's good, sir. Better'n good."

"Money we're likely to not live to see if we take that girl with us," said Mal. "If her tale's true, then these fellas felt safe enough to send one of their number out in broad daylight to kill her daddy. And what do we know about them, huh? The Collier gang, she calls 'em—what's that? Three of them? Ten? Fifteen? And you ain't tellin' me those fellas ain't mean—but how mean? Mean as Badger? Mean as Niska? Point is, we don't *know*."

"We finished off Niska, sir."

"Not before one of us here died!" shot back Mal.

"They killed her daddy, sir," said Zoë. "A good man. They shot him dead in the street and walked away like they done nothing." She was shaking her head and had that stubborn look on her face which sometimes filled Mal with confidence and sometimes with dismay. "It ain't right, sir."

"Whole 'verse of things that ain't right, Zoë, and we ain't in the business of fixin' 'em all." He eyed Book. "You're quiet, preacher man."

"Well, I can see the points you're making, Mal."

"But ain't in the way of agreeing?"

Whatever opinion Book had on the matter, Mal did not immediately get to hear. Someone was trying to wave them down. He slowed the Mule down to take a closer look.

"*Āiyā*," said Mal. "Do my eyes deceive me, or is that Kaylee Frye there by the side of the road?"

"Not only Kaylee," said Zoë. "That looks mighty like my husband with her."

Sure enough, there was Wash, waving his arms and jumping up and down.

"Oh my," said Book. "There'll be a tale to tell here, no doubt."

Mal slowed the Mule to a stop and let his two crewmembers come to join him. "Wash, Kaylee—*zěn me le*? Something wrong? Where's the others?"

Kaylee, who was out of breath from running, said, "They're coming…" She jerked her thumb behind her, gesturing back up the road. "On their way…"

Mal, getting out of the Mule, looked further up the road. Sure enough, Jayne, Simon, River were all heading in their direction.

"Circus has come to town, I see," murmured Book, coming to stand beside him. When the rest of the crew arrived, Mal looked them up and down.

"A sorrier-looking bunch I ain't never seen in all my days," he said. "Nor was I expectin' to see, neither. Thought I told you to stay on board *Serenity*. Not sure I could make an order more straightforward than that, but I'll try harder next time." He eyed them all, one by one. "Make this good."

"We aren't on the ship," said Simon, with some asperity, "because there isn't a ship to be on."

Kaylee rolled her eyes. "Simon! I told you that I'd tell him!"

"Tell me what?" said Mal.

"They took your ship, Mal," said Jayne.

"The who did what now?" said Mal.

"Coupla men from the port authorities," said Jayne. "Came and took a look round *Serenity* and impounded her."

"I said *I'd* tell him!" said Kaylee. "Don't be sore, Cap'n," she said. "I'm sure it's all a misunderstanding." She flushed red. "They said the starboard compression coil weren't up to scratch! Said she weren't safe to fly! *Gǒu shǐ*, some of my best work's been done keepin' that that gorram coil held together! Those fellas ain't got no idea what I done there—"

"Hold on," said Mal. "Back up a second now. I thought you went off to get yourself a catalyzer to fix the compression coil—"

"I *did*!" said Kaylee. "Brought the thing back to start work and the ship was already locked up! This lot hangin' 'round outside like a set of skittles just been hit by the bowling ball."

Mal heard the Shepherd suppress a chuckle. "But if you have the catalyzer," said Mal, "can't you just up and fix the coil?"

"There's a fine," said Wash. "We got to pay that first before we can get back into the ship, but we spent what we have getting the catalyzer, and there's nothing left to pay the fine to be able to get on board to get to the compression coil to start fixing it—"

"Husband," said Zoë. "You need to be quiet now."

"Yeah," said Wash. "I'm lookin' at Mal here, and I'm thinkin' that you are, as ever, completely right."

Just in time. Mal exploded. "*Rén ci de fó zǔ*, them *wáng bā dàn* have taken my gorram *boat*?"

"'Bout the size of it, Mal," said Jayne. He patted the huge gun that was slung over his shoulder. "Took a coupla minutes to pack though. Where's this job we come for? I'm in the mood for shootin' anything gets in my way."

"There ain't no job," said Zoë.

"No job?" said Jayne. "How we gonna pay to get the ship back?"

"Second thoughts yet, Mal?" murmured Book into his ear.

"Nobody," said Mal, "and I mean *nobody*—lays a hand on my ship."

"I do," said Wash.

"Honey," said Zoë, "hush."

"Where's Inara?" said Book.

"Back at the docks," said Simon. "I think they drew the line at impounding a Companion's shuttle."

Book nodded. "Might come in handy…"

"We ain't callin' on Inara to get us out of this," said Mal.

"There's a simple way out of this, I suppose," said Book. "Mal?"

Mal hesitated. Tempting, he thought, to take this job, make himself felt in these parts. Nobody touched his gorram ship and got away with it. But you had to be realistic. What could three of them—four, if Book was minded to help, and maybe even five, if River could be relied on—do to take on a gang of men running rings around the sheriff of Yell City? "Ain't so simple, preacher—"

"Take the job, sir," said Zoë.

"Zoë, you seen that girl—"

"I have, sir. And that's why I meant it when I say, you either take the job, or I will—without you."

There was a pause. "Wife," said Wash. "You're beautiful when you're angry."

"Quiet now, husband."

"Zoë," said Mal, "is this mutiny?"

"First time for everything, sir."

"I don't like it."

"Don't like it much myself either, sir. But that's where we are."

"Huh."

"I swear you've never looked so beautiful as you do now," said Wash.

"Keep that for later," said Zoë. "We got work in the meantime."

"What's the problem with the job?" said Simon.

"There's a few complications," said Book.

"Complications ain't the half of it," said Mal.

"You'll see when you meet Miss Annie," Book finished.

"Now I missed this moment when I said we were going back," said Mal.

"We are going back," said Zoë. "Sir."

"Much as I hate to interrupt this lovers' tiff," said Wash, "but in my experience, when Zoë has that expression on her face, it's simplest to go with the flow."

"Wise words, husband," said Zoë.

"I honor and obey," said Wash.

"Mal," said Book. "She's eighteen years old. Her father's died and she thinks there's some powerful people did the deed. Girl needs answers, and she's payin' to get them. And besides—how else are you plannin' on coverin' that fine? Plenty enough beggars out on these streets already."

When you thought of it that way...

They were back at the Roberts house—all eight of them—within twenty minutes. The maid, Maisie, opening the door wide so they could all troop in, took one look at them as they filed past and said, "I'd better put the kettle on."

"Maisie?" a voice called from above. "Who is it?"

Mal looked up. Annie Roberts was standing at the top of the stairs.

"This is the kid wants to come with us?" hissed Jayne. "Mal, you're not gonna bring her, are you? Tell me that ain't happenin'."

"Maybe talk to her before judging?" said Simon. "Teenage girls can surprise you. Or did you mean something else?"

"Don't need to talk to her to know she'll be a gorram liability!" said Jayne. "Just *look* at her!"

"Hold your tongue, Jayne," snapped Zoë. "Girl's lost her father. Show some respect."

"Respect? She'll get us all gorram killed!"

"You'll show some respect," said Zoë, "or I'll make you show respect."

Jayne shut up, unhappily. Annie came down the stairs, stood before Mal, and lifted her chin. "Look what the cat dragged in," she said. "Must say as how I weren't expecting you to darken my door again."

"Well, here I am, Miss Annie, like the proverbial good penny, and I brought my crew with me this time, so's you can take a good look at them, see what you're hirin'," said Mal.

"It's a bad penny, as I recall," said Annie. "Anything else you have to say for yourself, Captain Reynolds?"

"And I'm, uh... here to negotiate terms," said Mal.

"Terms," muttered Book, with a snort.

"Captain," said Annie Roberts. "Let's us be clear on this score. You're here to accept terms. Two hundred platinum was my initial offer, but looking at you now, I think I'll open again with one fifty."

From right behind him, Mal could hear the Shepherd chuckling softly.

4

Well, I wasn't expecting any of 'em, but there they were, all standing in my hallway. Some looked a mite more sheepish than others at intrudin' on me. That big fella with the orange hat— he made himself at home straight off, eyin' up Maisie as she dashed about and lookin' round, for the whisky bottle or something similar no doubt. Jayne Cobb was his name, and one I ain't likely ever to forget. Mother of mercy, that man. There was another fella in the most hideous shirt I ever seen who seemed to be hidin' himself behind Zoë—his name was Wash, and he turned out to be married to her. Funny who people choose to wed. There was a younger fella—pretty, I guess—with good manners. Turned out to be a doctor. There's always need for a doctor. A young woman, name of Kaylee Frye—not ashamed to say I liked her straight off; big smile and friendly ways. I saw nothin' over the next few days to disabuse me of this first impression and I came to mightily regret besmirching her skill with a catalyzer. And there was one other—a young girl, looked not much older'n me, but there was something off about her, something not quite right. She moved like a ghost, and she wasn't wearin' shoes. She drifted round, half-here and half-elsewhere. I said a little prayer when she went past. Not sure if it was for her or for me.

"This your lot?" I said to Captain Reynolds. Maybe they could help me sort through all that jumble in the hall. Might as well make themselves useful.

"There's one more," he said.

"Only one?"

"Only one. Her name's Inara." He looked around. "Any chance we can send her a message, let her know where we are?"

"She vital to carryin' out the job?"

"She might be. You never know."

"You got *two* lady gunslingers on your team, Captain?" I wasn't complainin'. The more of us could handle a gun, the more likely Young Bill Fincher would be swingin' within the week.

He laughed out loud. "No, only Zoë fits that bill. Inara's a Companion."

"Oh," I said, and perhaps there was something in my expression, because Captain Reynolds frowned back and asked, "That a problem, Miss Annie?"

Well, I ain't so sure about Companions. Ain't so sure that it's a right and good way to go about livin' your life, but when I used to say this Daddy would laugh and call me old-fashioned. "I'll take you to the Core one day," he said. "We'll visit your mamma's folks." I guess he would see my expression whenever he said this, because he'd go on, "You'll have a good time, Annie, I promise. Broaden your mind."

Sometimes folks broaden their minds so far that everything of consequence slips out, and, besides, I liked it here on Abel and had no wish to visit the Core, which seemed to me on the whole to be all shiny on the surface with nothing of substance underneath. But I wasn't goin' to call a halt on these proceedings over someone else's morals and, besides, it weren't none of my business. I turned to the Shepherd, who had been listening to this conversation, and said, "Do you mind this Companion, preacher?"

"Oh, I could never mind Inara," said he. "And if you don't mind me sayin' so, Annie, seems to me more'n'more that the trick to getting by in this world is to hold to your principles, but not so rigidly that you can't move with circumstance."

Well, that was me told and no mistake. There ain't many that I'd take such chastisement from. My Daddy was one, and it turned out that preacher was another. Sometimes, recalling that man, I think he might've been one of the wisest fellas I ever met. That kind of wisdom, you know, you can't learn that from study. Comes from bein' in the world, livin' in the world. I've wondered, many times, what life that man musta led before he became a preacher. Not least because he turned out to be handy with a gun too.

"If the Shepherd here don't mind her," I said, "then I don't mind. You can get onto the Cortex in Daddy's study, send a message to her from there. Come on, I'll show you the way. There's a file too, everything Daddy put together on the case before he died. You oughta take a look. "

"Best not to go in blind," said Captain Reynolds, and followed me to Daddy's study. Shepherd Book, Zoë and the doctor came too. The others went off to the morning room, where Maisie was layin' out a spread for breakfast. When Captain Reynolds was done leavin' his message for this Companion of his, Inara, he turned to me and said, "Well then. 'Spose we ought to hear more about this case your daddy was workin' on."

I took him over to Daddy's big desk where I'd laid out all the documents, and handed him the case summary. This kinda thing ain't much of a struggle for me. I been reading Daddy's cases since I could pick sense out of letters. A is for Attorney, Daddy used to joke, and B is for Brief. But some people can't make head nor tail of it. Captain Reynolds took a flick through the pages and said, "Might need some help here, Miss Annie."

The young doctor—Simon, his name was—held out his hand. "Can I take a look?"

"You familiar with legal cases, doc?" said Captain Reynolds. "You got a malpractice suit or two you never saw fit to tell us about?" Still, he passed over the file.

"No," said the doctor, calmly. "But I took a couple of graduate-level courses as insurance. Everyone does."

"You ace 'em?"

"Top three," said the doctor.

Well, this exchange was interestin' to me. Somethin' between these two made them like chalk and cheese. They didn't like each other much, but they respected each other. And the young doctor... Well, you could tell from his voice, all clipped and careful, that he weren't from the Rim. Sounded like my cousins. What was he doin' out here?

"So you didn't *ace* 'em," said Captain Reynolds.

"I got by." The doctor turned to me. "Mister Jackson L. Carson versus First Commercial Bank of Yell City Inc. Was it a foreclosure?"

"Somethin' like that," I said. "Daddy was suin' the bank for breach of contract. Jacky lost his farm to the bank after the drought hit, but his claim was that the clause shouldn't have come into force because the bank had promised support from a relief fund and never came good. Said he woulda made it with that money. I ain't so sure, given how the weather's been the past year or two, but Daddy said there was a case to be made either way and he would make it. *Pro bono*, of course." I sighed. "Sometimes I wonder whether Daddy ever got paid."

"People lose their farms all the time," said Captain Reynolds. "And by the looks of things, that's happening all the time these days here on Abel. So what made this case so special?"

"Here," I said. "Take a look at this."

I showed them the map I'd made.

Thing was, Captain Reynolds wasn't wrong. Awful lot of farms went under then, because of the drought, but not every piece of land that came up for grabs as a result attracted the same kind of interest.

"Here," I said, pointing to a little plot of land with a red border round it. "That was Jacky Colson's farm. And this whole area, with the green border," I traced it with my finger, "that's all been bought up over the past coupla years. Daddy didn't like it. Was lookin' into it. Same purchaser."

"Go on, Annie," said the Shepherd.

"Off-world company, name of Rising Sun Enterprises."

"Off-world," said Captain Reynolds. "Bet the folks who own it are back at the Core."

"Some," I said. "But First Commercial is local. Coupla other companies involved too, and you look through the directors of those, you'll soon see a few familiar names. If you know Yell City as well as I do, I mean."

"Runs deep," said the Shepherd.

"Always does," said Mal.

"This is why I think what happened was more than Young Bill Fincher shootin' off his mouth and his gun," I said. "Someone wanted to stop Daddy fightin' his case. Because the bank woulda lost. And that would have… Well, who knows. But someone was worryin' about that happenin'. That's what I reckon. Whatever's going on, something to do with this land out there. I heard the Collier gang been camped out that way, if you're lookin' for a place to start."

"Doc," said Captain Reynolds, "been readin' a while. Drawin' any conclusions?"

"Oh," said the doctor, and a stammer crept into his voice. "Ah, um, Mal, I'm not… I'm not a *lawyer*—"

"Top three," said Captain Reynolds.

"Not this branch of law—"

"Whatever the branch of law you're practicin' on the side, top three's the best we got available. Shepherd'll help."

"Don't mind takin' a look," said the Shepherd, easily.

Captain Reynolds turned to me. "Well, Miss Annie. Looks like we'll be takin' on this job for you, after all. But we got to have a conversation now—and a serious one—about you comin' along for the ride."

I set my jaw. "I ain't debatin' that."

He looked at me with a fair deal of frustration. "These are bad fellas—"

"They shot my daddy dead."

"Miss Annie," he said, "what you don't seem to be in the way of understandin' is—"

"No, Captain Reynolds," I said. "What *you* don't seem to be in the way of understandin' is that these are my terms, and I ain't makin' 'em lightly. I ain't a fool. I ain't a child. I can use a gun and I'm a fair shot. Most of all, I ain't afraid of bein' hurt. I been hurt once, bad," I held up what remained of my left arm, "and I lived through that. I ain't scared. My mind's clear on what's involved— and my mind's made up too."

Captain Reynolds threw up his hands. "*Gǒu shǐ*, girl, are you always this gorram difficult?"

"Yes," I said. "And you keep a clean mouth while you're under my roof, Captain Reynolds, or you'll be sleepin' in the midden with the rest of the filth."

I felt a hand upon my good arm. It was Zoë. Somehow I didn't mind her touchin' me. "Annie, would you show me to the kitchen? I'd like to check on that husband of mine."

"I'll ring for Maisie."

"You know," said Zoë, and I caught a note of something in her voice, "I think you should take me to find him. We'll leave these fellas here to talk about what they've learned."

"Very well, Miss Zoë," I said. "Come this way."

I led her out into the hall.

"You got a big garden here, Annie?" she said, when the door was closed behind us.

"A big garden and a fine one. Why you askin'?"

"Got a mind to do a little test," she said. "But we'll need a fair amount of space." She winked at me and patted the pistol holstered at her side. "*Dǒng ma?*"

I felt a little old smile creep over my face. "Like I said, a fine big garden. I think you'll find everything we need."

Mal, watching them go, didn't give the pair another moment's thought. He turned back to Book and Simon, and said, "What do we think?"

"Think you might find yourself making some powerful enemies here, Mal," said Book.

"Changin' your tune, preacher?" said Mal. "I thought you were all for helpin'. Take care of the widows and orphans, ain't that what your scripture tells you?"

"It certainly does," replied Book. "But you can't do much in the way of caring for them if you're dead."

"Do we think that's likely?" said Simon. "I... I... I mean, I'm all for helping, if she needs help, but not..." His hand strayed— unconsciously perhaps—to the spot where Jubal Early had put a bullet into him.

"Don't worry, doc," said Mal, with some compassion. "You won't be anywhere near the shootin' this time."

"Well, I thought that about being on *Serenity*," said Simon. "Somehow the shooting always seems to find us, doesn't it?"

"You're welcome to leave, whenever you choose," said Mal. "Might find life worse when you're no longer on *Serenity*."

"I know..."

"Not going to lie to you, son," said Book. "Helping Miss Annie's likely to put us on the wrong side of a gang of fellas already shown themselves willin' and able to kill."

"Not obliged to involve yourself, doc," said Mal. "Stay here, keep your head down, no shame in that—"

"No, I'll help," said Simon. "If I can. She's... she's not much older than River, is she?"

"No," said Book, putting his hand upon the young man's arm. "Difference is—River has plenty of folks behind her."

Simon gave him a grateful smile.

"Talk me through what we've learned so far," said Mal.

"Need to be sure in a situation like this that we don't go jumpin' to conclusions," said Book. "So let's stick to the facts. We know who killed Isaac Roberts—Bill Fincher. We know he runs with a gang who are causin' the devil's own trouble out beyond the city. We know the sheriff won't go after him while he's runnin' with this gang—but we don't know why the sheriff is so reluctant. Annie says he claims he's overstretched. There's no reason not to believe him, given we know there's been trouble out on the streets in the last few months. As for everythin' else..."

"We know Roberts was about to go to court in opposition to some powerful people here on Abel," said Simon. "So there's motive to have him killed, I guess?" He sounded doubtful. "I don't know, Mal. It all seems very circumstantial."

"Maybe. But Roberts might have got himself on the wrong side of more'n people on Abel," said Mal. "We can see the hand of some players back from the Core in all of this."

"We're surely moving well into conjecture now," said Book. "We'll need a mite more proof before we start throwin' accusations like that around. I'm guessin' we'll need to make some friends here on Abel. Difficulty will be workin' out whose on Annie's side, and who's on the side of Fincher's paymasters."

"If they really do exist," said Mal.

"What do you mean?" said Simon.

"That girl out there, she's had a bad shock. Lookin' for payback, can't blame her for that, believes there's enemies at the door. Sometimes life ain't so complicated. Bad man walks up to a good man, shoots him dead because that's the kind of man he is. Sometimes a sheriff don't get the job done because he can't."

"You think she's seeing a conspiracy where there isn't one?" said Simon. "I think I agree."

"Guess we won't know 'til we find out, will we? And that's what Miss Annie is paying us to do." Mal tapped his fingertips against his cheek. "Some of us need to go out and about askin' a few questions. Talk to this Jacky Colson, for one. Get his opinion on the whole business. Do we even know if his case is still going ahead?"

Simon shrugged.

"Speaking for myself," said Book, "I'd like to know a little more about Rising Sun Enterprises. Interesting name, isn't it?"

Simon, browsing through the files, said, "They've got offices here in Yell City. We could send someone along there?"

"Need to send someone they'd want to speak to," said Mal thoughtfully. "They'll close the door in the face of a man like me. We need someone speaks pretty, looks pretty..."

Simon sighed. "Please stop."

"You offerin', doc?"

"I'd said I'd help, didn't I? What do you want me to do?"

"I'd say turn up there sayin' you've a tidy sum of platinum you'd like to put in the pot," said Mal. "Money opens doors like that—and you lookin' all Core and shiny as you do, doc, reckon you'll have them eatin' out of the palm of your hand."

"All right, all right, please, stop... *talking*," said Simon. "I'll go. But what are you planning to be doing in the meantime?"

"Me, Zoë, Jayne—we'll be getting down to business. Go find Bill Fincher."

"Any thoughts where he'll be?" said Book.

"I'm thinkin' we'll start by takin' a look up near the Colson farm," said Mal. "Miss Annie said she heard the Collier gang holed up there. Might be worth seein' what's happenin' out there anyway. All that land. Someone must have plans for it."

"Um, one question?" said Simon, raising his hand like he was in some kind of seminar room or something. Book and Mal exchanged a look. One day, perhaps, he'd shed some of these manners. Or perhaps not.

"Knock yourself out, doc," said Mal.

"You said you, Zoë and Jayne going out?"

"That's my thinkin'," said Mal.

"Wasn't Annie pretty clear about going along too?" said Simon. "I… I mean, she more or less said that we wouldn't get paid unless—"

"I appreciate her grit and I understand her anger," said Mal. "But no."

"Oh," said Simon, glancing at Book.

"You got a problem with that, doc?"

"I… No…"

"Good."

"I'll leave you to break that news, Mal," said Book. "Though I wouldn't mind a ringside seat while you do it."

"Thankin' you as ever for your support, Shepherd."

He was heading over to the door when it opened. Zoë looked in. "Sir," she said. "Got something to show you out here."

"Your husband and Jayne ate poor Miss Annie out of house and home yet?"

"Not yet, sir. But it ain't that." She nodded at Book. "Thinkin' you might like to see this too, preacher."

Zoë led them down the hall, with Simon tagging along

behind, through the kitchen (where Wash and Jayne were feasting) and out into a big garden. "Pleasant here, Zoë, that's for sure," said Mal, "but I ain't much of one for sittin' outside."

"This way, sir. Ain't plannin' on doin' any sittin'.."

Zoë led him over the grass to the far side of the garden. On the back wall, someone had hung up a target. Mal went to inspect it. The two central circles were pocked with near two dozen neat round marks from a pistol. "You been practisin', Zoë?"

"Ain't me," said Zoë.

"Then who…"

"I ain't foolin' when I say I'm comin', Captain Reynolds."

Mal turned to see Annie Roberts standing there, Zoë's pistol in her one good hand. His eyes narrowed. "Zoë?"

"Set up a little test, sir," said Zoë. "Curious to see what she could do."

"I can shoot," said Annie. "That's what I been tryin' to tell you—"

"Zoë!"

"She can shoot," said Zoë, and shrugged. "I say we take her."

"That's plain foolishness and you know it," said Mal.

"I still say we take her," said Zoë.

Mal turned to Book. Here, surely, was someone he could rely on to speak sense. "Shepherd," he said. "Tell her."

"I'm inclined to agree with Zoë," said Book.

"Huh," said Mal. "Zoë, are you sure that's all her own work?"

"Sir, I stood here and watched her put every single one of those into that target. Wouldn't be disappointed with that myself."

"That's some good shootin'," said Jayne, coming out of the kitchen towards them, holding the biggest gorram sandwich Mal had seen in some time. "You been practicing, Mal?" He saw both Mal and Zoë glance over at Annie. "No way," he said. "No gorram way—"

"Why do I get the feeling that I've been set up?" said Mal.

"Might be because you have been, sir."

"Ain't that the gorram truth." Mal turned to the girl standing by. "Well, Miss Annie, looks like you're comin' with us after all."

"*What?*" said Jayne. "Now hold on a minute, Mal—"

"If that's the case, Captain Reynolds," said Annie, "looks like you and your crew's hired."

Simon burst out laughing. He quickly covered his mouth. "Sorry," he said and gestured at Jayne. "It's funny, that's all."

Watching Captain Reynolds tryin' to get his people to take his orders was a sight to behold, and I will admit that there were moments during our discussion when I thought my decision to hire this fella and his band weren't perhaps one of my better choices. Eight of 'em, all hunkered round the big old kitchen table, most of 'em with an opinion, most of 'em willing to talk over the rest of 'em to get that opinion out there and none of 'em willin' to do much in the way of listenin'. It was noisy and certainly a long way round to gettin' the job done, because, in the end, Captain Reynolds shouted at everyone to shut up, and when everyone *did* shut up, he then told 'em that he was the one in charge and they could do what he said or else they wouldn't see a penny from this piece of work. I know as well as anyone that money talks, and money certainly talked louder than anyone around that kitchen table that day. They all shut right up.

"Here's what's happenin'," said Captain Reynolds. "Me, Zoë, Jayne…" He glanced at me, shook his head, but carried on. "*And* Miss Annie here—we're off to find Bill Fincher. We'll start with the old Colson farm, see what's goin' on up there, and whether the trail leads to the Collier gang. Meanwhile," his eye fell on the doctor, "Inara, when she arrives, will be approachin' the local Guild with an eye to gettin' introductions into polite society for her friend, the wealthy investor—that's you, doc, in case you'd forgotten."

"Yes," said the doctor, not entirely happily. "Yes. Right."

"You got one of those covers of yours all set up, ready to go?"

Now that piqued my interest. Sounded like this young man was in the habit of using a cover story—but why? There was a tale there, I was sure. I wondered who would tell me, and then wondered whether any of 'em would. For all their bickerin' and quarrelin', Captain Reynolds' crew seemed very tight, in their own way.

"Yes," said the doctor, "that's all fine. Kaylee's been very helpful—"

Kaylee beamed at him. You didn't need half a brain to see what was goin' on there. I suppose the doctor was nice enough. Bit pretty for my taste, and awful gauche too. She was welcome to him—if she could get near him, poor girl. He looked the kind that scared easy.

"Glad to hear that," said Mal. "Kaylee—you and Wash head down into town to find Jacky Colson, get his side of the story."

"But Ca'pn—!" said Kaylee, and while she had been claimin' that she didn't want to get stuck goin' around the rougher parts of town, even I—who'd only known these folks half-a-day at the outside—could see that it was more because she wasn't going to hang around with her young doctor. Harder to tell whether he minded or not, since he was mostly keepin' an eye on his younger sister.

"Kaylee!" said Captain Reynolds, putting a finger to his lips. "What have I said about arguin'? You're going with who I tell you and that's final."

She stopped talking, though she sulked for a while. Sulkin' ain't the best of qualities, but I'll say this for Kaylee Frye: she weren't the kind to stay miserable for long. It was like she carried the sunshine round with her, and she couldn't stop it from lightin' her up.

"What about River?" said the doctor, uneasily.

Shepherd Book put up his hand. "Me and River will rub along together fine here at the house," he said. "We're used to each other's comp'ny these days, aren't we?"

I say there were eight around the table, because that girl, River, hadn't sat down during this whole conversation. She'd been wanderin' round the kitchen, openin' the cupboards, lookin' inside, and I thought, Is she after food? But the table's full... What's she after? And then she found the kitchen timer, a silly old thing that Daddy got for Mamma for her birthday one year, silver and shaped like an apple, and she sat in the rocking chair in the corner, hunched over this with her hair all hangin' down like curtains, and we didn't hear a peep from her for a good while after that. When Book spoke her name, she looked up and held the apple out for us all to see.

"Temptation," she said. "Everyone tempted. Want more than they've got. Core's rotten. Rotten to the core." She twisted the timer round, and the bell went off. She burst out laughing. "Pretty!" she said. "So pretty!"

I didn't know what to make of any of that. As for the crew—that was harder to tell. Seemed like they were used to River, and the way she talked, and yet, at the same time, it was hard not to be unnerved by her. The doctor—her brother—was looking at her with an anxious expression on his face.

"Yep," said Captain Reynolds. "She's stayin' here, and I'll be much obliged to you, Shepherd, if you mind the house."

"That's no problem, Mal," said the Shepherd. "No problem at all." He turned to the doctor. "Happy with that arrangement, son?"

The doctor sighed. "I guess." Remembered his manners. "Thank you."

"Good," said Captain Reynolds, and with that business was concluded. Assignments given; tasks handed out. Everyone went off to get what they needed. Zoë and Jayne went to fill up the

Mule with supplies and everything we'd need for our journey. The doctor went upstairs to borrow some of my daddy's clothes to play his part. And Kaylee and Wash set off into town in search of Jacky Colson. I'd given them the address from Daddy's files and a map. As for myself, I had some packing to do too. I was halfway to the stairs to go up to my room and change into travelling clothes when someone called out my name.

"Annie."

I turned to see Shepherd Book comin' toward me. "Something the matter, preacher?"

"Wondered if we might have a word."

I had an inkling where this conversation might be heading, but I led him into Daddy's study. We went and sat over in the curved window formed by the tower—Grandpa's folly, Daddy called it—in the window seat. I'd spent many hours sitting there reading while he was working, late into the night. Sometimes he'd come and sit beside me, and we've have our 'chats', as he called them, and he'd laugh sometimes and call me his funny old girl. I ain't sentimental, but sitting there with the Shepherd did put me in mind of those times, and how much I'd loved being there with my daddy and how much I wished I could be again... Stop that, now Annie Roberts, I told myself, because those days are done and they ain't comin' back.

"You got somethin' to say to me, Shepherd?"

"Uh-huh. And I reckon you know what it might be. I'm thinkin' you might consider stayin' here with me—"

"Shepherd, that ain't happening, and I'm surprised you're askin'."

He looked awful sad when I said that. "Don't want to see you hurt, little girl," he said. "Seen too much of that, recently..." And I guessed he was thinkin' of that other girl now driftin' around my house. The doctor's sister.

"What happened to her?" I said. "To River?"

He'd been lost in thought, but when I asked that, I saw his eyes sharpen up, quick as you like. Found myself wonderin' again, had he always been a Shepherd? Some fellas, they're born to it, called before they were thought of. Others take a longer road. Seems to me you can tell the difference. Saints and sinners. I ain't sayin' one's better than the other. Seems to me we need both kinds. Remind us of what we can strive toward. Remind us of where we've been.

"I can't rightly say," said the Shepherd. "You'd need the doctor to tell you that, and you might get more of an answer than you bargained for." He smiled at me. "Some people did River great harm, and she's still not right, as you can see. I'm… not sure she'll ever be right again. There's people in the world without pity, Annie, and I don't want any harm to come to you. That's all."

"Already happened, preacher," I said back to him. And I didn't mean what had happened all those years ago, in the crash that killed Mamma and left me the way I am now. I meant Daddy, and what had happened to him, and I saw on the Shepherd's face that he understood. He reached for my hand, and took it between both of his.

"All right," he said, and sighed. "Well, against my better judgement…"

On a whim, I leaned over and planted a kiss on his cheek. I ain't sentimental, by no means, but maybe I'd gotten fond of this fella, saint or sinner, whatever he might have been.

"Pray for me, preacher," I said.

"Already am, little girl," he replied.

5

Everyone was busy after that, gettin' ready to set off on their various assignments. Captain Reynolds was keen to be gone within the hour. "No point hangin' around," he said. "Get the job done." We were almost on our way when there was a knockin' at the door. I could see that the captain was hopin' this would be his Companion friend, but I'd had a string of visitors since the funeral, and didn't see why today would be any different. Wouldn't mind so much if everyone who came brought something for our collection drive, but not many did.

"Maisie," I said, as she went to answer the door, "if that's company, be sure you don't let 'em near Daddy's study." I knew everything was still laid out there, you see, and I didn't want pryin' eyes looking over what I'd been showin' the captain and the Shepherd and the doctor. Maisie came back after a minute or two to say that Mayor McQuinn of all people was there to see me, and she'd shown her into the parlor. "Excuse me," I said to the company, and went to go and see what the mayor wanted. Captain Reynolds followed me down the hall.

"Mind if I tag along?" he said.

"Any particular reason why?" said I.

"This mayor of yours," said he. "She powerful? Or she one of them officials ain't got nothing more than a loud voice and a big hat?"

"Hard to say," said I. "She's not been mayor more than a coupla months. Nobody expected her to win. The old mayor, he was the favorite. In with the de Cecilles, and those rich old families."

"Your daddy liked McQuinn?"

What kind of a question was that? "My daddy liked everyone."

"Huh." A frown settled on that craggy face of his. "Well, wouldn't mind a look at her, see her first hand."

"Fine by me. But mind yourself, please. This is my house and my rules."

He touched his brow. So, he did have some manners. "I'll try, Miss Annie. I'll surely try."

Together we went into the parlor. Mayor McQuinn was sitting over by the window, and when she saw me come in, she smiled and rose to her feet. Good manners, I'd give her that, but then politicians always put on a good show. When she saw Captain Reynolds behind me, she covered her dismay pretty darn quick.

"Annie," she said. She had a nice voice, deep for a woman, measured, and her accent made clear she was from Abel too. A point in her favor. "I didn't realize you already had comp'ny."

"This is my friend Captain Reynolds," said I.

"Pleased to make your acquaintance, ma'am," he said to the mayor, very prettily, and I couldn't fault him there.

"May I ask…" she eyed him. "May I ask why he's here?"

"You may ask," I said, "but it's my business, ma'am, and mine alone."

"Uh-huh," she said. "Well, Annie, I've been speakin' with Sheriff Peters, and he seems to think that this gentleman here in the brown coat is goin' lookin' for Young Bill Fincher for you."

"Like I said, ma'am," I said, "my business is my own."

She was looking most uncomfortable. Lowerin' her voice, not that it would make much difference, she said to me, "Do you remember what I told you, the day of your father's funeral?"

"It was the day of my daddy's funeral, ma'am," I said. "I ain't likely to forget a moment of it."

"I made a promise to you," she said.

"And that was kind of you, but I ain't seen any sign of that promise coming true."

"Annie—"

"Everyone knows who killed Daddy and nobody's liftin' a finger to bring Fincher to justice. So I'm seein' it done, and done right. Ma'am, I ain't bein' rude, and I ain't bein' awkward. But this is between me and Captain Reynolds now."

"Ah yes," she said, looking over at him. "Captain Reynolds. You know, I've been askin' around, tryin' to find out a little about you."

"Woulda thought you were a busy woman, Mayor," he said. "City to run. Gangs on the loose. Plenty more for you to be worryin' about than me."

"You're right," she said, "the city's my concern. And I don't like seein' freelancers—offworlders—comin' in, getting involved in affairs that they might not know well enough to leave alone—"

"Miss Annie here asked me to come," he said. "And I have to say, ma'am, it ain't a pleasant sight, to see a young woman like this, left to take care of herself, and it's an even less pleasant sight to see a mighty powerful person like yourself comin' to her door in the middle of her mournin', tryin' to lean on her."

"Lean on her?" said the mayor. "You think that's—"

"Ain't thinkin' anythin', ma'am," he said. "Sayin' what I see."

"Are you now? Well, Captain Reynolds, shall I say to you what I see?"

"Free city, ma'am, and you're the mayor of it."

"Well, then. I see a buncha rogues, takin' advantage of those in distress."

"You think that's—"

"Ain't thinkin' anythin', captain. Sayin' what I see."

"Mayor McQuinn," by the Good Lord, I was angry now, "I'm going to have to ask you to leave now."

"Annie!"

"Miss Roberts, please, ma'am. We ain't on first-name terms. I know you knew my daddy, but you don't know me. Or else you wouldn't have come here today and spoken like this."

She looked from me to Captain Reynolds, and back again, and then she stood. "Miss Roberts," she said. "I've offended, and for that I would like to apologize." She nodded over to the captain, but I'd say her look to him was a darn sight frostier than the one she gave me. "And to you, Captain Reynolds. That's not why I came—quite the opposite." She looked again at me, and I got the impression she was worried. "Annie…" She sighed. "Miss Roberts. Your daddy counted me a friend. I hoped you would too but… I plainly have some work to do yet on that score. I don't want to see you hurt—"

"I won't be."

She sighed. With a shake of her head, she seemed to decide she could take my word as final, and was about to take her leave, when there was a knock at the door, and Maisie looked in. "Miss Annie," said she, "there's a lady here to see Captain Reynolds."

"A lady friend, captain?" said the mayor.

"Says her name's Inara Serra."

"She's a friend," said the captain. "The last of my crew."

I knew who it was now. The Companion.

"Last of your crew?" said the mayor. "How many of you under Miss Roberts' roof right now?"

Well, that got my hackles risin', and right then I didn't care if she were a Companion or no, this Miss Serra was welcome in my house. "However many there are," said I, sharply, "they're my guests and my business. Show her in, please, Maisie."

I won't forget the sight of Inara Serra comin' into the parlor; she put me in my mind of one of them poems Mamma loved so much and used to say to me. *She walks in beauty, like the night…* She came over to me, took my hand and looked me right in the eye, and said, "Miss Roberts, I'm very grateful to you for allowing me to visit."

"Well," said the mayor. "Goodness me."

Miss Serra turned to her, all grace and poise. Captain Reynolds cleared his throat. "This is, er, Mayor McQuinn, Inara," said he. "She's, er, the mayor—"

"I gathered that, Mal," said Miss Serra. "Mayor. I'm very pleased to meet you."

"Well," said the mayor. "Yes. I mean… Likewise."

"The mayor here," said Captain Reynolds, clearly enjoyin' her discomfort, "is concerned that Miss Annie here has fallen into bad company."

"You mean she's been talking to you, Mal?" said Miss Serra, and though she gave a laugh that sounded like silver bells, I heard a little edge underneath. I don't think Mary McQuinn caught it, mind you. She was still flabbergasted at this wondrous sight that had come from nowhere into our midst. "Mayor McQuinn," Inara said. "I've known the captain for several years now, and let me assure you that he is a man of… honor, and whatever promises he has made Miss Roberts, he will keep. You have my word on that."

"Oh," said the mayor. "Well." She looked at me. "Miss Roberts…"

"You may call me 'Annie'," I said.

"Annie." The mayor sighed and shook her head. "I still say— it would be best if you leave this well alone."

"My mind's made up, ma'am."

"Then thank you for your time, Annie, and I hope this…"

She looked at the captain and Miss Serra. "I hope none of you come to any harm." She nodded. "I'll see myself out."

She left, and we waited till the front door closed. Then Captain Reynolds said, "Have to say, Inara, you hit the ground running there, and for that I'm mighty—"

"Mal," said Miss Serra, with more than a touch of irritation in her tone. "*What* is going on?"

"They took my boat," he said. "They took *Serenity*."

Seein' his face, I felt pretty bad about my hand in that. But I kept myself steely. How else would I have got him to do things the way I wanted? Once this job was done, and I'd seen Bill Fincher brought to justice, and whoever else lay behind this—well, then I'd add the fine to his fee, and he'd be no worse off. In the meantime, best I kept my cards close to my chest. After all, I'd only met this fella for the first time this morning.

"Oh Mal," said Inara, softening ever so slightly. "I suppose we'd better get her back." She looked away. "For Kaylee's sake, I mean."

"Yes," he said, after a moment. "For Kaylee's sake."

Whatever lay between these two (and it was plain something did), it didn't stop Ms Serra falling in with the captain's plans straight away. And that was that. Within the hour, we were in the Mule and on our way, out into the country—Captain Reynolds, and Zoë, and that big fella, Jayne, who I assumed was goin' to prove his worth at some point (size of that gun promised much but might yet deliver little). And me. Anne Imelda Roberts, headin' out into the country, to bring her daddy's killer to justice.

"Why do you and I always get the *lousy* jobs?" grumbled Kaylee.

Wash, looking down Main Street, kind of agreed. Yell City's main drag had that faded look towns get when the money is running out. Flashy old signs saying things like SALE! SALE! and BIG

BARGAINS HERE. Tattered posters for Blue Sun luxury goods that surely nobody could afford. Nothing to fill you with confidence that Abel was an up-and-coming world with a bright future ahead.

"Do we get sent to the *fancy* bits of town to talk to the *fancy* kinds of people?"

The whole place looked like it was one bad piece of luck shy of falling apart.

"Oh no. Not us. We get to go to the *slums*. Wash, is that really what the cap'n thinks of us? His *engineer*. His *pilot*. Are we the *slummy* ones?"

Wash, perhaps unwisely, said, "At least we're not going hunting after a gang of cold-blooded killers. If I get to not be the one doing the cold-blooded killer-hunting, I'll take being slummy."

"Huh," said Kaylee. "You say that *now*. But look at this place! Think this isn't full of rascals and scoundrels... and, and... people that do shenanigans?"

Shenanigans?

"And if we get *hurt*, it's not like we have a *doctor* with us to do anything about it."

Now Wash knew what was going on. It wasn't that Kaylee was cross about heading for what you might call the less salubrious parts of Yell City. It was that she wasn't doing it in the right company. Wash tried to think through his options here. He could try to cheer Kaylee up, but there wasn't much he could see that would be helpful in the cheering-up-of-the-Kaylee. The clothes in the shops looked like they were all second-hand and that would be more in the line of enraging-the-Kaylee-further ("Not even *new* clothes for us, Wash!"). He could try to pretend he couldn't hear her, but that was... kinda *hard?* Also, she might get cross about him ignoring her, and Wash didn't like people being cross with him. So, there was only one thing left to do.

"Um, Kaylee..."

"What?"

"Er, I have a confession to make."

She eyed him. "What is it?"

"I think I've had the map upside down…"

"*What*?"

"I think we've been going in the wrong direction? Maybe? Maybe not? Map's a bit confusing?"

"Oh, *Wash*!" Kaylee reached over and took the map from him. "If you want a job doin'," she muttered, turning it round until she knew where they were. "This way…."

Wash followed her. Yes, a distraction. That always worked, and Wash didn't mind playing the fool because most people thought he was something of a fool anyway. Which, in fairness to them, he probably was, but in what he hoped was a *nice* way.

"Oh, well, at least we haven't gone too far out of our way," said Kaylee, after a minute or two. Which, well, *no*—since Wash wasn't a fool, actually, at least when it came to map-reading.

"But we need to go down there," said Kaylee, pointing to a side street on the other the road.

"You're the boss," said Wash.

"You betcha," said Kaylee. As they crossed the road, dodging a couple of beaten-up hovercars and passing a fairly greasy-looking diner, Kaylee elbowed his arm. "Hey you," she said.

"Hey me?"

"You're okay."

"Back atcha."

"Ugh," she said, looking down the side street. "*Miserable*."

"I know," he said. "Stuck with the lousy job. So let's show 'em what we're made of."

She took a deep breath. "Okay."

* * *

If Main Street was shabby, the further away they got from it, the more desperate the town became.. A couple of people stopped them as they walked past, asking for money, and Wash soon emptied his pockets. "Damn," he murmured. "This is *sad…*"

They walked for about half an hour through narrow lanes of tenements before they got to the street they were looking for. "Number twelve," said Kaylee. "Can't be too hard to find…"

Turned out to be harder than they'd thought. None of the buildings were numbered. The only thing that seemed to distinguish them was a red symbol spray-painted on some of the walls. A five-pointed star, with one of the diagonal lines, from top right to bottom left, missing. Wash, pointing it out to Kaylee, said, "What do you think that is?"

"Dunno."

"And why is it on only some of the buildings?"

"Wash," she said. "I really don't know."

"Okay, okay… Just wondering, that's all…"

On the steps of one building stood a young woman looking out over a couple of kids playing. Kaylee went over to ask her directions, but after only a brief chat the woman shook her head and turned her back. Kaylee, coming back to join Wash, said, "She wouldn't talk to me. Wouldn't say a word. I said Jacky Colson's name and she clammed up."

"People might be scared, given what happened to his lawyer…"

"'S'pose," said Kaylee, looking round. "Maybe we're just lost."

Wash looked down at the map. This was definitely the right district. This was definitely the right street. But why was the right building proving so difficult to find? He glanced up and saw a few people dotted here and there, watching them. He smiled and waved. Tried to look unthreatening. Did they think he and Kaylee meant trouble? He couldn't think of two people less likely to cause anyone trouble. Still, he couldn't shake the feeling that folks weren't keen on having them around.

"Wash," said Kaylee, nudging him hard.

"Ow. What?"

"I got an idea." She pointed across the road where a little girl, maybe six or seven, span around on her heels, looking bored. "Let's see what she'll tell us."

They crossed the road. The girl, seeing them approach, stopped spinning and stood stock still, staring at them with big eyes. Her face was grubby and her shirt, a couple of sizes too big, had been patched up too many times to count.

"Hey!" said Kaylee, kneeling down to speak to her. "You know where we can find number twelve?"

The kid stared at her.

Kaylee reached into her pocket. "You know what I got in here?"

The kid shrugged.

Kaylee brought out a little silver chain. Nothing she'd miss too much. The boy who'd given her it was nice enough but not really anything special either. Kaylee's tastes were a mite more sophisticated these days. The girl's eyes lit up at the sight of such treasure. "How d'you like this? Shiny, huh? You take us to number twelve—it's yours."

The girl's eyes narrowed. She stuck out her hand: *Give it to me now.*

"Nuh-huh," said Kaylee, shaking her head. "Paid when the job's done. That okay? Look, you take this hand of mine, and I'll hold the chain in the other, and you'll see I ain't plannin' on cheatin' you."

The kid hesitated, and then took Kaylee's hand, dragging her— and Wash in tow—down the street. Halfway down, she stopped and pointed at the nearest building, and then held out her hand.

"Number twelve?" said Kaylee.

The kid nodded.

Wash took a look at the building. Nothing to distinguish it from the rest, not even that piece of red graffiti. Place wasn't deserted though.

Outside the front door was a man sitting on a plastic chair. Mid-thirties, short black hair, wearing a black t-shirt. He was working at fixing what looked like a piece from a hovercar engine—grav stabilizer, Wash thought—and yet watching them closely.

Kaylee pooled the chain into the kid's hand. "See? I promised. You done a good job. Thank you."

The kid stuffed her prize in her pocket and followed behind as they went up to the house. The man sitting there shook his head.

"Well, well, well. I admire your courage, mister."

"Courage?" said Wash, anxiously. Courage was the last thing he wanted to be mistaken for having.

"That's a mighty brave shirt."

"Oh," said Wash, tugging at it. "Thank you. One of my favorites."

"Huh," said the man.

"Does Jacky Colson live here?" said Kaylee.

The man's eyes narrowed. "Why you askin'?"

"We're here to help—"

"Help?"

"We're working for Annie Roberts," said Kaylee. "Isaac Roberts' daughter. You heard of Isaac Roberts?"

"Everyone on Abel's heard of Isaac Roberts," said the man. "What's his daughter hired you for? Heard she ain't one spends money freely."

"Well, she ain't happy about the circumstances surroundin' her father's death," said Kaylee. "Asked us to look into 'em."

"Asked you two?" said the man. There was a note of disbelief in his voice that Wash didn't find particularly complimentary. He might take umbrage, whatever that was.

"Our whole crew," said Kaylee. "But us," she patted her chest and nodded at Wash, "we're investigatin' whether there's more to the killin' than meets the eye."

"And you want to speak to Jacky Colson."

"That's right," said Kaylee.

This, thought Wash, wasn't going anywhere. He made a move towards the door. The man stuck out his leg to make it clear that the way ahead was shut.

"I mean," said Wash, "we don't *have* to come in, but we'd *like* to. If that's okay? Is that okay?"

"No," said the man.

"Hey!" said Kaylee. "We don't mean no trouble. I mean— *look* at us! Do we look like trouble? I fix the engine on a ship, and he flies the ship. We are perhaps the *least* troublesome people on Abel right now."

"And yet here you are, on my doorstep, takin' up my mornin'."

"We're here to help," said Kaylee. Her eye had fallen on grav stabilizer. "You know," she said. "You're makin' a real mess of that. You're gonna break it for good. Let me do it." She reached over and plucked the part from the man's hand.

"Hey!" he said. Oh no, thought Wash. Oh, no, no, no…

"You gotta handle these gently, you see," she said. She bent a few wires, twisted a few others. "You watchin'? It'll happen again and you'll want to know how to do this. Got it?" She handed it back. "All shiny now! Mr Colson home?"

"Huh," said the man, after looking it over a couple of times. "Miss…"

"Oh, Kaylee's fine."

"Well, Kaylee, thank you for your assistance. So you want to talk to Jacky?"

"Yep."

"Despite knowing full well what happened to the last fella who tried to help Jacky Colson?"

"Um," confirmed Wash.

"I'll take that as a yes," said the man.

"We know," agreed Kaylee, with a sad smile. "Really. That's why we're here to help."

"Hired by Annie Roberts, huh?" The man looked at them thoughtfully. "Sheriff Peters given up on the case?"

"Ain't passin' any comment on Sheriff Peters," said Kaylee, smiling brightly. "But maybe he needs a helpin' hand."

The man's lips twitched into a smile of their own. Then he spoke to the kid, who was still hanging around and been listening to the whole conversation. "Nance," he said. "Go find your daddy. Tell him he's got visitors."

The kid turned and ran off at a fast pelt.

"Meantime," the man stood and pointed to the door. "Miss Kaylee and, er… you there, fella, with your shirt, kindly follow me."

Inside, the building was bare. Never good, thought Wash, when the main decoration in a place was the damp on the walls. Their guide led them up three flights of stone steps to the topmost landing. There was a door on each side, and he tapped on the one on the right. "Lucy," he said. "It's Ryan. Some folks here with me. Come to see Jacky."

"Jacky ain't here," called a voice from within.

"I know, Luce," he said. "Sent Nance to get him."

The door opened a crack. A young woman peered out. "Who've you brought here, Ryan?" she said. "I don't know these people."

"Please," said Kaylee. "We're here to speak to Jacky. We think we might be able to help."

"She seems okay to me," said their guide—or Ryan, as Wash could now call him, though of course they hadn't been formally introduced... "Can't say much more about this fella other than no-one tryin' to be unnoticed wanders round in a shirt like that."

"Are you Missus Colson?" said Kaylee.

The woman glanced at Ryan, who nodded. "I am."

"I'm Kaylee Frye, and this is Hoban Washburne. Wash to his friends, and I hope you'll soon be countin' us as friends. We really are here to help."

"Jacky said not to open the door to strangers," said Lucy Colson.

"I'm here," said Ryan. "These two ain't gonna be a match for me. And it might be worth hearin' 'em out at least."

There was a pause, then the woman opened the door fully. Wash looked round a room that somehow managed to feel cramped without much in the way of furniture. An empty table; couple of chairs; kitchenette. There was a baby in a highchair, and another scrap of a kid playing with some blocks in the corner who looked up at them with huge eyes. The woman—Lucy Colson—was leaning with one hand on the table, the other resting on the bump on her stomach. *Ah hell*, thought Wash.

She said, "What do you two want with my Jacky?"

Kaylee glanced at Wash. He nodded. You do the talking here, Kaylee. He was glad it was the pair of them that had come. The least-threatening among *Serenity*'s crew. Imagine Jayne walking in here...

"Missus Colson," she said. "We're from off-world. We're here on account of Miss Annie Roberts—"

"Annie *Roberts*?" Lucy suddenly looked frightened. "Ryan, I don't think this is a good idea—"

Wash opened his mouth to speak, but he didn't get the chance. Footsteps outside, coming up the stairs. A man bursting into the room. Looked frantic; looked scared. Waving around what looked like a pistol... *Lǎo tiān yé*, thought Wash, that really *was* a pistol, and the way this fella was swinging it around he might do someone some real damage—

"Get out," cried the man. "Get the *hell* out of here!"

"Cover stories," said Inara. "You're turning into quite the undercover agent, Simon."

"I hope not," said Simon, tugging off the latest tie he'd tried on and throwing it onto the bed. "They're... Well, it seemed like something useful to have in my pocket, that's all. If Mal was going to keep on pulling me into his schemes. Which..." He threw up his hands. "Despite my better judgement, here we are again."

"It's a very good idea," said Inara. She reached for the tie which Simon had so unceremoniously discarded, and began to roll it up.

"It was the Shepherd's idea. He had some good advice on how to set things up too."

"Of course," said Inara, putting the tie away in the drawer. "Doesn't every preacher have a full set of cover stories in their back pocket?"

They gave each other that look, often shared among *Serenity* crew, that said something on the lines of: If he was always a preacher, we're more of a ship of fools than we look. Still, it was part of the unspoken pact on board Mal's ship that the crew didn't scrutinize other people's personal histories too closely. A custom which Inara approved of warmly. She wasn't sure she was going to find a place anything like *Serenity* again in a hurry... She turned her attention to the contents of the drawer and plucked out another tie. "Try this."

"They make me look like a lawyer," grumbled Simon. "Worse, they make me look *fifty*. Aren't I supposed to be some kind of sophisticated man of money from the Core?"

"That will come mostly in performance," said Inara. "But clothes certainly help." She went over to the wardrobe and rummaged around. It was generous of Annie Roberts to let them use her late father's clothes. Annie hadn't struck her as the sentimental type, but she plainly loved her father very deeply, and even the sturdiest person might baulk at seeing someone else in the clothes of someone they had loved and lost. Inara thought she might delay letting Simon back downstairs until she was sure Annie was on the road.

"Any luck?" said Simon.

"Give me a moment…"

Inara soon found a suit at the back of the wardrobe which might do the trick. From the quality of the material and the precision of the cut, far better than anything else she'd found so far in this wardrobe, Inara was fairly sure this hadn't been made on Abel. Hadn't Annie said something about her father studying at the Core? Maybe he'd had this made out there. The only worry now was that it would look hopelessly out of date. She turned to hand the suit over to Simon. He had taken off the previous one, and Inara could see the scar on his leg, where the bounty hunter, Jubal Early, had shot him. She touched her lip. Early had hurt her too, but nowhere near as badly as he'd hurt Simon.

"I hope I can do this," Simon muttered, pulling on the new suit. He'd had to guide Zoë through operating on him to get the bullet out. There was no doubt Simon could be annoying at times, and smug (and he had made some *bad* mistakes with Kaylee), but you certainly couldn't say he lacked courage, or conviction.

"You'll be fine, Simon," said Inara, gently.

He put on the tie. "Well?" he said. "Satisfied?"

"Oh yes," she said. This suit was much more the kind of thing she'd been hoping for. Well made, good fabrics, and—to her relief—a classic style that never went out of fashion. You could wear this back at the Core, and not look out of place. You'd look serious, someone who wasn't careless about their appearance, but wasn't vain. Someone who was focused on what was important. Was that the kind of young man that Isaac Roberts had been?

The suit made a difference to Simon too. He relaxed, and began to look like he was inhabiting the part. Someone for whom everything had come easily. Someone who expected the world to present them with good things. Someone for whom doors opened and the way ahead was clear. Simon had been that kind of person, like Inara too had been—once upon a time.

"It looks good on you, Simon," she said. "Shall we go?"

In the kitchen, Book and River were playing chess.

"How do I look?" said Simon.

"Splendid," said Book, distantly, entirely focused on the board.

"Live man walking," said River. "Dead man's clothes."

Simon sighed. "I'll take that as a seal of approval from both of you. Although I do find myself wondering why people keep on challenging River to games."

"Humility's a virtue, son." Book looked up. "Yes, very smart, both of you."

River, picking up the little silver apple timer, twisted the two halves round. The bell rang. "Time's up, preacher man," she said. "Make your move, or surrender." Book reached out for one of his bishops, and River giggled. Inara, who could see that Simon was starting to fret, put her hand on his arm and moved him gently away.

"They'll be fine," she said. "Come on. We have work to do."

Outside, their hired hovercar was waiting for them. Simon put on his shades (Inara knew that they helped him bypass retinal security scans), and they were soon on their way.

The buildings used by the Companions' Guild were located not far from the Roberts' house. Security seemed to be unusually tight. A couple of guards, issued with pistols and wearing uniforms bearing a Rising Sun logo, politely but firmly prevented their hovercar from entering the grounds, and they were subjected to a series of checks and questions. They were instructed to leave the hovercar before being granted admission. They complied and were allowed access to the House. Inara, leading Simon up the steps, was beset by the usual mixed emotions that she felt whenever she visited such a place these days. The sense she always had of coming back to somewhere familiar, but complicated now by the feeling that homecomings were no longer in her reach. Her shuttle, maybe; *Serenity*, perhaps, and the people there, people like... No. She wasn't going to pick at that particular scar.

At the Guild House, Inara gave her name, and there was another round of security checks. At last, however, they were taken through to a comfortable room to await the head of the house. Their cover story was straightforward enough: they were travelling here on business, but their bags and other identificatory details had been mislaid in transit, and they were hoping that the Guild House could lodge them until they had been found. The head of the house, Meya Vitale, was thrilled to have a visit from a Sihnon-trained companion, and went out of her way to help. As they sat together in Vitale's rooms, drinking tea and making charming conversation, Inara felt a pang of guilt at the subterfuge. Simon, at least, was playing his part beautifully: Lucas Amery, an angel investor based on Londinium, who had heard there were opportunities on Abel these days.

"I was surprised to see so much security around the house," said Simon. "Have you been having trouble here?"

Vitale refreshed his cup of jasmine tea. "The House hasn't been targeted—not yet, at any rate. But the situation in Yell City has been getting steadily worse this year, and tempers flared up over the summer."

"Flared up?" Simon gave the kind of frown that a wealthy man might give on discovering that the place in which he intended to invest was not such an easy market. "That doesn't sound promising. Was there serious trouble?"

"I'll be honest with you," said Vitale. "It's been a difficult couple of years here on Abel, particularly for the farmers. The drought brought many of them to the city, and there isn't enough work to go round. The farmers are willing to undercut the locals, work for pittance. It's all very tense, and one has some sympathy with the locals too. Why should they accept a cut in their standard of living? But what else are the farmers supposed to do? It's that or camp on the streets."

"We saw a glimpse of that on our way over from the space docks," said Simon.

"So very sad," murmured Inara. She had been keeping a low profile in this conversation, letting Simon establish himself and his credentials. She thought he was doing very well. His body language was completely different. He sat relaxed in his chair, open and confident, nothing like his usual buttoned-up self. If she didn't know better, she might even think he was enjoying himself. "I saw children…"

"It's desperate." Vitale shook her head. "Abel was always such a pleasant place. Good weather, relaxed way of life. Came through the war with hardly a scratch. One would have thought good times were coming. But something has gone wrong." She eyed Simon. "We need investment, you know, and urgently, if the situation isn't going to deteriorate further."

"I guess that's why I'm here," said Simon. "Although naturally I want a return on investment. I don't want to be throwing platinum away. But why do you think the Guild might be a target?"

"People are finding grievances wherever they can," said Vitale. "There seems to a feeling among some in the city that the Core isn't helping. That either the money isn't coming in, or it's going to the wrong people. The Guild is tarnished by association."

"So why choose Rising Sun to look after the place?" asked Simon. "Doesn't that make you look more pro-Core? Wouldn't you be safer with people from the sheriff's office at the door?"

Vitale laughed. "I wish! Poor Ned Peters is just about keeping his office afloat. I've never seen a man so eager for retirement. But perhaps you're right and using Rising Sun might make us a target. I should give that some thought."

"There are many independent operators out there," said Inara. "I imagine that if you went on the Cortex, you'd easily find someone to hire to look after the place."

"Sounds like the Collier gang," said Vitale.

"Who?" said Simon, innocently.

"Local bunch of vigilantes." Vitale shuddered. "I'd hate to hire anyone like that to look after the place."

"Indeed not," said Inara, sweetly.

"You know someone might take on the job?"

"If I think someone suitable, I'll let you know," said Inara.

"There are some real rogues out there," said Simon. He drained his cup and put it to one side, then draped his arm casually across the arm of the chair. "You might be better off with what you have."

Vitale sighed. "It's so difficult. Some of the people looking after the place—they lost their farms in the drought. It's not their fault they've taken whatever jobs are on offer. I can't exactly fire them… I suppose I could ask them to take off those badges…"

"It's not their fault either if Rising Sun is offering the same service as the sheriff's office, but at a cheaper rate," said Simon. "Perhaps this is the shake-up that Abel needs to start running itself more efficiently." He gave a rather chilly smile. "It's better for everyone, in the long run."

Inara's eyebrows almost lifted. He really was getting to grips with the part. She wondered who he was channeling. She sipped her tea and stayed quiet. How easy it was, these days, to let the lies slip out, she thought. Another reason to get away from *Serenity*. Everything was becoming blurred. Everything was slipping out of focus. This feeling that she was losing herself—couldn't be allowed to continue. She let Simon carry the bulk of the conversation, and, by the end of the meeting, they were all on very cordial terms, with Inara invited to use the House as her base while she was in the city. Better than that, they had been promised introductions to Abel's elite. There was a charity event that evening, in fact, a recital at City Hall followed by a drinks party, for which an invitation would be procured. In the meantime, Vitale said, they should relax.

At last, they went up to their rooms. Simon kicked off his shoes, yanked off his tie, and collapsed onto the nearest chaise longue. "I'm exhausted," he said. "And *starving*. I'd forgotten how tiring small talk can be."

"Don't switch off entirely," said Inara. "We have a party to go to later."

Simon groaned. "Parties… We'd be better setting up a meeting with someone from Rising Sun Enterprises—"

"Don't underestimate events like this, Simon," said Inara. "They're sources of excellent information—"

"Gossip, you mean."

"Intelligence," she insisted. "You'll see. There'll be someone from Rising Sun there, and we'll get inside much more easily if the introduction seems to arise naturally, rather than us tracking them down. Make them feel that they're courting us, rather than the other way round."

"I guess," said Simon. "I suppose we will learn something. If there's anything *to* learn, that is…"

"What do you mean?"

"I'm… I'm not sure there's really some big conspiracy at work here, Inara. Don't get me wrong, I think what's happened to Annie Roberts is appalling. But she's grieving, and it's natural for her to look for someone to blame. But that doesn't make it true."

"You don't think there's anything for us to find?"

"At the very most, someone might have suggested that Abel would be a better place without Isaac Roberts taking on uncomfortable cases—"

"That sounds like a conspiracy to me, Simon."

"Murder, yes. Conspiracy? Let's see. But there won't be anything in *writing*, Inara. It's not like whoever it is sat down with Collier and Fincher and drew up a contract. We'll never be able to *prove* anything."

"Still," she said. "At least we get to go to a party."

"Oh yes," he said, grimly. "What fun *that's* going to be."

There was a knock at the door, and two of the younger Companions arrived, arms full of clothing and other accessories for them both. Inara sifted through the clothes, which, whilst not quite the quality she was used to, were nevertheless well made and tasteful. She could certainly pull together a more than suitable outfit from them for the occasion. "Come on," she said. "See what you like in all this."

"What?" said Simon, peering up her, and sounding completely confused.

"For tonight. You need to pick something to wear for tonight."

"Not another suit… Do I really need to change into another suit?"

He was trying on a third outfit—and looking very close to mutiny—when there was another knock at the door. This time it was Vitale, looking somewhat anxious.

"Something the matter, Meya?" asked Inara.

"The event this evening," she said. "It's been cancelled."

Simon looked up, just about hiding his relief. "Any particular reason why?"

"That's what's worrying me," said Vitale. "The organizers said they were concerned about security round City Hall."

"Yell City is turning out to be somewhat more febrile than advertised," said Simon, snapping back into his cover persona. "Is this an everyday occurrence?"

Vitale went to some length to assure him not, but she wasn't entirely convincing. Reading between the lines, Inara sensed that the trouble was running deep. An event like this would be an understandable target, thought Inara, in a city where poverty was out there for everyone to see on almost every sidewalk. The sight of those untouched by it, dressing in their finery and enjoying luxury food... One could see how that might make people angry.

"It was supposed to be raising money for local charities," said Vitale, unhappily.

Which might make the idea rather worse. "Don't worry," said Inara, warmly. "I'm sure there'll be other occasions very soon."

When Vitale was gone, Simon let out a huge sigh of relief, sounding for all the world like a man whose sentence of execution had been commuted, pulling at his tie like he was loosening the noose. "Can we get on now with trying to set up a meeting with someone at Rising Sun?"

"In a moment," said Inara, turning back to the pile of clothes. She handed him yet another suit. "Try this on first."

"Inara!"

"Try it on!"

"But if we're not going to some stupid recital, why do I need to get changed?" he complained. "*Again?*"

"Simon," she said. "You know as well as I do that you can't wear the same thing to a drinks party that you would wear for a business meeting. *Do* try to enter into the spirit of things."

6

It was a sad old journey out into the country, and no mistake. When I was a little girl before we lost Mamma and things changed for me, I recall many happy times out in these parts. The three of us went, a coupla times, to visit my great-aunt, out on her farm in Wilder County. Great-aunt Brenna bred horses, and even though I was small for my age, she insisted I ride with the rest of them. Oh, there's a joy to ridin' you don't find anywhere else! The wind in my hair... Felt free. You can see why people love the kind of life keeps them out here in the country. You can see why people don't want to come to the city. Breaks my heart, thinkin' of all those farms out here can't make it any longer. But if the rains don't come, the rains don't come—and they ain't been comin' for three years now.

I hadn't been out this way for many years because in time the old lady died—as old people are wont to do—and Daddy didn't think he could do the farm justice, so he sold everything to her steward, Old Ted Doughty, and his son, Young Ted. Nice pair of fellas, but I would bet my new black boots that Daddy didn't take anywhere near the real price of that old ranch. Daddy told me Old Doughty died right before the drought began, maybe four or five years ago, and I got no idea what happened to the ranch. Mamma died not long after Great Aunt Brenna, and we didn't have the heart—me and Daddy—to do the things we all used to do when we were three of us, so we didn't leave the city much after that.

Still, God has given me a good brain, and the sense to use it, so I knew how bad things had gotten out in the country. Like I say, there hadn't been a rainy season for three years now, and it had been fairly dry for a coupla years before that. My, but the land was parched. Weren't a patch of green in sight—and this was the fall, remember! When Abel was terraformed, the seasons were made to be reliable and temperate, good for farming. Should have been some rain by now. No wonder all them farms was failing. No wonder Yell City was full to overflowing with those poor fellas lost their lands and their livelihoods, and tryin' to find some work to keep themselves and their families fed. And no wonder too how those city born and bred were blamin' these folks for their own troubles. Lack of work, and gettin' crowded and rundown. Ain't pleased about McQuinn becoming mayor either. Said it weren't fair, her winnin' because of all them farmers comin' into town. Daddy told me there was some talk of preventin' them from votin' in future and you'd have to show you'd been born in Yell City to choose the mayor. That sounds like a fiddle to me, and Daddy agreed.

Captain Reynolds, up front in the Mule, said, "*Lăo tiān yé*, this is a sad old place."

I weren't fond of all this cussin' and blasphemin', but neither did I want to get to quarrelin', so I said a little prayer askin' for forgiveness and instead said, "You a farmin' man, Captain? I mean, before you got into the bounty huntin' business."

"Grew up on a ranch," says he. "Horses. Was a good life." But one he'd chosen to leave behind, seemingly. I wondered what the story was there, but I doubted he'd tell me freely. A shame. I liked to hear 'bout horses. I thought maybe when this was business done and dusted, and Fincher in the ground, I might get myself a little horse. Start to ride again. Well now! Writing this down now, I see that was the very first time that I started to think what life might be like, after all this. After Daddy.

We passed a few abandoned homesteads, boarded up and left to rot. Sorry old sights. You think of the hope people musta had, coming out to these pieces of land, intendin' to live peacefully, plant their crops and earn a livin'. Watch their children grow and thrive, and leave them somethin' good at the end. Somethin' to start them off in life. But those hopes had turned to dust. All flesh is as grass, the Good Book says. I don't say you always find comfort in scripture, but you do find truth.

Coupla hours out from Yell City, we took the road that led up to where the Colson homestead had been. The land out here was as bad as it came. You couldn't eke a livin' from soil this dry. No wonder poor Jacky Colson's farm had failed. My daddy had come out here once or twice, preparing for the case, and when he came home from those trips, he was more fired up than ever. "It ain't fair, Annie," he said. "That young couple worked their fingers to the bone, and they ain't got a thing to show for it but debt. The people who shoulda helped failed 'em. I won't be counted among that number, that's a promise." I guess I'd inherited that promise, in a way, along with everything else. If I could see Jacky Colson done by fairly in turn, that would be a good thing, I thought.

Well, Old Man Sun was past his height by the time we got to what had been the Colson farm, and I could see a faint sheen of one moon in the bright blue sky. It was gonna be a clear fair night, though warmer than we might prefer this time of the year. Zoë pulled the Mule to a halt outside the door to the farmhouse, and she and Captain Reynolds and myself got out for a closer look. That big fella Jayne Cobb stayed put; said he didn't want to leave his guns behind, all lonely like. Never seen no-one as attached to his weaponry as that fella, but I suppose what's been left out in the case of brains has to be made up in brawn. Wouldn't be surprised to learn he had names for each and every one of 'em.

The farmhouse was all shuttered up, front and back, but we found a key beneath a stone by the back door. Captain Reynolds opened up and we entered the kitchen. Oh, that was a sight to break the heart! Jacky and his wife had left the place spick and span, like they were only plannin' to be away for a weekend or something. All the surfaces scrubbed clean, and I was sure as I could be that if we went round the rest of the place, we'd see the same thing. They'd clearly loved this little house. Peeking out through the window, I saw a kitchen garden. A single apple tree, fruit on the branches goin' unpicked, with a tiny swing swaying to and fro in the breeze. I recalled Daddy telling me they had children. Was it two or three? That musta been where they played. All of a sudden, I felt as if I was intruding. That I had no right to be here.

"Captain Reynolds," I said. "We ain't got no call to be here in this house. Let's be movin' on."

"Feelin' like a burglar myself," he said. "Zoë? You done?"

"Can't see any need to stay, sir."

We left, and locked up behind us. But I wasn't quite done here yet. I walked through the kitchen garden into the back field. Zoë caught up with me. "Don't go off by yourself," she murmured.

"I can manage."

"I'd say the same to him," she said, jerking her thumb behind her, meaning the captain. "And to Jayne. We cover each other. Got that?"

"I got it."

We walked across the field. Captain Reynolds caught up with us. At length, we came to a big wire fence, separatin' what had been Jacky's property from the next one along.

"Coupla signs up over there," said Zoë.

"Let's take a look," said Captain Reynolds.

One of them signs was clear enough. You can't get much clearer than: PRIVATE PROPERTY KEEP OUT. And I recognized another sign too. Red lines on a white background, spreading out like the sun in the morning. Red sky morning; shepherd's warning.

"That's them Rising Sun fellas," I said. "But what's this?" I pointed at another sign. Blocky letters, blue and white, over a blue half-circle, with blue characters underneath. "You know this one, Captain?"

"Oh yes," he said. "Blue Sun Corporation." His eyes went real hard when he said that. "*Qǐng wā cāo de liú máng!*"

"Captain Reynolds!" I said. "There ain't no call for talk like that!"

"In this case, I'd say there is," he said. "Gorram Core companies, coming out to the Rim, stealing livelihoods!"

"Think they're the ones behind this, sir?" asked Zoë.

"Feel it in my bones."

Well, I wasn't my father's daughter for nothing. "Feelin' it in your bones ain't gonna stand up in a court of law," I said.

He looked at me. "What you thinkin'?"

"I'm thinkin' we take a pair of wire cutters to this," I patted the fence. "And take a good look round."

"That's breakin' and enterin'," said the captain. "God-fearing girl like you, shouldn't get mixed up in business like that. Shouldn't be havin' ideas like that neither. You'll need to have a long talk with the Shepherd when we get you home, Miss Annie."

"Captain Reynolds," I gathered up my dignity. "I'm servin' a higher purpose. You got some wire cutters in that big old Mule of yours or not?"

Maybe it should have crossed Wash's mind sooner that marrying a lady gunslinger would mean that his exposure to, well, *guns* would become much more frequent, but it wasn't like he went out and about with a gun of his own, and therefore he was of the opinion that he should be able to walk around town and pay a courtesy visit to a young married couple without one of said couple coming running into the room and waving a pistol into this face.

"Woah!" said Wash, holding up his hands. "Hang on there, fella! No, no, no… *absolutely* no need for that!"

"Jacky!" cried Lucy Colson. "The kids!"

"Jacky," said Ryan, his voice quiet but stern. "Don't be a gorram fool."

"I want these folks to go!" said Jacky.

"We will!" said Kaylee. "If you want, we'll go—right now! You don't have to wave that… that *thing* around! We ain't here to cause trouble!"

The kid in the corner, who wasn't old enough to understand what was happening but could certainly pick up on the distress of these grown-ups filling the room, began to wail.

"Jacky, please!" cried Lucy.

The young man wavered—and then the matter was taken out of his hands. Ryan, who had made his way quietly to stand right behind him, grabbed hold of Jacky's wrist, and, through greater force, easily removed the pistol from the other's man grip. Jacky lunged for it, but Ryan held him back. "Leave it, Jacky. Let's sit down and talk this out."

Jacky burst into tears. Wash, who knew how to exert a little quiet authority when necessary, said, "Everyone in this room needs to take a really deep breath and calm *right* down."

"With you there, fella," said Ryan. He checked the pistol over, powering it down. "Goddammit, Jacky," he said, shaking his head. "Where the hell did you get this?"

"Bought it off Bryce at Stacey's Bar," said Jacky, through gulps and sobs.

"In that case, your main worry was it blowin' up in your own face," said Mick. "*Gǒu shǐ*, Jacky! Whatever did you think you were doin' burstin' in here like that? The *kids!*"

Lucy fell into a chair at the table, her head in her hands. Kaylee said, "You know what? I'm gonna make some tea, *dǒng ma?*"

"Good idea," said Wash. "Jacky," he said, putting his hand on the young man's shoulder, "why don't you sit down too?" He gently pushed him towards one of the other chairs. Jacky collapsed into his seat and reached across the table for his wife's hands. "Sorry, Luce."

From across the corridor, a voice called out. "What in the name of the devil himself is goin' on over there?"

Ryan, leaning out of the door, said, "Missus Greyson, any chance you could you take these kids for a little while?"

"You know I will, Ryan Hunter," the voice called back. Less than a minute later, a tiny woman, with a sharp but not unkindly look to her eye, was there, gathering up the toddler and handing the baby to the little girl, Nance (who had seen this whole thing... *Poor kid*, thought Wash). Missus Greyson nodded at Wash and Kaylee, and said, "Who are these two?"

"Friends," said Kaylee, firmly, putting the teapot down on the table. "Here to help."

"'Bout time," said Mrs Greyson, and went on her way, children in tow.

There was an audible sigh of relief from everyone who remained in the room. Kaylee sat and poured out the tea. Wash took the seat over from her. Ryan closed the door and leaned back against the wall, folding his arms. "Well," he said. "You two have caused some trouble."

"Not *really* our fault," said Wash. "I mean, you brought us up here. And—you know—we weren't the ones waving the *pistol* around."

"Fair," said Ryan.

"You said you were here to help us," said Lucy, wearily. "What exactly do you mean? What help you got for us?"

"It's like this," said Wash. "Our crew's been hired to go after the man who killed Isaac Roberts. Our captain, Mal Reynolds, he's off right now trying to track him down."

Jacky looked interested. "Sheriff Peters doing something at last? Didn't think he'd resort to usin' bounty hunters—"

"No-o," said Wash. "Not the sheriff. We've been hired by Annie Roberts."

"Huh." Jacky frowned, thinking that over. After a while, he said, "Suppose I mighta guessed it weren't comin' from the sheriff's office. But ain't Annie Roberts a kid?"

"She's eighteen," said Kaylee. "In possession of a decent fortune and the will to spend it. And so she's hired our crew to bring Bill Fincher to justice. And… and she's asked us to look into who paid him to kill her daddy."

Jacky went white. Ryan gave a short, bitter laugh. "Told you it weren't a spur-of-the-moment thing. Told you there was somethin' else goin' on."

"We don't know that yet for sure," said Wash, holding up his hands to slow things down. "That's why we came here—to ask about the case and find out whether there's something we're missing, or something we can learn—"

"I think you'd better go," said Jacky, very quietly. He looked at his brother-in-law. "You shouldn't have brung 'em here, Ryan."

"Jacky," he said.

"I said to you again and again, I don't want me and Luce and the kids messed up in that world of yours."

What world, thought Wash.

"Ain't like that, Jacky," said Ryan. "Thought they could something for you all—"

"Jacky," urged Lucy, "they said they want to help. Maybe… maybe we can get the farm back—"

"Farm's gone," he said. "It ain't comin' back."

"Jacky, we can't stay here—"

"We're gonna have to, Luce—"

"We can't live this way—"

"You know how hard I'm tryin'—"

Wash looked away, embarrassed to witness this. He caught Kaylee's eye. She was biting her lip, plainly feeling the same way.

"Jacky, I can't go on much longer—"

"Please," said Kaylee. "Jacky—Mr Colson. We're good people. We want to help."

"You know what happened to the last person tried help me, miss?" said Jacky. "Someone walked into his office, shot him dead, and went on his way." He was close to tears again. "Isaac Roberts was maybe the best-loved man in Yell City. They shot him dead in broad daylight, and nobody—*nobody*—been held to account. You think they'll stop for a second before comin' after me? Comin' after Luce, and the kids? You folks want to help? Then keep outta this and leave me and mine alone!" He turned to Ryan. "Same goes for you."

Wash had no answer. The man was making a very good point.

"Jacky," pleaded Lucy, "please, let's hear what they have to say."

But Jacky was shaking his head. He stood up, brushed himself down, gathering together the last shreds of his dignity. "Kind of you to visit," he said, "and kind of you too, miss, to make tea and take care of my Luce in this way. But I'd like you both to go now. And please—don't you ever come back."

Lucy was crying, very softly. Kaylee reached over and squeezed her hand. Then she stood up. "Guess that's clear enough."

"Kaylee?" said Wash.

"We ain't stayin' here if they don't want, Wash," said Kaylee. "Can't force yourself into a fella's home, can you?"

"No," said Wash. "I guess you can't." He got up too, and followed Kaylee out of the door. "Look," he said, turning back. "Maybe we can tell you where to find us? If you change your mind?"

"I won't change my mind," said Jacky.

"Annie Roberts," said Kaylee, to Lucy. "You can reach us through Annie Roberts."

"Go," said Jacky.

They went. Ryan followed them out, closing the door behind them.

"You seein' us out?" said Kaylee. "You don't have to. We're off."

"Seein' you out?" He shook his head. "I'm takin' you for a drink is what I'm doin'."

"Not to Stacey's Bar, I hope," said Wash.

"Not if you want to keep that shirt on your back and your money in your pocket," said Ryan. He was about to head back downstairs when the door across the corridor swung open. Mrs Greyson looked out.

"How're them two poor kids?" she said, nodding over to the other door.

"Give 'em an hour or two, will you, missus?" said Ryan.

"You know I will," she said, and went back indoors.

Ryan took them back down and outside. They walked down the street, turned the corner, and crossed the road. There was a small bar there (not called Stacey's, as promised, Wash saw with relief), and Ryan led them inside. A few people greeted him, eyeing his guests with interest. They sat in a small booth with Ryan on one side, Kaylee and Wash on the other, like they were interviewing each other.

"In case you hadn't worked out," he said. "Lucy's my sister."

"Saw the likeness," said Kaylee.

"Jacky's a good fella and don't deserve any of what's happened to him. But he's going under."

"Yeah," said Wash. "You could see that." He looked round. They were attracting some attention from the other patrons. Not ideal. "Is there anywhere more private where we can have this conversation?"

"No secrets here," said Ryan. "And you might find some folks able to help. People are fond of Luce and Jacky. And they respect me."

Wǒ de mā, thought Wash. He's a gangster, isn't he? "You know," he said, "we've probably caused you enough trouble today."

"Wash?" said Kaylee, with a frown. "What's the matter?"

"I mean, you looked really busy back there on the step, sitting on your—er—chair. Chair-sitting's a frantic activity—"

"Wash?"

Wash made a move to stand and Ryan, reaching over the table, put his hand on his shoulder and pushed him down again, gently but firmly. There was a very big man—Jayne-big (looked like he might be Jayne-nasty too)—blocking the way out of the booth and, when Wash looked back over his shoulder, he could see the door back out onto the street was closed, with another Jayne-sized oaf standing in front, his arms folded.

"Sit down, little fella," said Ryan. "Time the three of us had a real talk."

After everyone left, Book settled down in Roberts' study with River and the chess board. Maisie—nice young woman—came in with fresh tea and tiny cakes, as if that breakfast hadn't been enough. On the whole, Book couldn't complain about how this particular job was panning out for him. The chess tournament was another matter.

"Well, little girl," he said, laying his king down flat. "You got me beat again."

"Another?" suggested River, hopefully.

"You've won three in a row already," Book said, mildly. "And I have the strangest feelin' you'd best me no matter how many games we played."

River lowered her head, concealing her face behind her long hair. She rested her fingertip upon her queen (she was playing black; Book even had the advantage, not that it counted a mite), and began to spin the little piece around. "Queen's going," she murmured. "King's falling."

Book sat back in his seat and contemplated her. River was so much better these days, so radically altered from the traumatized young woman who had emerged screaming from that box all those months ago. He'd prayed hard on that score; hoped that had made some difference. Even now, odd as she was, with these strange things coming out of her mouth, which meant something to her (and were likely to mean something to you too, given time), she was much improved. Nobody on *Serenity* made the mistake of underestimating or ignoring her, these days.

"I've often wondered," said Book, "whether you get bored."

"Bored?" River looked up at him. Well, that had got her attention. Brought her to here and now, the present moment. She was so often off a wanderin' somewhere else.

"Nobody's a match for you, are they?" Book said. "Not even your brother."

River didn't answer right away. She kept spinning the black queen round and round. The chess set—which was being used with Annie's blessing—was particularly fine. Hand-carved, and, if Book was a judge of this kind of thing, had come all the way from the Core. Weren't cheap.

"Preacher," River whispered at last, "*everything's* a match for me."

Book gave her the space to carry on.

"Feel it all," she said. Her hand closed around the black queen, hiding her from his sight. "See it all. No rest… No rest from the noises, the noises in my head. Hear 'em out there on the street with their banners and their slogans and their rage. No rest for the good and no rest for the wicked… No way of stopping it, stopping them… Stopping the buzzing and the whispering and the talking and screaming… I can hear the trees shrivelin' and the crops dyin' and the water boilin' and everything is going in reverse… Simon!" she cried. "I need to tell Simon! Everything's in reverse!"

Ah, but now she was getting upset. That had certainly not been his intention. He reached over the table to still her hand. "It's all right. I'm sorry, River. I didn't mean to upset you."

She pulled a face; a scornful expression. "*I'm* not upset." Her voice was, suddenly, perfectly normal. She opened her hand. The piece was gone. "Queen's here."

Book heard hammering at the front door. Maisie, the maid, hurried past the open door of the study to answer, murmuring, "Oh, now who can this be…"

Book turned back to River. "Did you spirit her away?"

"Who?"

"The queen?"

"She'll try to do that herself."

Maisie came back, looking very flustered. "Shepherd, sir, I don't know what to do…"

Book turned and gave her an encouraging smile. She was a nice young woman, clearly fond of Annie, and had laid on a splendid breakfast for the whole crew, at the drop of the hat. "Can I help, Maisie?"

"It's… there's a visitor, sir…"

"For Annie?"

"Yes, sir. And I don't know what to say to her, I don't know what to do…"

Book stood up. "Want me to see her?"

"If you could, sir, please?"

"Who is it?"

"It's…" Maisie's voice lowered to a whisper. "It's *Madame de Cecille…*"

It was clear that this was supposed to mean something to him, but the name hadn't come up in anything that Book had read so far. Still, he could make a few educated guesses. Worlds like Abel, out on the Rim, for all they made a play of being homespun and no-nonsense, almost invariably had their own oligarchies. And many of these liked to style themselves as aristocrats. Remarkable, he thought, as he smoothed down his shirt, straightened himself up, how many barons and baronets, lords and ladies and suchlike you found out on the Rim. Book wasn't convinced that their family trees would bear much scrutiny. In fact, he was sure of it.

"I think I can find a polite word or two," said Book. He looked at River. She was laying out the chess board again. Perhaps she intended to play against herself. Maisie led him round the bags in the hall into the parlor, and announced him.

"Shepherd Book, ma'am," she said.

Madame de Cecille, who had been standing by the window looking out into the street, turned to greet him.

Now here was a wealthy woman. Rich clothes, haughty manner, natural beauty enhanced by what Book assumed was considerable expenditure throughout the course of her life. Jewels like that didn't come cheap. Smart too, he guessed; from the way she was looking at him that it would be foolish to mistake her for a perfumed doll.

"*Shepherd?*" she said.

"Yes, ma'am."

"I was hoping to speak to Annie," she said. "Where is she?"

"She's unavailable at present," said Book. "May I be of some assistance?"

"Unavailable? Why?"

"Indisposed." Book asked the Good Lord to forgive him that one.

"I'm very sorry to hear that. I didn't know she'd been ill—"

"Grief," said Book, "can bring the best of us low." That, at least, wasn't a lie, so there would be no penance to be sought for that.

His guest, however, was certainly not pleased. "Well, this is an annoyance."

"Perhaps I could pass on a message?" offered Book.

The lady frowned, and studied him closely, as if considering him properly for the first time. "Who *are* you, exactly?"

Book opened out his arms. "I am, as you can see, a preacher."

"I can see that. Where from?"

"Lately of Southdown Abbey, ma'am."

"I haven't heard of it."

"No surprise, ma'am, since we ain't been aimin' to make a name for ourselves."

"No? May I ask what has brought you to Abel?"

"I've been out of the world for a spell." His prepared speech. "Walkin' it a while."

"And you walked all the way to this house?"

He nodded. "That's right."

"May I ask in what capacity you're here? As a minister?"

"A minister, yes. Also, I'm Miss Roberts' guest."

"But she is… indisposed."

Book nodded again, very slowly. He'd found, since leaving the Abbey, that lies didn't in general feel so bad if you didn't say 'em out loud, and he promised the Good Lord that would make amends later for all this prevaricating.

"Well," said the lady, with a sigh that communicated more than a little of her dissatisfaction with this interview, "I wonder if I might leave this, for Annie." From her bag she took out an envelope—thick, creamy, card-like paper, covered in a bold script—and placed it on the nearby table.

"I'll let her know you were here," said Book, "and I'll be sure your message reaches her."

"There's some urgency," said Madame.

"I'll be sure it reaches her soon."

She tilted her head, a small gesture of gratitude, and allowed Maisie to lead her out. When Book was sure that she was gone, he picked up the envelope and opened it. Inside was a thick piece of card, on which was printed, in cursive script, an invitation to a charity lunch that day. Embedded in the bottom left-hand corner of the page was a tiny hologram depicting what seemed to be a rising sun.

"Huh," said Book. Charity lunch. That kind of thing wasn't particularly within the Shepherd's expertise, but he could take a guess at the substance of the event. Lots of fancy folk payin' over the odds for admission, swannin' around with each other in their fancy clothes eatin' fancy food, tellin' themselves it was all for a good cause when it was as much a chance to be seen in the right place and seen to be doin' the right thing. Well, this might not be Book's milieu, but he knew a couple of people might find the event useful.

There was a writing desk by the window, so Book rustled through the drawers until he found more or less the right kind of paper and a nice fountain pen. After that, was a matter of minutes to assemble something similar. Easy enough too to prize out that hologram and fix it in position. On a separate piece of paper, he scribbled a few notes explaining the significance of their hosts. He addressed the envelope to Ms Inara Senna and Lucas Amery, Esq. (care of the Guild House, Yell City), then called for Maisie, who arranged for the thing to be sent directly over. When that was done, Book looked at the original, cannibalized invitation. He could probably fix up something to replace that hologram, but Annie was hardly going to be back in time to attend. Mal wasn't *that* efficient a bounty hunter. Besides, Book had a sense Annie would have no desire to attend such a thing. If the state of her hall was anything to go by, her charitable work was geared towards the practical. He popped the thing into his pocket to dispose of later. This one could stay between him and his Maker.

Back in the study, River was still absorbed in chess. Book, looking down at the board, saw that the pieces were laid out as if for a game, but they were all mixed up: black and white pawns, alternating; a white castle next to a black knight. What did she see, he wondered. What was in her mind?

"Queen's going," said River.

"Queen's gone," said Book.

"No," said River. "Not yet." She wrinkled up her nose. "Her perfume."

"What about it?"

"I didn't like it."

Book gave a smile. "It *was* strong, wasn't it?"

"Not strong," said River, very certainly.

"No?"

"No," she said. "*Rotten.*" She looked up at him and sighed, like a disappointed parent presented with a naughty child. "Have you been telling fibs again, preacher?"

He winked at her. "Only a coupla small ones. Not so's anyone would notice."

"Except your god."

"Except Him."

"Interfering with the mail too?" said River.

"Not so's anyone mortal would notice. You keepin' score, River?"

"Someone has to. But I'll wipe the slate clean," she winked back, "if you make it best of seven."

7

"Relax, fella," said Ryan, as Wash fell back into his seat. "I only want to talk. Find out who you really are and why you've come such a long way to help Luce and Jacky. Ain't nobody does somethin' for nothin', and like Jacky said—the last fella tried to help got shot. I want to know what the catch is."

He waved at the big man, who nodded, and faded away.

"So you're not, um…" Wash was struggling to find a way of asking without offending.

"Not what?" said Ryan.

"Not, well, *gangsters*."

Ryan's expression on hearing that was completely blank. *Āiya*, thought Wash, mighta made myself an enemy here? Then he realized that Ryan was trying to stop himself laughing, and attempt which quickly failed. He roared.

"I don't like it," said Wash, gathering up his dignity, "when people laugh in my face. Which happens more than it should to anyone of my amazing talents."

Ryan started to get control of himself. "Oh, *wā*," he said. "You don't want people to laugh, you shouldn't be so funny."

"All right," said Wash, cautiously. "Thank you? I think?"

"They ain't gangsters, Wash," said Kaylee. "They're organizers." She gave Ryan a bright smile and pointed at the wall. It was covered in stickers bearing slogans like, *Rise Up* and *No Pasaran* and *Workers of the 'Verse Unite* and more than a few with the red symbol they'd seen sprayed all over the walls of the tenements, "You're the union, aintcha?"

"Oh…" said Wash. "Oh!"

"Which one?" said Kaylee. "Not the farmers, I'm guessing."

"Not the farmers, no, though those fellas should start getting themselves organized and stop takin' every scrap of a job Rising Sun sees fit to throw their way. Associated General Workers of Yell City. Transport, logistics, power, communications—the folks that keep this place running." Ryan smiled. "One flick of the switch, and we can bring Yell City to a standstill."

"So definitely not gangsters," said Wash.

"That's the other side," said Ryan. "Them fellas struttin' around places like Westerly district, and Keyside, and that little warren of buildings backs up against the Summertown space docks. Kickin' down doors and pullin' in danger money. They've been tryin' to take over parts of the city, and we've been doin' our best to hold 'em back. Had our candidate on the ballot for mayor—and then…" He snapped his fingers. "Mary McQuinn goes and wins."

"You got a problem with the mayor?" said Kaylee.

"Don't know anythin' about the mayor, that's the problem," said Ryan. "All those people who've been comin' into the city from the farms, she was their person, really. I guess it's funny in a way. All them powerful folks around Yell City thought their fella was goin' to walk the election. And turned out the people they'd foreclosed on, forced out of their farms, they'd all come here in droves, and they're the ones put McQuinn into City Hall." He began to laugh again. "All those big rich folks, they were furious. Serves 'em right. So that's one reason not to mind McQuinn—but I'd rather our girl had won."

Seemed like there were three sides to this, thought Wash. The old opposition—wealthy folk working with Blue Sun. Ryan and his people—the ordinary city workers. And then an unexpected complication—the farmers and their mayor, McQuinn, hungry for work—literally, in some cases—and, from what he could work out, undercutting the city workers' wages.

"You and the farmers," he said. "You think you'd have a common cause."

"You'd think so, wouldn't you?" said Ryan. He sounded exasperated. "I blame the homesteading lifestyle. Makes people believe they can get by on their own. And I ain't sure about McQuinn. Heard she's been talking to Blue Sun about putting private security on the streets."

"Mal didn't like McQuinn," said Wash, thoughtfully.

"Who's Mal?" said Ryan.

"Cap'n of our ship," said Kaylee. "He met the mayor earlier. Said she's tryin' to bully Annie Roberts into sendin' us away What do you think, Ryan? You think there's more goin' on than meets the eye?"

"Jacky surely thinks so," said Ryan. "All that I'll say is that if you folks want to lift up that stone and take a peek at what's crawlin' underneath, you've got my blessin'. Anything that'll help poor Luce and her Jacky and those kids. And no doubt you'll be doin' everyone on Abel a service. But some of the creatures livin' round here—they ain't good people."

"We've worked that out already," said Wash. "I guess... what we don't know is the whole picture. Why this has happened now."

Ryan leaned in. There was a gleam in his eye that Wash wasn't so sure about. He'd fallen in with some activists in his younger days working kitchens, and those fellas were *scary*. Ryan was reminding him uncomfortably of those days. They kept coming knocking on his door, asking him to help them with leaflets and things and Wash had never quite known how to say no. Exhausting few months. Finished him in the hospitality industry too.

"Drought started it," said Ryan. "Though the fault lines have been there since the end of the war."

"As a matter of interest," said Wash, thinking of Mal, "whose, er… whose side were you folks on?"

"Weren't on any side. Alliance? Bunch of graspin' kleptocrats. Independents? Bunch of starry-eyed romantics—they were never gonna win, were they? We ain't here to fight losin' battles."

I'll not mention this part of the conversation to Mal, thought Wash, and caught Kaylee's eye. She nodded her agreement. "So the drought came?" he prompted.

"Drought came; farms failed; city began to fill up—and some folks started to take advantage of that. Setting old-timers against newcomers. Places like Westerly, Keyside—so much trouble folks are scared to walk around. Fellas like Frankie Collier takin' advantage. People don't feel safe. Makes you wonder—who's payin' those fellas, and all those struttin' around town right now totin' some expensive pistols and makin' it clear they think they're above that law. That must be suitin' someone. And next thing you know—same old story. In come the big guns from the Core, those Rising Sun fellas for one, promisin' new jobs—well, ain't that convenient? And I'll tell you what comes next—what happens next here on Abel. Folks in need take the company credits, sign on the dotted line, on the promise that they and their families'll be safe. But they'll find they've signed their rights away. Lost their freedoms—can't draw a line at your workin' hours or can't say what they think without losin' their livelihoods. That's where Abel's headin', and me and my people? We're here to stop it."

Sounded to Wash like the usual kind of conspiracy theory, but Kaylee's eyes were sparkling.

"Anyway," said Ryan, smiling at her. "Our day will come—

and sooner than any of these folks realize."

"Go on," said Kaylee. She was looking far too delighted about all this, thought Wash. "Tell me what you got planned."

"The mistake these people always make," said Ryan, "is forgetting who keeps a city up and running. Who keeps the lights on. And who," he patted his chest, "can switch those lights off."

"Oh," said Kaylee. And then, "*Oh*... You're goin' on strike. When?"

He tapped the side of his nose. "Sooner than you might think," he said. "Let's see McQuinn and Peters keep law and order in a blackout. Let's see if those Rising Sun fellas that have been sniffin' around Abel makin' promises about what they can do come good when it comes to the crunch. My bet is they won't. And soon the mayor will have to come askin' us what it is we want, because this city won't be workin' until she does."

"What do you want?" said Wash, doubtfully.

"Fella, what does anyone want in this 'verse? A decent wage and a decent place to live, and to be sure that it won't all be stolen away at the whim of someone who's already got more than enough. I want guarantees there'll be no more talk of Rising Sun steppin' in to fill the work done by our people. I want the terms and conditions and pay on that work made clear. And if I'm givin' you my wishlist, I want those folks from the countryside who have ended up here to realize that when they undercut us, they're harmin' themselves in the long run. I want McQuinn to show me that she understands that."

All of which sounded peachy, thought Wash, but so far as he could make out, the root of the trouble was the drought—and not even the best organized union in the 'verse could go on strike against the weather.

Ryan smiled at Kaylee. "You and your crew and your cap'n, you've walked into a city on a knife edge, Kaylee. So take care, will ya? Don't go wanderin' about and, er…" He winked. "Especially later tonight."

What? Wash looked round the bar. More and more people coming in. Some of them in one corner making banners. Real buzz about the place. "Oh," he said, shaking his head. "I don't like the sound of this—"

"This trouble's been brewin' for a while, fella," said Ryan. "We ain't the ones been bringin' it, but we're the ones that'll be stoppin' it. You'll see. We're always there first. In the meantime— you go about your business. And if you bring the killers of Isaac Roberts to justice—and I mean the real killers, not that idiot Fincher, doin' other people's dirty work—then you're doing me a favor. You lift that stone, I hope you bang it back down hard on any creature you find crawlin' underneath." His face hardened. "They've made Lucy's life hell, and they're wreckin' this world. We want 'em finished too."

That big fella, Jayne Cobb—turned out he weren't so keen on that sweet little plan of ours to cut through the fence and head into corporation territory for a good look round.

"Blue Sun, Mal," he said, shakin' his head. "They're big news. Powerful. Plenty of money."

"And I'm wonderin' why that's a problem all of a sudden?" asked Captain Reynolds. "Ain't ever been the kind of thing that's bothered your pretty little head in the past."

"I dunno," said Jayne, giving a shrug. "Plenty of friends up high, I'd guess. That's all. We're likely makin' enemies enough here on Abel without addin' more back at the Core. Never mind the ones we picked up already along with them strays…" He looked at me and seemed to change his mind about sayin' more. "You know what I mean."

"Strikes me," said Captain Reynolds, "that they're the kind of fine upstanding people already made themselves my enemy."

Now all of that was mighty interestin', you can be sure of that, and I thought I might like to know the story behind all of this one day. Doubt I ever will.

"Fly under the radar, you always say," said Jayne. "And then we always end up doin' a gorram damn fool thing like this. War's over, Mal—"

"Ain't no call to be bringin' that up, Jayne," said Zoë. "You don't like the idea of comin' with us, you stay here on the farm. Ain't nobody will think you're any less of a man if you do."

I saw what Zoë was doin', of course. Mention of the war—I'd worked out by now that seemed the quickest way to rile Captain Reynolds. Make him do somethin' dumb. I certainly weren't gonna mention it. T'was none of my business what them fellas got up to all them years back. But I wasn't havin' that fool Jayne Cobb interferin' with our plans.

"You can all stay put here quarrelin' until the sun boils Abel dry as far as I'm concerned," I said. "I'll cut that fence and go that way myself if I have to."

Captain Reynolds smiled at me. "Ain't no need for that, Miss Annie. Zoë and I'll be with you. Can't speak for Jayne Cobb, mind, since it seems this little blue sun over here's put the scarifiers on him—"

"Zāo gāo, Mal, you know as well as I do that I ain't stayin' behind!"

"I know," said Captain Reynolds. "You got your cut to earn for one thing."

Thing about platinum is that it quickly puts paid to all kind of nonsense, and soon Zoë and the captain were busy cutting at that wire and rollin' it up so's we had a hole big enough for the four of us. Weren't easy, scramblin' through, and I let Captain Reynolds give me a helpin' hand. I'm proud, I know, but I ain't a darn fool. When we was all through, we walked some towards a clump of trees. From there, we saw a bunch of buildings, far in the distance.

"Let's head for there," said Captain Reynolds. "See what we can find."

"Bunch of barns, most likely," grumbled Jayne. "You plannin' on fillin' *Serenity* with cows again, Mal?" But while Jayne hardly stopped complainin', he still kept on walkin'. I guess that fee of mine was an even better motivation than I'd thought. Was a fair walk across those fields, and the sun rose up in the sky as we went. The day was warm for the season. Not right. I said to Captain Reynolds, "You notice something about these fields here?"

"What you seen, Miss Annie?"

"Ain't no fences, leastways, not where I'd expect 'em. This place—it's huge. Wonder what they're plannin' on plantin' here."

"Maybe they're not plannin' on plantin' anythin'," he replied.

"What d'you mean by that, Captain Reynolds?" I said.

"Sometimes," he said, "there's more value below the soil than in it."

Now, I have to say, that was something that I hadn't thought of. Abel was—to my mind, to everyone's mind—a farming world, after all. Crops, in the main; some livestock, and plenty of horses, of course, in Wilder County and beyond. Was that what was happenin'? Was that enough of a motivation to steal Jacky Colson's land and livelihood –enough to take my daddy's life? I glanced across at Jayne, glowerin' away as he walked. Some men, after all, it's money what gets them out of bed in the morning.

After mebbe half an hour or more, the sun was getting higher in the sky, but everything was still. Them buildings were at last close enough for us to take a proper look. They were strange old constructions—nothin' like what I was used to seein' here on Abel. Most of the builds out here in the country are farmhouses and so on, wooden. These seemed to be some sort of plastic. Musta come from the Core. Five or six long, low huts, laid out in two rows. Smelled like when you take the wrapper off a new piece of fancy kit. I couldn't see no lights on inside of 'em, and nobody movin' around. More than a mite uncanny.

"Place looks deserted," muttered Zoë.

"Or not open for business yet," said Captain Reynolds.

That Rising Sun logo was everywhere, on the walls and such, and, here and there, smaller, the Blue Sun, stamped beneath windows and so on. Weapons drawn, we walked between the two blocks, lookin' round, ever so careful, on the lookout. When we came to the end of the blocks, Captain Reynolds sent Jayne and Zoë off to cover the far side of the left-hand row, and he and I went round to check the back of the other row. But we seen nothing. Blinds down in the windows. Even in the sunshine this place was creepy. I ain't superstitious—ain't no place in God's good world for such stories—but I didn't like it there, not one jot. I didn't like how bare it was, how lonesome. Them plastic buildings felt detached, like they wasn't part of the land here. Nothin' like poor old Jacky Colson's farmhouse. That, I knew for a fact, had been abandoned— and yet you still got that warm feelin' that came from knowin' it had once been a home, full of love and laughin'. This place was chilly. Cold, like old bones. I didn't like it and I wanted to leave.

"Captain Reynolds," I whispered. "We ain't stayin' here much longer, are we?"

"Huh?" He was tryin' one of the windows.

"I said, we ain't stayin' here much longer?"

"Awhile yet, Miss Annie," he said. "I want a look inside one of these blocks, don't you?"

"No," I said. "I don't like it here, and I don't see how pokin' around will bring us any closer to Bill Fincher—"

Which is when the shootin' started.

"*Tā mā de hún dàn!*" hissed the captain, and I was so shocked at what was happenin' that I forgot to check him for his filthy manners. Barely seconds passed before Zoë and Jayne came runnin' round the side of the buildin'.

"Zoë," snapped Captain Reynolds, his voice all clipped and soldierly, "*zĕn me la?* What in the gorram 'verse is going on?"

"Think we found our fellas, sir," she said, voice laid back but her body all taut and ready. "At least, there's half-a-dozen of them, the other side of those far buildings."

"Well," said Captain Reynolds. "Least we know now we've come to the right place."

"Musta seen us comin' a mile off," said Jayne. "Lay low, let us come close and split up. I said we shouldna come here, Mal!"

"Jayne," said he, "we're tryna *find* these fellas!"

"But not so's they can take pot shots at us!" Jayne spat on the ground. "They know how many of us there are, most likely taken a good look at our weapons—oh, yeah, and they know that one of us is a green kid who's only got the one good hand!"

And that's when I slapped him, hard, across the face, with that one good hand. "You keep your junk mouth shut!" I said to him. "*Fèi wù!* You ain't nothin' in this world!"

He looked about ready to hit me right back, Zoë laid her hand upon my arm, and Captain Reynolds got between us, and he said, "*Bì zuĭ!* You stop this! The pair of you—you stop this right now or I swear to God—"

"What you plannin' on doin', Mal?" snarled Jayne. "You're gonna need me to get you out of this, not some kid with one arm missin'—"

Oh, but that was a mistake. Captain Reynolds got up close in his face, real close, and he said, "You thinkin' of payin' another visit to an airlock, Jayne?" I ain't got no idea what he meant by that, and I don't think I ever will, and from Zoë's face she didn't know either, but that Jayne Cobb knew, that's for sure, and those words had some power over him.

"*Zāo gāo*," he muttered. "All right, Mal! All right." He looked at me, with hate in his eyes and, I daresay, his heart too, whatever he had that passed for a heart. "Gorram kids," he said. "Gorram girls—"

"Thinkin' I might take a look round the corner, sir," said Zoë.

"Thinkin' you're right," said Captain Reynolds. "Jayne— cover her."

I saw Jayne make the calculation—did he want to poke his nose round the side of the building and risk getting' shot at, or did he want to get stuck with me—and he went off after Zoë. Captain Reynolds, busy checkin' his gun, said, "I ain't sayin' you weren't provoked, but that's an end to it. Nothin' else like that, or you go straight home. *Dǒng ma?*"

"I understand," I said.

"Well, good," he said. "Because we got more to be worryin' about right now." He nodded to the other side. "We'll take a look thataway. You follow me, Miss Annie, and you keep behind me, and if anyone starts shootin', you get yourself right back here."

We inched round the side of the building. Captain Reynolds was ahead, gun out and at the ready. When we got the corner, he poked his nose round. I heard him curse under his breath. He waved his hand, tellin' me to move. Once we were back behind the building, I said, "What you seen, Captain?"

"Fella there's wearing a brown coat," he said. Looked a mite shocked.

"Yes," I said. "That's Frankie Collier. Fought for the Independents during the war. Didn't you know?"

"No," he said. "I didn't. I didn't know that at all."

"Does it make a difference?" I said, somewhat warily. It had been my observation over the years that those brown-coated fellas stuck together. The captain, I noticed, hadn't answered my question, and his face had gone all thoughtful. "Captain," I said again. "Does it make a difference?"

When the invitation to the charity lunch arrived at the Guild House, Simon could cheerfully have murdered Shepherd Book. Inara snapped immediately into action. While she assembled yet another outfit for him, Simon read the preacher's briefing on their hosts.

"Monseigneur and Madame de Cecille," he said. "Probably the richest people on Abel? And this is a charity lunch at their home to raise money for people who I'm sure would rather just be given the money directly—"

"Perfect," said Inara, firmly. "We'll meet the right kind of people at this, Simon. There's sure to be someone from Rising Sun."

Simon turned the invitation around in his hands. "I wonder how the Shepherd managed to get hold of this?"

"I wouldn't ask too many questions, Simon. We're in, and that's what matters."

Inara called to arrange for a hovercar. Simon, accepting his fate, morosely followed her downstairs. Even as a medical student, he hadn't been the kind who often went to parties (well, there were a couple of notable exceptions to this rule, but surely even someone like him was allowed to kick back after graduating in the top three percent of his year). He preferred to spend his down time with a couple of friends, kicking back, talking, the sort of thing he did these days with Kaylee, now he came to think about it. Simon shut that train of thought down, quickly. Best not to think about that… His parents, however, were exactly the kind of people who liked to host dinner parties, and drinks parties, and cocktail parties, and they also liked to parade their gifted children. As a result, Simon had more experience with small talk than perhaps many of his crewmates might have imagined. There was something about being on board *Serenity* that brought out a stammer, that made him misspeak. It hadn't been like that back home. (Simon still thought of the Core and Osiris as home, and he didn't honestly think he would ever be able to think otherwise.)

Back at home, Simon was usually tasked to talk to the older women, who found him charming company, a handsome young man with perfect manners who was willing to listen to long stories about their children and grandchildren. River would perform—some music, usually—and then be kept at their mother's side, without much opportunity to speak. There had been, on reflection, a great deal more consideration about the feelings of polite company than perhaps Simon had noticed at the time. Funny the perspective you got, with distance.

Today, however, it seemed he was to be admitted to the company of the men. Money did that—or, at least, the performance of money. Simon didn't have a bean these days, but everyone assumed that Lucas Amery was a rich man. Funny how he hadn't had to provide any evidence of that, thought Simon. All he'd had to do was use the right kind of voice, and put on the right kind of clothes, and made the right kind of conversation. You could see how conmen found their marks.

The de Cecilles' mansion was certainly splendid by Abel's standards, although Simon's parents' house was a little bigger, and he'd had several school and university friends who would consider this on the small side for even a second home. Still, this was the Rim, after all, and you couldn't deny that the reception room into which they were brought looked pretty splendid. The big surprise was the Alliance flag, which was prominently displayed at the far end of the room, above the string quintet.

"Huh," murmured Simon.

"What?" asked Inara.

"I thought Abel was on the side of the Independents in the war."

"I think it was complicated," said Inara. "Maybe... we won't mention it?"

"Good idea," said Simon.

The server announced them: *Mr Lucas Amery, of Londinium and Ms Inara Serra, of Sihnon.* From out of the company, two figures emerged—richly dressed, about the age of Simon's parents, at ease. Their hosts, it transpired—Monseigneur and Madame de Cecille. They greeted them both with considerable interest. Some small talk followed, about how helpful the Guild had been, about how Lucas was exploring business opportunities in Abel, which were rumored back in the Core to be significant, and then Madame de Cecille, taking Inara's arm, said, "Let me introduce you to my friends," she said. "They would certainly like to make the acquaintance of such a charming woman as yourself."

Simon watched as Inara let herself be led away, deep in conversation with and Madame.

"Women, eh?" said de Cecille. "Daren't interrupt their business. They'd run the whole planet if they were allowed."

"I imagine they would," said Simon.

De Cecille was studying him with interest. There was a bluff directness to him, almost roughness, but his eyes were sharp, and Simon guessed it would be a mistake to think his manner meant the man was not clever. "So," said his host, "you're here to spend some money?"

"If I can," said Simon. "We don't know the Rim well, back at the Core. But I've been increasingly thinking that there are opportunities out here—for all of us." He glanced pointedly at the Alliance flag. "Now we're all on the same side. Seems to me it's long overdue for some of what we have at the Core to flow this way."

Mal, he thought—not without pleasure—would explode hearing him talk like this. But, in fact, Simon wasn't lying when he said these things. Everything would improve if people could try and put the war behind them, and get on with making life better for all citizens of the Alliance, whatever their opinions had been on Unification. And this little speech seemed to have struck a chord with his host. The Monseigneur was nodding.

"You're not the only one," he said. "Come on, let me introduce you to Emory Scarlett. He's from your neck of the woods."

"From Londinium?" Simon went on alert. He knew Londinium fairly well—every schoolchild in the Core visited Parliament at some point or another—but perhaps not well enough to fool a local.

"Yes, Londinium, I think… Maybe Sihnon?" said de Cecille. He laughed. "All those Core worlds," he said, winking broadly. "They're much the same, aren't they?"

Simon made sure to laugh at his joke, and followed de Cecille across the room. Inara, he saw, was embedded with a group of five or six other women, including Vitale and Madame. Hopefully, she was learning something of value.

Emory Scarlett stuck out like a sore thumb. The clothes, the gloss, the manner, the corporate badge—this was absolutely not a man from the Rim. De Cecille made the introductions and, after some chat, said, "I'll let you fellows get better acquainted."

Scarlett smiled, thinly. They watched him go. Scarlett sipped some champagne. His lip curled slightly, as if he did not like the taste. "Well, Mr Amery," he said. "How do you like Abel?"

"I think I like it in much the same way as you," said Simon.

Scarlett gave a low laugh. "These Rim parties," he said. "There's something rather homespun about them, *dŏng ma*?"

Simon laughed too, but something twisted inside his gut. He was glad Kaylee wasn't here to listen to this conversation. It took him a moment to find a name for this feeling. Shame. Travelling around the Rim hadn't been easy for Simon—but there had been many unexpected kindnesses and generosities, without which he and River would not have survived.

Sorry, Kaylee, he thought, wretchedly.

"How long are you staying out here?" said Scarlett.

"Depends on whether or not I find anything worth staying for," said Simon. "Yourself?"

"Well, the Rising Sun project will, I hope, be around for many years yet," said Scarlett. "And I'll be overseeing at least the first phase. Keen not to get embedded here, of course." He tried another sip of champagne, grimaced, and put down the glass. "Couldn't stick the wine for one thing."

"Rising Sun," said Simon. "I've heard that mentioned in several places now."

"I'm glad the name is getting recognition," said Scarlett.

"I've had a little difficulty understanding the nature of the business," said Simon. "What's it all about."

"Oh, we have a diverse portfolio of interests," said Scarlett. "They vary, of course, depending on the specific planetary context. Here on Abel we're primarily operating in agronomic services, looking to attract inward investment in that area."

He sounded uncomfortably like Simon's father. "Well," said Simon, trying to sound enthusiastic, "that sounds like the kind of thing that might persuade me to stay on Abel a little longer."

Scarlett gave a smile. "Why don't you come over for drinks this afternoon?" he said. "Hear a little more about what we're doing?"

"I'd like to."

"How do I reach you?"

"You'll find me at the Guild House." Seeing Scarlett's expression, he gave an embarrassed laugh. "I'm travelling with a Companion. Our bags and ID got lost in transit. The Guild House here on Abel have been helping us out."

"Oh," said Scarlett, who was plainly not interested. "Well,

I'll get my assistant to send time and location via the Cortex. You are free this afternoon, aren't you?"

"I'll make myself free."

"Good." Scarlett nodded over the room. "This your Companion coming over?"

Inara was indeed heading their way.

"That's Ms Serra, yes."

"Sweet," said Scarlett, looking her up and down.

Inara, approaching them, had her hand up against her brow. "Lucas, might I have a quiet word?"

Scarlett smiled. "I'll leave you to it," he said. "See you later."

"Yes, I'm looking forward to it…" Simon turned his attention to Inara. "Inara, are you all right?"

"I'm afraid," she said, loud enough for Scarlett to hear, "that I'm feeling rather ill."

"Ill?" Simon studied her face closely. She *looked* okay…

"I think I have the start of a migraine—"

"I didn't know you got migraines, Inara," said Simon, starting to get worried. "There's prescription medicines that can help—"

"Might we discuss this in the hall?" said Inara, her tone bright and brittle. "The noise in here…"

"Yes, of course," said Simon, and took her arm. She leaned heavily on his arm as they left the reception room. "I mean it, Inara," he said, quietly, as she asked one of the nearby servers for their coats and to call for a hovercar. "Migraines are very treatable. We'll run some tests when we're back on the ship. You know, I think you're the only member of the crew who has never had a full medical. Let's do that." He glanced back at the party. "That champagne, probably. Common trigger—"

"Simon!" hissed Inara. "*Bì zuǐ!* Stop being so… *Simon-ish*!"

There wasn't very much he could about that, thought Simon. "Inara, are you okay?"

"I'm perfectly all right!"

He gestured back into the reception. "Then, ah, why... I mean... Why are we...?"

"We have to go," she whispered.

"I was beginning to enjoy myself—"

"We're not *here* to enjoy ourselves!"

"No," said Simon, with a sigh. "We never are, and I never do. What's the matter?"

"The mayor's about to arrive. Mary McQuinn."

"So? Won't she be someone worth talking to?"

"Almost certainly. Unfortunately, she and I have met today already," said Inara. "Back at the Roberts' house. I arrived when she was in the middle of quarrelling with Mal—"

"Mal quarrelling with someone? Oh, this story can't be true..."

"Exactly. She knows I'm with Mal. Or Mal is with me... Whichever way, if she sees me, our cover is blown."

"Then I guess we have to go," said Simon. He hesitated. "I ought to say goodbye to the de Cecilles, thank them for their hospitality. Don't want to get on the wrong side—"

"Don't worry, I've done all that already. Please, put your coat on and move!"

Simon pulled on his coat and helped Inara into her wrap. Outside, a couple of hovercars were pulling up outside. They hurried down the steps into the midday sun. One of the de Cecilles' staff was opening the hovercar door for them. From the other car, a woman was emerging.

"It's her," hissed Inara, turning and dipping her head. "McQuinn."

The mayor, pausing for a moment to smooth out the skirt of her dress, caught Simon's eye. "Never a good sign when guests are leaving early," she said. Her voice was laidback, almost a drawl.

"Oh, well, um..." Simon held up his hands. "Busy day."

"I hear you on that." McQuinn eye's drifted towards their car. Inara was in the far seat. Had she seen her? She wasn't saying anything, if so. "See you around," said McQuinn, and went up the steps into the house. Simon got in beside Inara.

"Did she see me?" said Inara.

"I... I honestly have no idea," said Simon. The door closed, and the car moved on, back to the Guild House.

"*Gǒu shǐ*," Inara was muttering. "Mal will *kill* me..."

8

Captain Reynolds still hadn't answered my question when Zoë and that big fella Jayne came back. Their news weren't good.

"Four of them over our side, sir," said Zoë.

"Uh-huh," said the captain, but his mind was still on that wretched brown coat, I could tell.

"What did you see, Mal?" said Jayne.

"Three of 'em on ours," I said.

"Them odds ain't good, Mal," said Jayne. "What we gonna do?"

"Collier's a Browncoat," mused the captain.

I could see where this was goin' and I did not think much of it as an idea. I looked round our position, usin' the eyes that God gave me, and I had an idea. So I put in, "Why don't we—"

"Sir?" said Zoë.

"Frank Collier," said Captain Reynolds. "He fought with the Independents."

"So?" Jayne spat on the ground. "War's long over and I ain't ever interested. What we need to worry about is that those fellas are shootin' at us right now. Gorram stupid idea coming over here," he muttered. "Walked over more or less in broad daylight. Musta seen us comin' a mile off."

"Thinkin' I might go and have a word with him," said the captain.

"What?" Jayne wasn't happy. "Mal, that's a dumb idea!"

I was inclined to agree, and, besides, I thought I had a pretty good idea. "All's I want to say is—"

"Hush, please, Miss Annie!"

"You think he'd been open to listenin', sir?"

"Thinkin' it might be worth a try."

"Another dumb idea on top of a whole day of dumb ideas," grumbled Jayne. "No good ever came of walkin'. Better'n that, shoulda not bothered comin' over here in the first place. Said we shouldn't. Sittin' ducks."

"He ain't shown us much in the way of consideration as yet, sir," said Zoë.

"Does he know we're on his side?"

"He ain't on our side, Mal! Keep tryna tell you that!"

And, once again, I agreed with Jayne Cobb. Who says there's no such thing as miracles. That darn war. Over years ago, and still these fellas talkin' like they was still fightin' it. I was done with all this, but nobody listens to you when you're my age and particularly not given the way I am. They all seem to think I musta lost my brains when I lost my arm. It's my experience that when folk don't start listenin' they ain't ever gonna listen, so you may as well get on with what you think is best. I lifted up my little pistol, the one Daddy got me for my fourteenth birthday, and I fired straight at the corner of the nearest window. I'd noticed, you see, that this was a particular kind of reinforced glass, and the thing about this particular kind of reinforced glass: you shoot in the center there's a big explosion you get yourself covered in shards and risk all manner of cuts and damage. You shoot dead on the right spot in that bottom corner and—*phwock*. It kinda implodes on itself. I read that on the Cortex once. There'd been a scandal; folks installin' the stuff and then findin' it weren't as secure as they thought. People buy cheap, they get cheap. I'll drive a hard bargain, but not at the expense of quality. Anyway, that window, it went:

Phwock.

It sure was a satisfactory sound, and I was kinda glad, too, to discover that what I'd read turned out to be true because if it hadn't I'd have just given away our position without any benefit. There was a brief silence—and then we heard voices, shoutin', from around the other side of the building, callin' out to head our way. As for Captain Reynolds— well, I thought he was about to explode.

"*Gǒu shǐ*, girl, what do you think you're gorram doin'?"

That filthy mouth of his again. I hoped that Shepherd of his prayed hard for him, because he was surely in need of a good word or two with his Maker. I said, "I figured we needed cover and since we're standin' right next to a big buildin', made sense to get inside somehow. You comin'? 'Cause I think those fellas are on their way here."

"I'm in," said Jayne. He took his gun and thumped away at what was left in the window frame, making sure there weren't any sharp edges would catch and cut us. He was inside first, and then Zoë, who gave me a helpin' hand to clamber through the window. Above us, the lights started to come on, musta been on motion detectors, and Jayne shot 'em out. He was crossin' the room to the door. That was locked, but it surely didn't stay that way for long. Jayne shot that open too. He was comin' in handy.

Zoë and the captain threw a few chairs underneath the window so that any of those fellas comin' after us wouldn't have it too easy climbin' in after us, and we all dashed out of the room. Captain Reynolds was draggin' one of them chairs what spin around after him, and when we got out into the corridor, he hooked it up under the door handle. Struck me then that maybe these folks I'd hired weren't so hot at plannin'. Seemed there was an awful lot of thinkin' on the fly. 'Cause the Collier gang weren't gonna waste time climbin' through that window, were they? They were comin' through the main door.

"Sir," said Zoë. "We need a plan."

Mighta rolled my eyes at that.

"I'm thinkin'," said Captain Reynolds. The door behind us was rattlin', so he sent a few shots through. I most certainly heard someone shriek, and there was some choice language too. More fellas in need of prayers, though if this was some of the Collier gang comin' after us, I daresay a little cussin' weren't the worst of what they'd done.

"That way," said the captain, pointin' down the corridor—and then we saw someone turn the corner down there and start headin' toward us. The captain shot him. "No," he decided, "*this* way!" He was pointin' in the other direction. Zoë ran, and I ran after her. Figured she was the one that I wanted to be standin' next too, if this came down to a shootin' match. She had that look of one who would still be on her feet long after everyone else had fallen down. The captain was next, and then the big fella, Jayne, walkin' backwards down the corridor, firin' as he went. Good job, too, cause a couple more of the gang were comin' after us. I think he hit 'em both; don't know if he killed 'em. That was three we'd hit—but we knew there was seven of 'em at least. I was strugglin' to see how we could work these odds in our favor.

That corridor ended in a door, which the captain shot open. We dashed into a big room, all filled with long tables, workbenches, I guess. The room looked like a big classroom to me. There weren't much to put in front of the door to use as a barricade, but the workbenches kinda worked as defensive positions. Zoë pulled me behind one of them and said, "Keep your head down." She placed herself behind the one in front of me. We heard runnin' outside the door. Some shots were fired. I ducked down, but as I did, I misjudged the distance and gave my poor head the most awful bang against the side of the bench. Lord, that hurt. The captain and Jayne, nearer the door, had done the same, but soon as they could, they popped up again like jack-in-the-boxes, firing through the door down the corridor. Good job we weren't hopin' on using that door as a shield, it was as pocked full of holes as one of them fancy cheeses.

I will say—with time and distance and a little thought—that I didn't see how we woulda got through this. I guess maybe the captain was hopin' that he'd get that chance to speak to Collier face-to-face, but there'd been a fair amount of shootin' by then, and I didn't see how Collier was goin' to be well disposed towards us, Browncoat or no Browncoat. I had a feelin' that the plan wasn't going to amount to more than 'let's make a run for it', and I didn't think much of that. And when we heard the sound of a hovercar approachin' outside, my first thought was that Collier musta called for some back-up. Or maybe we'd tripped some alarms and security were arrivin'. We were gonna have a hard time explainin' the cut wire and the broken window in that case. I felt a fool, like I'd made a promise to Daddy, and then been and gone and hired this fella, and he'd turned out to be no darn use. That engine outside got very loud, and then I heard an explosion.

"Sir," said Zoë. "Them's splinter grenades."

At the time I didn't know what that meant; only later I discovered that whoever had arrived was usin' some serious firepower to shoot at the fellas on the ground outside. The shootin' stopped beyond the door. We heard shoutin', and some more gunfire, and then the sound of hovercars headin' away. After that, things went kinda quiet. The captain, popping up his head, opened the door with the barrel of his gun. Nobody shot off his hand.

"Huh," he said.

"Where they gone, Mal?" said Jayne. He was checkin' out his left leg, which looked to have some blood on it.

"Ain't got no idea," said Captain Reynolds. "Maybe that it's got something to do with them splinter grenades we heard."

"Who is that?" I called out from where I was still hunkered down.

"Better not be the sheriff's men," said the captain. "We might have some explainin' to do."

"They shot first," said Jayne.

"Only because we was trespassin'," said Zoë. "Sir, you want me to go take a look outside?"

The captain, comin' out from behind his cover, swung the door wide open and looked down the corridor. "Huh." He moved away from the door, so's his back was protected by the wall, and turned to look round the room at the rest of us. "Huh." Then he lifted his gun and pointed at the wall near me. "Back door," he said. "That's handy."

I looked. He was right. Another door, maybe four or five feet from, leadin' back outside. Fire escape, maybe, that kind of thing. I was about to move over to try the handle, when someone shot it open. I turned. Jayne was standin' there, smirkin'. "Thought I'd save us some time," said he. The captain gave him a look that said, Do that again and you'll be the one shot at, and walked over to me. Laid his hand on my shoulder as he came past.

"Handled yourself pretty good there, Miss Annie," he said. "Didn't lose your nerve."

Well, what had he expected? I was here to get the job done, same as him. My head was surely hurtin', though. The captain pushed the door open, and I followed him outside. I didn't miss how Zoë put herself between me and Jayne. That fella sure was junk.

Wasn't hard to find our savior. There was a big hovercar – pristine and very fancy, not the kind of thing much seen out here on the Rim—parked up round the side of the building. Next to it stood a woman dressed all in black, carryin' almost as much firepower as Jayne. She held up her hand—palm out—as we drew nearer, something between warnin' and greetin'.

"Hi there," she said.

"Hello there, ma'am," said Captain Reynolds. He could certainly manage good manners when he wanted. "And how may we be helpin' you this fine day?"

She looked past him into the wrecked room. "I was about to ask you the same thing."

Shepherd Book, at rest in Isaac Roberts' study, closed the files he had been reading, and sighed, deeply. Across the room, River was curled up on a deep and comfortable sofa, fast asleep. Book stood and crossed over to the bay window in the curve of the tower, and looking out into the street. Early afternoon, and everything quiet, almost uncannily so. Wash and Kaylee had checked in earlier, to let him know that they were among friends and working on finding out more about the trouble in the city and how it connected to their business. There'd been nothing from Mal, and nothing, to Book's surprise, from Simon and Inara. He'd been expecting the young doctor to check in on his sister well before now.

As if catching his thoughts, the console on Roberts' desk chimed softly. Book stole across the room to check. Incoming message from the Guild House. This he could take with impunity, since it was, most likely, for him, and not for Annie Roberts. He accepted the call, and two familiar faces appeared on the screen.

"Inara. Simon," he said. "Good to see you. And before you ask, doctor—River's fine." He saw Simon's shoulders relax.

"*What's she been doing?*"

"She put away a substantial lunch and came up with a new way of playin' chess to keep herself amused." There'd been three boards out in a line at one point, River going from one to the next murmuring to herself. Kings and queens. "And now she's sleepin'. So I won't disturb her, if you don't mind."

"*All right,*" said Simon, although he looked disappointed. "*I guess that's best…*"

"How was your lunch? Learned anything to our advantage?"

"*I'm not sure,*" said Simon. "*Though our cover was nearly blown.*"

"Ah," said Book. "Not that invitation, I hope?"

"*That was fine—*"

"Problem with your credentials? We can take a look at that when you get back."

"*It wasn't Simon's fault,*" said Inara. "*Mayor McQuinn arrived. She met me when I arrived at the Roberts' house.*"

"Did she see you at the lunch?"

"*We're not sure,*" admitted Inara.

"Unfortunate," said Book.

"*Nobody's yet come hammering on the door to drag us away,*" said Simon. "*I think we may have got away with it.*" He frowned. "*I hope so.*"

"The mayor does seem to turn up at all kinds of unwelcome moments," said Book. "What's our thinking on that score?"

"*I didn't really get a chance to speak to her,*" said Simon.

"*She was certainly giving Mal a piece of her mind earlier,*" said Inara. "*Which would usually be a point in her favor… Have you heard from Mal?*"

"Not a peep out of him so far," said Book. "I'm sure everything is going swimmingly."

"*Oh yes,*" said Simon, dryly. "*Because it always does. Would we even know, if he was—*"

"*Don't, Simon,*" said Inara, quickly.

"Indeed," said Book. "But was there anything you found out at your party worth exploring further?"

"*We're meeting a man from Rising Sun later,*" said Simon. "*I think he's going to make my fortune.*"

"Good work, Simon," said Book.

"*I did manage to spend a little time talking to some of the women here,*" said Inara. "*Always an excellent source of information. They're worried about Annie Roberts, and intent on... 'drawing her out', as one of them put it. You may have a stream of visitors this afternoon, Shepherd.*"

"Forewarned is forearmed, Inara, and I thank you. I shall think up a good excuse as to why she is not available to see them."

"*A migraine works,*" said Simon, somewhat enigmatically. "*Any word from Kaylee and Wash?*"

"Not a peep from them either," said Book. "As for me... I've been diggin' a little deeper into Abel's history. Tryin' to learn some more about how things stood here before and during the war."

"*The Alliance flag was displayed fairly prominently at the de Cecilles' earlier,*" said Simon.

"I guess they know which side their bread is buttered these days, at least," said Book. "But I'm not so clear how generally that enthusiasm for the Alliance is shared in these parts, however."

"*You think there's some holdouts here?*" said Inara.

"Mm, not entirely. But perhaps not everything from the war has been entirely resolved."

Simon, he saw, was looking pensive. "*I wish I could speak to River...*"

"She's fine. Like I say, we played a fair amount of chess. Well, she wiped the floor with me."

That made the young man smile. "*Good. And... there was nothing... nothing troubling her?*"

Book thought about that. She hadn't liked the de Cecille woman much, but then neither had he. And then there'd been that moment when she'd got upset... "She said something about the world being in reverse. That mean anything to you? Somethin' you've talked about in the past?"

"*The world in reverse?*" Simon shook his head. "*Doesn't mean a thing.*"

"She particularly wanted me to tell you that."

"*Thank you anyway,*" said Simon, with a sigh. "*I'm sure I'll realize what it means at some point. I usually do in the end.*"

They each bid the other farewell, and the call ended. Light-footed, Book crossed the room to the sofa, and stood for a while looking down at River. Good to see her so peaceful. She didn't look that way often enough. Tenderly, with great care, he placed a cover over her. Suddenly, her eyes opened.

"Shepherd?" she said. "Did you tell him? Did you tell Simon?"

"I did," he said.

"Good." She closed her eyes again. She seemed contented. "Good." As he turned to go back to his seat, he heard her murmur, "War ain't over, Shepherd. You'll see."

Now whatever could that mean? Book went back to his reading. He'd ploughed his way through local news from the past year or so. Learned about the election of Mayor McQuinn earlier in the spring, and how that had come as a shock to pretty much everyone in Yell City. Read about the hot summer (summer of discontent, they called it) and how those tensions between the city folks and the incomer farmers had flared up into fighting. Learned some about the unions on Abel, and their frustrations. Saw the mayor give a talk about cleaning up the city. (And how, he wondered, was she planning to go about doing that?) Saw the reports made about Isaac Roberts' death and read, over and over, how he was the best-loved man on Abel. Opened up the lawyer's obituary—

And saw something he most certainly didn't want to see.

"Heaven preserve us," murmured Book, rubbing his eyes. Best-loved man on Abel, it transpired, had supported Unification.

Not so far as to put on a uniform and get out there shootin' Browncoats, but enough to make sure that when it had come to the point that his world had to make a decision, Abel had come down on the side of the Alliance.

Book stood up and went to stare out at the still afternoon. That war, that *terrible* war... From this distance, it was, in Book's opinion, getting harder and harder to see who had been right and who had been wrong. Yes, the cause of independence had been good, and righteous—but there had been things done in the name of the cause that been cruel, and wicked, that had hardened men. Turned them cruel. Drove them to bad acts. A man who chose to walk down that path was not likely to find it easy to return. As for the Alliance—was it possible, Book wondered, to have supported that cause in good faith? Increasingly, he believed so. A man like Isaac Roberts—perhaps he looked to the Core, which he knew, into which he'd married, and saw benefits to that way of life. Perhaps a man like that could indeed look towards the Core and think, Yes, that's how I want the 'verse to be. There's good there, good in which we all should share...

Book could see how a good man might come to such a conclusion. For himself, he would always prefer the Rim, its rough edges and hidden corners, which to his mind supported the diversity, the eccentricity of life which mattered so much to him, but hard-won experience told him the sides weren't quite so black and white as he once might have wished them to be. Weren't so black and white as Mal, for one, still saw them. And that intransigence—what could that do to a man? Defeat was a bitter draught, one that could sour you if you drank too long and too deep. Same with anger; same with hate. Once upon a time, Book had been heading in that direction, until he found himself on another path. Book had struggled to forgive his enemies, and to forgive himself, and he knew in his heart that there was no future in war, no future in keepin' on fightin' these old battles. You had to find your way to peace, and that might mean makin' some strange alliances…

He looked back over his shoulder at River, sleeping deeply. Such hurt she'd taken, that little girl. There were bad folks out there who'd harmed her, and Book didn't care what side they'd fallen on during the war. Chances were the people who had done this harm didn't care either. Cared only for the power that victory had brought them. These were the kinds of fellas Book considered his enemy. Those would do harm to a girl like this, and consider it necessary, to hold onto whatever power they had.

Still, he thought; he would not mention Isaac Roberts' affiliations to Mal. Not until they were paid. Not until they were far away from here. Perhaps never. Weren't a lie, as such. More a kindness.

The woman with the guns and the big shiny car looked at us one by one. I didn't like the way her eyes rested on me, takin' in my whole self, before movin' on to the others. Who did she think she was? I mean, apart from the person who had saved all our sorry lives, but that didn't give her permission to look at us that way. After she'd taken the measure of us all, she said, "Any of you injured? I've a medical kit in the hovercar."

My head was sore, but I figured I was going to be fine and I didn't want no fuss to be made, so I said nothing 'bout that. Jayne was starting to look real sorry for himself, however, and Captain Reynolds turned to him and said, "What about that leg?"

"'M all right," said the big fella, and then: "*Zāo gāo!*" he hissed, the moment he tried to walk.

"Do you want me to take a look?" said the woman.

"Think maybe someone should," said the captain. "But perhaps a few introductions might be in order?"

The woman smiled at him. "You go first," she said.

I was becomin' mighty sick of this, the truth be told, since the sun was high now, and those boys that had been shootin' at us were either gettin' away or busyin' themselves to come back. Besides, my head was by now buzzin' like a hive o'bees, so I said, "My name's Annie Roberts, and for my sins I've hired these people here to bring my daddy's killer to justice. The killer's name is Young Bill Fincher and he runs with the Collier gang. These folks are Captain Malcolm Reynolds, and she's Zoë Washburne, and the big fella there with the gammy leg—his name is Jayne. Girl's name, I know, but there we are. That's us and that's what we're doin' here."

"I ain't a girl!" snapped Jayne. "And it's Cobb. Jayne Cobb."

"*Āiya*, Miss Annie!" said Captain Reynolds. "You mighta held *somethin'* in reserve!" He looked horrified, but someone had to start things movin', otherwise we'd all be here till the sun went down.

"Turns out we have one thing in common," said the woman. "We're all interested in Francis Collier and his people." She didn't sound like she was from Abel. She sounded somewhat like Mamma, as far as I can remember, like she was from the Core, but at the same time, I caught a few cadences in her voice, like she knew the Rim. Maybe she'd spent time out here. "You know," she said, looking straight at Jayne, "I really think that before we start telling camp stories, we should do something about that leg of yours."

Jayne turned out to be ready to have somethin' done, so, with the captain on one side and Zoë on the other, he hobbled over to the woman's hovercar, and he let them all take a look and Zoë fell to doing what needed to be done. As Zoë patched Jayne up, the captain said to the woman, "Now we're all nice and friendly, perhaps you might see to givin' us your name?"

"Amy Lin," she said. "You can call me Amy Lin."

That, I thought, wasn't the same as tellin' us her name, but at least we had something to call her. "You're not from Abel, are you?" I said.

"No," she said. "Where I'm from doesn't matter so much as what I'm here for."

"And what's your job?" said the captain. "What's your interest in the Collier gang?"

"My job…" She smiled. Not givin' us much this one, and not ever likely too, I thought. "As I'm sure you know, there are a lot of bad people out here in the Rim these days. And I'm paid to stop them."

So what did that mean? Another bounty hunter? Or somethin' else? I thought, I wonder why Sheriff Peters didn't mention her name when I came knockin' at his door askin' for people to hire… but since Sheriff Peters wasn't there, I wouldn't be gettin' an answer, so I put the question in my pocket for later. I saw Captain Reynolds and Zoë exchange a look, and I wondered whether they considered themselves to be 'bad people'.

"Uh-huh?" said the captain. "Who's payin' you?"

I watched as her eyes took in his brown coat. Captain Reynolds didn't miss this either.

"That's need to know," she said. "And—"

"Yeah," said the captain. "I got the rest already."

"If you're after the Collier gang," she said. "We're on the same side." She looked round us all again, her eyes landin' on me. "So you're paying for this?" Her lips twitched. "Something of an odd job."

That made me see red. I said, "There ain't nothin' funny about what happened to my daddy, Miss Lin."

"No," she said. "There certainly isn't." And then I saw her face screw up into a frown, and she was movin' forward to grab hold of me, and she said, "Are you all right, honey?" Because I don't know whether it was everythin' that had been happenin' or else maybe it was me gettin' angry with her, but suddenly all that I could see was a blur, and, my goodness, I felt awful dizzy.

"I'm *fine!*" I said, before the world turned black.

Yes, I am most sorely ashamed to say that I fainted.

When I came back round, I was lying down alongside Miss Lin's car, and Miss Lin and Captain Reynolds and Zoë were all leaning over me, looking mighty concerned.

"What happened?" I said, as Zoë helped me sit.

"Annie," she said. "Did you bang your head?"

"Maybe a little," I said, Lord forgive me for that lie. "How long was I out?"

"Few seconds, nothin' more." Zoë looked up at the captain. "Concussion, I guess."

"We won't rightly know till the doc takes a look at her," he said. And if I hadn't been so brain sore I mighta seen where this was headin'. Captain Reynolds stood up and turned to Miss Lin.

"Well," said he. "Sounds like we're in the same game, so perhaps we might pool resources."

"I suppose we could," said she. "Not least because…" She looked at Jayne and sighed. "I think you're a man down."

Movin' my head all careful like, I saw Jayne sittin' on the ground. His leg was bandaged up, but he looked mighty pale. "Lookin' that way," said the captain. "Any information you care to share with us? They likely to come back to this place? Or they somewhere else they like to hole up?"

"I don' think they'll be back," said Miss Lin. "There's another place, further inside the compound, which they seem to have been using as their main base. I'm planning to fly by there. You're certainly welcome to come along. There's a few more of them than I was expecting."

"Uh-huh," said Captain Reynolds. "You'll forgive me for bein' blunt, Miss Lin, but if I'm bringin' a handful of people to the party, I want to know I'll be remunerated."

"You will," she said, and nodded over to us. "But only you and Miss Washburne here. Those two need to head back to town."

"What?" said Jayne.

"What?" I said. "Captain Reynolds, that was *not* our agreement!"

The captain muttered something under his breath that I am glad that I was not able to hear. Mother of mercy, that man's language! "Now, Miss Annie," he said, "don't go you tryin' my patience—"

"Tryin' *your* patience?"

"Annie," said Zoë, in a quiet voice. "We think you're concussed. You need to go back, see the doc, let him check you over—"

"And we'll do that, soon's I seen Bill Fincher good and dead—"

"Annie," she said again. "You ain't comin' any further."

I knew then that I wasn't gettin' my way. If Zoë wasn't supportin' me no longer, there wasn't much I could do—not here, at any rate. But I kept on tryin'.

"Captain Reynolds," I said, through the buzzin' in my head. "We had an agreement. You go after Bill Fincher, and I come with you."

"Annie—"

"You go back on our deal, and I ain't payin' you a single brass coin—"

"*Hú chě!*" he snapped, and I did what I was told and shut my mouth. I hadn't seen him so angry. "This ain't games we're playin' out here, girl! One of my crew been hurt and you've been banged on the head! This is over, *dǒng ma*? You're headin' home and we'll be back when this job is done. And it will be done. I said it would, and I ain't minded yet to break that promise despite more than my fair share of provocations." He turned to the big fella. "Jayne. Back to the Mule. Take Miss Annie with you, and go to her house."

I saw what was happenin' dawn on the big lump's face. "Aw, Mal! Why'm I the one gets stuck with baby-sittin'?"

"'Cause you're the one with a chunk taken out of your leg," said Captain Reynolds. "I'm done with all this quarrelin'! There's eight, nine, maybe ten fellas out there do not mean us well, and we ain't got any sense of where they might be right now. You two get yourself back to the Mule and back to town. Miss Lin," he said. "Myself and Zoë here will be joinin' you, if you're willin'."

"Fine by me," she said, and went round to the front of her hovercar.

"Mal—" started Jayne.

"I mean it," I said. "Not a single brass coin—" And I did mean it. He could pay his own darn fine.

"No more," he said. "From either of you. We'll see you in town when the job's done."

And off he and Zoë went to join Miss Lin. Soon they were on their way. That big fella looked at me like I was muck on his shoe. Darn cheek of it. Only one of us was junk, and it weren't me.

"*Zāo gāo*," he said. "Gorram baby-sittin'. All right, girl, get movin'."

He stood up, with some effort, and I saw—to my horror—he was going to have to lean on me if we were goin' to get anywhere. Just my luck.

9

Mal watched with a sense of foreboding as Jayne and Annie headed off back toward the Colson farm. He didn't feel entirely good with himself about going back on his word to the girl, but there it was. She was hurt, and so was Jayne, and perhaps the mistake had been bringing her out with them in the first place.

"Made the right choice, sir," said Zoë, quietly, from beside him. "We're up against who knows how many, and we can't be lookin' out for someone might pass out on us any moment."

Lin came to join them. "You'll forgive me if I'm speaking out of turn," she said, "but I'm amazed you brought that kid with you at all."

Mal, watching the two figures disappear into the night, said, "Miss Lin, we didn't have much in the way of a choice."

"That girl can take care of herself," said Zoë. "Some fine sharpshootin'—"

"I can only speak about what I've seen," said Lin, "but my distinct impression was that she couldn't take care of herself. I mean, she got herself banged on the head back there, didn't she?"

Mal sighed. He knew in his head that what Lin was sayin' was fair and true, but she hadn't spent time with that gorram kid.

Annie Roberts had a way of answerin' back that left you with no argument—no surprise her daddy was a lawyer. Besides, he'd wanted to get paid. He'd been sure he could keep her out of harm's way. Didn't he do that all the time with River and Kaylee? They had their own strengths, true, River in particular, although not entirely reliable, and he'd thought, well, what was one more girl runnin' underfoot? But it hadn't worked out so well after all.

"She'll be safe with Jayne," he said, more confidently than he felt. Jayne had taken against her, but Mal was sure he wouldn't risk her life, nor his payday. Besides, that moment they'd shared—Jayne in the airlock, Mal threatening to let him fly—that would command his obedience for a while yet.

"I hope so," said Lin.

Mal turned to look at her. "You're mighty concerned about the safety of Annie Roberts. Any particular reason why?"

"I'm concerned about the safety and security of everyone on Abel." Lin gave him a thoughtful look. "Is this going to work?"

"What do you mean, Miss Lin?"

"We've only just met," said Lin. "I want to be sure you've got my back."

"For what it's worth, you've got my word," said Mal. "I'm here to see this job done and be at your side—or guardin' your back, as you prefer—until the job is indeed done. Whether you choose to believe me—that's a choice you have to make. I'm choosin' to believe you'll do right by me and my crew, Miss Lin. I hope you'll do me the same courtesy."

"Fair enough," she said.

"What's courtesy got to do with it?"

"I'm of the opinion that this 'verse would be a happier place, if folks from the Core were a little less grasping and a little more courteous."

"Hey," she said. "All I'm here to do is help the people of Abel restore law and order."

"So you say," said Mal.

"Sir," said Zoë. "Time to be on our way."

"I agree," said Lin. They climbed into her hovercar—that was a big and shiny machine, wasn't it? Man could get jealous of kit like this. Sometimes, Mal thought, the odds seemed stacked against fellas like him. Maybe that's why Collier had taken on the job of killin' Isaac Roberts. Maybe there was more to this whole business than anyone was lettin' on.

"This place we're headin'," said Zoë, from the back. "You care to tell us a little about it? Guessin' I speak for the captain as well as myself when I say I don't like goin' into places blind."

"There's a big compound a couple of hours ride from here," she said.

"Oh yeah?" said Mal. "Who owns it?"

The hovercar lifted smoothly into the air, and began to eat up the countryside beneath. Lin seemed to be considering her words and, eventually, said, "So, you know as well as I do that Fincher didn't casually kill Isaac Roberts. It wasn't as simple as a quarrel that got out of hand."

"Biggest open secret on Abel, so far as I can make out," said Mal.

"Yeah," said Lin, with a sigh. "So the question is—who paid to have Isaac Roberts killed, and why. You know about the Colson case?"

"Miss Annie took us through the whole thing."

"And so you know about Rising Sun Enterprises."

Mal shrugged. "Seen the name around. Little more information wouldn't go amiss."

"Rising Sun gets substantial benefits from Parliament," said Lin. "Tax breaks, funds for R&D. They've become a big player in the whole up-levelling program."

"The which now?"

"Captain Reynolds," said Lin. "I'm astonished to learn that you don't follow policy announcements from Parliament."

Since Mal was the kind of man that thought Parliament would, on the whole, be better shut down or, at least, severely limited in the kind of meddlin' it could do in the lives of other people, the answer was, no, he didn't, but he suspected that Miss Lin knew that already.

"Up-levelling?" said Zoë. "What's that supposed to mean?"

"The basic idea is to put money and resources into Rim worlds," said Lin.

"Rebuilding?" said Mal. There were some worlds been blasted to smithereens when the Alliance passed by.

"Not so much that," said Lin. "Not places that got hit badly, but places that, well, don't have the same standard of living as you'd expect at the Core. Now that we're all Alliance citizens, you see. Why shouldn't Rim worlds have the same benefits, the same way of life as folks elsewhere in the Alliance?"

"Sounds like they want to turn us all into pale copies of the Core," said Mal. "Do people fall for this *niú shǐ*?"

"Do people like being given platinum to make their worlds better places for their friends and family?" said Miss Lin. "Strangely enough, yes."

"What's in it for the Core?" said Zoë, bluntly. "What do they stand to gain? What does Parliament stand to gain, handin' out money?"

Lin gave a small laugh. "There's a lot of companies in the Core lining up to be the ones to build the infrastructure, open up premises, and so on—"

"And let me guess," said Mal. "A lot of Parliamentarians and their friends happen to be on the boards of these companies."

"I couldn't possibly comment," said Lin. "But you see the

worry, don't you? If one of these companies has overstepped the mark, is using Parliamentary money to—let's pick an example close to home—pay a local bunch of gangsters to kill a lawyer so that he doesn't cause trouble for them. That's a problem, to put it mildly."

The problem, in Mal's opinion, was them all being out here in the first place, stickin' their noses into the business of people who simply wanted to be left alone. Jacky Colson wasn't seein' much in the way of benefit from this up-levellin', was he? Nor Isaac Roberts, come to that. And how about all those others in Yell City right now, forced off their farms, so that some big Core company could come in and claim that they were makin' everythin' better? They weren't doin' well out of things either, were they?

"You don't approve," observed Lin.

"No," said Mal. "I don't approve."

"Guess that's what I'd expect," said Lin, eyeing his coat.

"What do you mean by that?" said Mal, temper rising.

"Nothing," said Lin. "Captain."

"The whole reason we fought," said Mal, "was so we could be left alone. Live and let live. Not have others come in, tellin' us how to lead our lives and what's best for us—"

"Sir," said Zoë, in a warning tone.

"All right, Zoë, I'm done," said Mal. "We'll leave it there."

They drove on silence for a while. "What I'm hoping to discover, of course," said Lin, "is that this doesn't in fact go all the way back to Rising Sun. That Francis Collier had some sort of personal grievance against Isaac Roberts. Which I guess is possible." She sighed. "Simplest all round."

But not likely, thought Mal.

"You ain't yet told us what this place is where we're headin'," observed Zoë. "Why do Risin' Sun want all this land?"

"It's listed in the planning documents as a research facility," said Lin.

"Not minin', then?" said Mal. "I thought maybe they wanted what was under the ground."

"Maybe they do," said Lin.

"Need to know, huh?"

"Need to know," she agreed.

And that was that. They drove on, over dry-as-bone land, into the unnatural heat of an autumn afternoon.

That big lump Jayne Cobb was not happy to be stuck with me, and let me tell you the feelin' ran both ways, and deep as the Murray River cuts through the Violet Mountains. I couldn't think of anyone in the entire 'verse that I would rather spend less time with than that fella. He was mean and he was uncouth, and I could not for the life of me think why Captain Reynolds put up with his nonsense. But I suppose he was handy with all them guns he lugged round with him, and I suppose in their kind of business you can't be choosy. I could take a guess and say Captain Reynolds musta decided it was better havin' that fella on the inside making his mess than on the outside. But the upshot is that neither of us much liked the other, and neither of us was happy gettin' stuck with the other and, if we had one thing in common, neither of us was takin' much pleasure in missin' out on the action.

"Gorram girls," he muttered away to himself. "Curse of my gorram life."

I imagine we musta cut something of a comical sight—the fella hoppin' along on his injured leg, propped up by a one-armed girl—but neither of us was doin' much in the way of laughin'. Quite the contrary, because, Good Lord in Heaven, I was furious. All of them promises Captain Reynolds had made me, that I would be there at his side when Young Bill Fincher was brought to justice, and first chance he got he sent me on my way. I was sad about Zoë too, since I thought she understood what it meant to me; she had seen I could acquit myself perfectly well. Oh, how these wounds festered! As I went along, proppin' up that big lump, I wound myself up into a fair old state. We weren't nearly halfway back to the Colson place when I came to my decision.

I wasn't havin' it. I wasn't goin' to be left by the wayside when I'd become inconvenient, and Captain Reynolds found himself fancier friends. I'd got this far—got within hand's reach, maybe, of Young Bill Fincher!—and I knew in my heart he was close by. I was goin' to see this job done, and there weren't no shabby old Browncoat goin' to stop me. The Lord was on my side, I told myself, because my cause was righteous.

"Gorram baby-sittin'..." mumbled that big fella to himself. I was of a mind that he would be better payin' less attention to his grievances and more to gettin' us back to the Colson place, but I weren't much interesting in squabbling. No point fightin' with a fool. They only turn you into a fool yourself. And I wasn't no fool.

"Gorram Mal..."

But in the end all of us reach our limits, and I'd reached mine. I stopped all of a sudden and dead still. He more or less toppled over. Came down to the ground with a bump. "Hey," he snarled. "What do you think you're doin', you gorram *jiàn huò*?"

"I'm done listenin' to your complaints."

"You're *what* now?"

"Think I want to be stuck haulin' your carcass around? 'Cause I don't."

"*Wŏ de mā*," he said. "You're a gorram harridan, aintcha?"

"You think I care one jot about whether or not I have your good opinion, Jayne Cobb? Let me tell you I cared more about the good opinion of my old grandma's hogs. They had more brains in their heads for one thing."

He sat there gawping at me.

"And you can lift your jaw back up too," I said. "You may be a fool, but you don't have to look like one."

"Well," he said, after a moment or two, "that ain't nice."

"No," said I. "And I ain't nice either, and you can be sure that Captain Reynolds will hear all about this when we see him again."

"Huh," he said, and I saw the thought goin' through his skull as to whether he should keep this quarrel goin' or else give it up as a bad job. In the end, he seemed to settle on the latter. I'm not sayin' that I beat him, 'cause I think the main thing that shut him up was the thought of what I might tell Captain Reynolds about him. I didn't much care either way because the main thing was that he shut up. I did wonder, though, like I did again and again over that time, what the hold was that the captain had over him, and how he got Jayne Cobb to do his biddin'. Not that I was thinkin' fondly of Captain Reynolds at that point; if he had appeared at that moment out of the darkness, I might have spat on his grubby old boots.

My word, I am not sure I have ever been as angry as I was at that time.

But the chief thorn in my flesh—Jayne Cobb's sulky demeanor and constant complaints—was at least dealt with, and we lumbered on back towards the Colson homestead.

We got close to the fence we'd cut earlier before someone took a pot shot at us. It was dark by then and I must confess that my head hurt more'n a little. I'm not sayin' I was concussed nor that the captain was right in givin' me my marchin' orders, but I was ready to sit down and drink some water and maybe have forty winks. And I'm guessin' Jayne Cobb was havin' the same thoughts, because—give that fella his due—I don't think under normal circumstances he woulda missed anyone creepin' up on us. I'm guessin' it was a warnin' shot, since it went over our heads, awful close.

"*Wŏ de mā ...*" growled Jayne, pushin' me down to the ground and swingin' his weapon round to fire off a few shots of his own. "Cover," he muttered. "Need some gorram cover..."

Now, I don't want you to go thinkin' that I'm the kinda person leaves a comrade in the lurch, but let me be clear as clear can be that I did not under any circumstances consider this fella a comrade. What I saw now was that I'd been given my chance. Jayne, pointin' with his gun, said, "Them trees over there. Get yourself to them." And I did what he said. I dashed off, and left him lumberin' behind me. But when I got to the trees, I didn't stop. I carried right on.

Lookin' back over my shoulder, I saw Jayne reach the cover of the trees.

"Gorram kid!" I heard him shout after me. I turned toward them buildings where we'd been shot at and met Miss Lin, and started to run that way like the very Devil himself was on my tail. What else did Captain Reynolds think I was gonna do? Leave him to get on with the job? I didn't think I could trust his word now. He'd promised me, I thought, as I ran. He'd *promised* me. I saw now I'd been a darn fool to believe a single word that came out of that Browncoat's mouth. Miss Lin had said she was here to see justice done—but what did that mean? Was her idea of justice the same as mine? Was she plannin' on seein' these fellas arrested? Takin' off somewhere to trial? I didn't want that. I wanted them to hang, here, on Abel. I wanted them punished for the murder of my daddy, not some other crime.

My head sure was hurtin', and I'm not sayin' that I was makin' the best plans as I ran away from Jayne Cobb that day and went back towards them buildings. But sometimes you have to stick to your purpose. These fellas—Young Bill Fincher, and Frankie Collier, and whoever it was paid 'em to shoot Daddy—they had done me great harm. All I wanted was to see them pay. That's what drove me, and when I ran out of puff to run, that's what kept me settin' one foot in front of the other as the afternoon started warming up.

All I wanted, you must see, was justice. All I wanted was vengeance. And the sad fact of this 'verse is that there ain't nobody out there will do a darn thing for you, there ain't nobody out there that you can trust to come good. Not even Daddy, who had taken on that darn case and got himself killed for his pains, leavin' me all alone in a world that cares not one jot for the widow and the orphan. I'd thought Captain Reynolds understood, but it seemed to me right then that I'd been mistaken. Got sentimental; trusted the first fella that came my way and treated me kindly. I surely wasn't going to make that mistake again. There was only me—Anne Imelda Roberts—and I was goin' to see this job through and see it done, all on my lonesome, as I had always been, as it turned out had been the case all along.

Simon and Inara had barely arrived back at the Guild House before a message came for them from Scarlett saying he'd "escaped" from the lunch, that his next meeting had cancelled, and he had a window of opportunity right now to meet for drinks. He was sending a company hovercar to bring them over to his hotel.

"Good of him to fit us in," said Simon, dutifully putting on a different shirt and tie. "I'm not sure I like Mr Scarlett much."

"You don't have to like him," said Inara. "You just have to get him to talk."

The hotel turned out to be a crumbling affair at the far end of Main Street, but the concierge gave them a fine welcome, and, when they gave Scarlett's name, had them escorted into the bar. This was shabby too, and old-fashioned, done out in plush but patchy velvets, with plenty of flaking gilt on the edges of seats and table. They were taken to a booth, where Scarlett was waiting for them. When he saw them approach, he got to his feet. He was very sharply dressed, standing out from the other patrons.

"Good to see you both," he said, nodding a welcome. "I hope this place is suitable."

"It's charming," said Inara.

"You think so?" They took their seats and Scarlett looked round. "I think it's as if they've had a hotel from the Core described to them, but never actually seen one."

Inara smiled. She was giving away nothing. Simon felt awkward, recalling occasions when he'd said similar things—and left Kaylee with hurt feelings. The problem was that Scarlett was right. These worlds were nothing like the Core—and Simon preferred the Core. He wished he could take Kaylee there—to Osiris, his home. Show her the sights. Make her see how beautiful it was, how comfortable...

The menus arrived. Scarlett flipped through it. "Don't hold out your hopes for much," he said, with some distaste.

"It can't be that bad, surely?" said Inara.

"Oh, I suppose not," said Scarlett. "But I have to say," he lowered his voice, "the sooner places like Abel can be brought up to scratch, the better..."

"I guess they're trying their best," said Simon.

"Don't get me wrong, it's all very... *quaint*. What I mean is, there's a world of difference in..." He paused to consider his choice of words. "... *opportunity*, and *expectation*, when it comes to worlds like this here on the Rim."

"I've seen worse," said Inara.

"Me too," said Simon.

"That's partly my point," said Scarlett. "Abel wasn't particularly affected by the war. And, until this drought began, it's been doing more or less all right. But the quality of what you can experience here..." He lowered his voice and shook his head.

"The Core worlds are in another league. I don't think I'm saying something *wrong* here. Merely observing."

"And is that why you've come here to Abel?" said Simon. "Is that what interests you most about a place like this?"

There was a brief lull as the waiter came to take their order. Scarlett sighed heavily as he ordered "bar snacks and whatever *decent* white wine you happen to have…" When the waiter left, Scarlett carried on.

"Raising up these places is the whole point of the Rising Sun program," he said. "You can't win a war and then hope the people on the losing side will simply knuckle down and get on with being losers. You have to spread some of the victory around. There are some out there who hope that one day their worlds will be independent again—but the reality is Unification is here to stay."

"Unification means Unification," agreed Simon. One of his father's favorite expressions.

"Exactly," said Scarlett. "So how do we make it a success?"

"You… spread a little of the victory around?" suggested Simon.

"That's right," said Scarlett. "Rising Sun is all about levelling up Rim worlds. Bringing some of that Core prosperity out to the Rim. And if some of us make a little money in the meantime?" He smiled at Simon. "Who would hold that against us?"

"Not me," said Simon. "If I happened to be the one making a little money."

"Well, quite!" He gave Simon a conspiratorial look. "I'll be honest with you, Amery, places like Abel aren't an easy sell. People come out here, they see this," he gestured round, "providing what passes for the best lodgings in town—and they retreat back to the comforts of the Core. A decent hotel would go a long way—"

"But Rising Sun isn't simply about building better resorts, surely?" said Inara.

"What? Oh no, no!" Scarlett laughed. "I'm not in the hospitality business! There are plenty of other people in that line of work. Our ambitions for Abel are much greater. Our primary interest right now is this drought..." He shook his head. "That's causing real concern. It's the main reason that we were approached by, er... well, let's say, many local worthies."

"Might that include our hosts earlier?" said Simon.

"Amongst others," said Scarlett. "The lack of rainfall here on Abel is starting to be a real threat to stability here."

"How so?" said Simon.

"Look, I don't want to scare you off..."

"I'd like to know what I'm getting myself into," said Simon, in a mild voice. "From someone who shares the same horizons as me. People on the Rim, I've observed, seem to have a much higher tolerance for violence in their day-to-day lives."

That, at least, was completely true.

The food arrived. Scarlett picked at it and frowned. "Everything's *fried*," said Scarlett. "You long for a decent salad, *dǒng ma*?" He laughed. "You should see the gym at this place, Lucas! Like a children's playground."

Simon, who hadn't managed to eat much at the lunch earlier, and was getting stuck in, thought the food was absolutely delicious. Perhaps living off *Serenity*'s reconstituted supplies had altered his tolerances. Still, and regretfully, he reined himself back. Didn't want to break cover.

"All right," said Scarlett, pushing his plate aside and reaching for his wine glass, "here's what's going on. The drought has brought a lot of people into town. You must have seen them— half of them sleeping rough." He shook his head. "Local law enforcement isn't on top of things. Parts of the city are a law to themselves these days. Next thing you'll see is people forming their own little militias... We're already providing private security services; you're staying at the Guild House, you must have seen. If the people of Abel don't start getting their house in order, you'll see more of that. Better than vigilantes running around, I guess."

"Will it come to that?" asked Inara.

His eyes drifted briefly over to her, but settled back on Simon. He smiled. "Let's say I've got a meeting with the mayor later." He stretched back in his seat, wine glass in hand. "The local sheriff's office is weak, overstretched. People are losing faith in him."

"Didn't some lawyer or someone get shot?" asked Simon.

"Oh, you heard about that, did you?"

"Hard not to," said Simon.

"Yes, and nobody's been arrested. All a mess. And a distraction from the real work here, which is getting this drought under control. If we can't guarantee climate security, we'll never attract interest from the Core." He glanced at Simon. "You're from Londinium, right?"

"That's right," said Simon. "But I studied on Osiris." He'd decided that it was easier to weave a few truths here and there, to help make the lies more convincing.

"Oh yeah? That's meant to be a nice place."

"I liked it," said Simon.

"The business school?"

Simon had visited the place a few times, when he was taking an elective on healthcare administration. "Yes."

"I don't know it," said Scarlett. "Why go to Osiris rather than stay on Londinium?"

"Why does anyone choose to study on a different planet than the one where their family live?" said Simon.

"Ah," said Scarlett, with a smile. "Like that, was it?"

Scarlett had no idea of the extent of the estrangement between Simon and his parents, but, yet again, that little grain of truth helped with the lie. "And, of course, it meant that I made my own fortune."

"Which was in?"

"Medical imaging technologies," said Simon; something that he could speak about knowledgeably.

"Hmm," said Scarlett. "Not something I know much about… And not particularly what we're looking for here on Abel."

"I sold my company a couple of years ago," said Simon. "I'm now in the business of making money from my money. And if it helps…" He gestured at their shabby surroundings, "…level up a world like this, then we're all winners, aren't we?"

Scarlett smiled and lifted his glass. There was a little more general conversation, and Scarlett, checking the time, said, "Look, I've got to go, I'm afraid. Can't keep McQuinn waiting." He laughed. "Well, I *could*. She needs me more than I need her. But… Hey, don't want to be rude." He put down his glass. "How long are you planning to stay here on Abel, Amery?"

"I can stay as long as I like," said Simon. "Is there more for me to see?"

"There could be," said Scarlett. "Maybe you could come out and see some of what we're doing in the countryside. The research lab we're establishing. See if that looks like something you'd like to put your money into."

"I'd like that very much."

"All right. Look, the next couple of days are likely to be busy, but if you can wait till the end of the week, I'll take you out there. I'll send you some information in the meantime."

"Thank you," said Simon.

Scarlett paid the bill, and they all got up to go. "One last word of advice," Scarlett said, in a low voice, as they went outside. "The situation here is pretty volatile. You might think about making sure you have a way of leaving quickly."

Simon and Inara looked at each other.

"I appreciate," said Scarlett, misunderstanding their look,

"that might not be easy, given your missing IDs and so on, but if you're stuck—let me know. I can get you away easily."

"Thank you," said Simon. They shook hands, and their hovercar arrived to take them back to the Guild House. Back in their rooms, Simon changed, slowly, thinking about all he'd heard. "The thing is," he said, after a while. "The thing *is*…"

"Go ahead," said Inara. "I won't repeat a word you say."

"All right," said Simon. "I… I wouldn't ever say this in Mal's hearing, but I think the man made some good points. Why shouldn't some of the wealth be spread around? Why shouldn't people on a world like this get to have the same standard of living as people back in the Core? I mean, we are all in the Alliance now, aren't we?" He caught Inara's eye and stopped. "Don't say I said any of that to Mal, will you?"

"I certainly won't," she said. "But, you know, Simon—I don't disagree." She smiled. "Promise you won't say that to Mal either, yes?"

"Of course not. But at the same time…" He shook his head. "Inara, he was *awful*!"

She began to laugh. "*Wasn't* he?"

"He barely even *spoke* to you!"

"That's sweet of you, Simon, but you were the one with the money. I wasn't expecting to be spoken to."

"He could have made *some* effort." Simon looked out of the window. The day was wearing on. A year ago, he'd never been to the Rim. Would have shared the same opinions. Had aired a few of them at the start of his time on *Serenity*. Wouldn't dream of doing that now. Spending time with Kaylee had broadened his horizons, he saw, in ways he'd never imagined. Had never even wanted. But here he was, far away from home, and everything had changed. His whole life—that safe, straightforward trajectory, that would have brought him more money, more influence, more status—all gone.

"What next?" said Inara.

The console on the desk chimed. Simon, going to look, said, "Incoming from Mr Scarlett. Oh look! He's sent me some corporate literature. I guess that's the rest of my day spoken for..." He sat down. "Let's see what secrets these reveal..."

"Are you starting to think there may be something to Annie's conspiracy theory?"

Simon shook his head. "No, Inara. I don't think so. Just... greedy people, out to make themselves richer than they already are." The kind of people, he thought, who might sell out their children rather than lose their standing. Didn't make it right. Simon stared at the screen, at the glossy pictures of green fields lit up by the rising sun.

Everything in reverse...

10

Wash, footsore and grouchy after a fruitless day tramping around the city, was looking forward to a shower and a nap. They had spent the day trying to reach more than half-a-dozen people who had at one point been involved in cases like Jacky Colson's, but everywhere they turned they met closed doors. There were a lot of worried people in this city. When he checked the time, he thought he might go so far as to count himself among them. Ryan, hearing their plans for the day, had advised them to get indoors before dark, and Wash was starting to see what he meant. Some of the shops and other businesses were closing early, the proprietors putting up the shutters with a hunted air about them. He'd seen a more than a few small groups of people hanging around, looking like they were biding their time, waiting for it to get dark before getting started on whatever plans they had for tonight. But Kaylee didn't seem bothered. She seemed set on trying one more name. So Wash did what he never did—or never did successfully.

"Kaylee," he said, stopping dead in his tracks. "I am putting my foot down."

She walked on. After a moment or two, she turned to look

at him. "Oh, sorry, Wash, did you say somethin'? I was trying to make sense of this map…"

So much for the foot-putting. "Kaylee, it's gonna get dark soon. Ryan said not to be outside when it got dark. We've got to get under cover." Also, he wanted that shower. And the nap. He particularly wanted the nap. He braced himself for an argument, but Kaylee sighed.

"Okay," she said. "I guess we're hittin' a brick wall, aren't we?" She looked up and down the street. "Huh. Everything's shut. Maybe we *should* hunker down? See what the others have turned up?"

Wash couldn't believe his ears. But he didn't argue.

Back to the place they were staying, on the main road that lay between Westerly and Keyside, he finally got his shower. Halfway through however, the power cut out.

"*Gǒu shǐ!* Typical of my luck!"

He stumbled around the bathroom—"*Ow! Ow! Ow!*"— hitting pretty much every sharp corner, hopping around as he tried to get into his clothes. Kaylee was waiting for him, sitting on the bed, flashlight in hand. Wash had a feeling she always had that kind of thing in her pocket. She looked miserable.

"Kaylee? Everything okay?"

"I think we should go back to Annie Roberts' place."

"Huh?"

"I ain't happy here. Ain't sure we're safe." She nodded over to the window. "Go take a look."

Wash, obediently, padded over to the window and twitched back the curtain.

"*Āiya!*"

Whatever had happened to the power in the hotel wasn't an isolated problem. There wasn't a light on in any building. Late afternoon, the sun racing down, and Ryan's people only getting started. The city would be paralyzed by the time it was full dark.

He saw a hovercar race past, music blaring, couple of folks hanging out of the windows. A couple of moments later, there was the unmistakable sound of a window being smashed, and a huge cheer went up. Not even dark yet and the looting was starting. Wash looked down at his shirt.

"You want my opinion, Kaylee? We're safer in here than out there."

"Been thinkin' about that. Thought Ryan might be willin' to help. I put a call through to him."

"Hasn't he got enough on his hands right now?"

"I'm sure he has. I just wanted to ask if he knew a way through town, keepin' clear of the protests—"

"I'm guessing he said that he couldn't guarantee our safety."

Kaylee flushed. Well, no, of course he couldn't, thought Wash. You shook up a bottle like this, then unpopped the cork, nobody could tell who would be in the firing line. Plenty of angry people out there weren't going to be sitting back taking orders from the Associated General Workers of Yell City. They'd be out and about letting off steam. There'd be more windows broken, and that was only the start... No way was Wash going out in the middle of this. Head down; see what the morning brought.

"What Ryan did say," said Kaylee, "was that he'd send a friend over in a car. But we got to get to a pick-up place first—"

"Oh, I see," said Wash. This, here, now, the words coming out of her mouth—they weren't a suggestion. They were instructions. "Did you think of talking this over with me?"

"It ain't far. Ten, fifteen minutes—"

"In a power cut. With the streets filling up of people intent on causing trouble."

Kaylee's mouth set. "You can stay here if you like. I'm going back. Want to make sure River's okay."

Ah, thought Wash, there it is. Not River though. Simon.

Outside, a little way across the city, a siren was blaring. Kaylee sat on the bed, holding the flashlight, not budging an inch. Wash knew when a battle was lost.

"Give me the flashlight," he said, yanking on his shoes. "You can be in charge of the map."

She jumped off the bed and hugged him. "You're my very favorite of everyone in the crew, you know."

"No, I'm *not*," he said. "That's not enough close to being true."

"Second favorite," she said. "Okay, maybe third."

Mal, Zoë, and Lin had been about hour on the road when the message came from Jayne.

"*She's gone, Mal. Gorram girl gave me the slip.*"

Mal, who had been dozing, was suddenly wide awake. "*Tā mā de*, what're you sayin' to me?"

"*The kid. Someone took a potshot at us, and she made a run for it. Guess she's plannin' on followin' you, best she can.*"

The stream of invective that followed this revelation would have shocked Annie Roberts into silence. "Now you listen to me, you *qīng wāo cāo de liú máng*," said Mal. "You find that girl straight away or you can forget about coming back on *Serenity* when this is done."

"*Mal, I ain't walkin' right!*"

"Ain't thinkin' right neither. You heard me, Jayne. That kid took a bang to the head, she could be out cold now and in bad trouble—"

"*Typical of you to think more some kid than the rest of your crew—*"

"Typical of you to forget that if that girl gets killed, we ain't seein' a penny of her money. Find her, Jayne. Or stay where you are. *Dǒng ma?*"

"*Mal!*"

Mal cut the comm.

"Trouble with the troops?" asked Lin.

"No more than usual," said Mal. "How long till we get where we're going?"

"Another hour or so."

They went deeper into the countryside. No movement anywhere, as far as Mal could see. The sun passed its height, and the afternoon began to lengthen. At last, after a couple of hours, a pale glow appeared on the horizon.

"That's the research base," said Lin, silencing the engine on the hovercar.

"Someone there already," said Zoë. "Collier gang?"

"Mebbe," said Mal. "Best not go in blind. Where we landing, Miss Lin? This car of yours seems quiet enough we could park on the front step, and no-one inside would be any the wiser."

"Let's give it a go, shall we?" Lin replied. Gently, Lin began the descent, bringing the car down within a few meters of the nearest building. They got out, weapons ready. Suddenly, Zoë swung about and fired off a swift, silenced, and deadly round of shots.

"Zoë?"

"Heard somethin'," she said. "Comin' up behind us."

They all froze—and caught the sound, someone groaning in pain, not far away. They moved quickly that way. A man lay on the ground, covered in blood. Not much to be done for this fella, Mal could see, but he might tell them something useful first. He knelt down beside him, put his hand upon the man's shoulder.

"Now listen," he said. "There's still a chance. Might be able to do somethin' for you. But nothin' I can do if there's more of you takin' shots at me. Anyone else here?"

The man looked up with hate in his eyes.

"*Qù nǐ de,*" he said. "Fuck you!" And then he died.

"Mal," said Zoë quietly. "Look at his coat."

Mal looked down. Browncoat.

"*Wǒ de mā* ... Zoë—one of ours!"

"Lookin' that way, sir."

"They're all Browncoats," said Lin, from behind. "Francis Collier, all his men—they were with the Independents during the War." She was looking at Mal oddly. "Didn't you know that?"

"Knew about Collier," said Mal, getting to his feet. "Didn't know the same was true for his whole crew."

"Half of them fought together," said Lin. "Same brigade. Battle of Sturges."

Bloodiest battle of the war, if you didn't count Serenity Valley. Mal, looking at down at this dead... comrade, he guessed, thought what he would do to someone who killed Zoë Alleyne. Zoë, who had been looking through the man's pockets, said, "Got his name here, Mal. Seth Robinson. We'll find his folks, see things done right."

"You all right, Zoë?" asked Mal, grateful that he had not been the one that had done the shootin' here.

"Ain't rightly pleased with myself, sir, but not much to be done."

"*Āiya*," muttered Mal, shaking his head. All been so simple, during the War. You knew exactly who your friends were; you knew exactly who you were there to shoot at and why. Those certainties had kept Mal goin' a long while. But now? Browncoats, takin' on work like this? Mal had taken on a fair few suspect jobs of his own since the end of the war; you had to make a livin', after all, in this gorram 'verse, and he was not so naïve not to think that some folks had come away from that war bent inside, twisted—but this? Scarin' folks off their land? Shootin' good men dead in the street? That weren't right.

"Captain Reynolds," said Lin. "You need to tell me—does this make a difference?"

"I don't know yet," said Mal, with complete honesty.

"'Cause you're going to have to make a decision very soon," she said.

"Sir," said Zoë. "This don't sit well with me, but the truth of the matter is we gave our word to Lin here. And to Miss Annie. We got a job to do, and we should see it done. Everything else will fall out the way it will."

Mal knew she was right. Still, though, he had to wonder, if he'd known that these fellas were all fellas like him—would he have taken on this job?

"Zoë's right," said Mal, to Lin. "We said we'd help, and help we will. Inside, I guess?"

"Inside," agreed Lin.

They moved quietly through the compound until they found what seemed to be the central building. Big glass front and low lights on. Mal, not eager to use Annie Roberts' approach to breaking and entering, was not displeased to learn that Lin was able to bypass the security. They went into a reception area, unstaffed and quiet. The building was arranged behind this space: a bank of silent offices stacked up like bricks in three storys, windows facing out over reception. All the lights were off except in one, on the second floor, to the left. They found the stairs and went up there.

From behind the door, they heard voices and laughter. Cautiously, Mal pushed the door open and walked inside. He found himself looking at a kind of recreation room. Three couches were laid out, and, lining the fourth wall, a kitchen area. A couple of low tables sat in the middle, covered in cups and plates and a few bits and pieces of kit. There was a pool table in the corner, and lounging on the couches were a man and a woman, looking up at him in surprise.

"Who are you?" said the man. On his shirt was a badge with a Blue Sun logo and his name, presumably, underneath. *Townsend*. "Haven't seen you before."

"You know this room is meant for base staff only?" said the woman. She was wearing the same badge, and her name was *Larsen*. "And you should knock?"

"What do you want?" said Townsend. "Are we being moved again?

"I don't want to move again," said Larsen.

Most likely it was the note of petulance in her voice, because all of a sudden Mal felt the rage upon him, and the red mist comin' down over his eyes. Weren't this the gorram truth of the 'verse? This pair, sittin' pretty indoors, feet up, sharin' a drink and laugh, and outside, some poor fella down on his luck paid to protect them, and he was the one lyin' dead on the ground, shot by his own side.

Mal strode forward, grabbed Larsen by her shirt, and pulled her up from her seat. "No," he said. "We ain't been sent by Collier. We been sent to find Collier, and the folks behind him."

"Hey!" said Townsend, jumping to his feet. "Leave her alone!" He made a grab for Mal, and Mal, with one swift swipe of his left hand, sent him flying. Townsend fell back against the couch and bumped, unceremoniously, onto the floor.

"Listen to me," said Mal. "You two are goin' to tell me what's happenin' here, and you're gonna tell me very quickly, or I will be gettin' into the messy business of causin' pain. And you'd better believe me—I'm mighty experienced at causin' other folks pain—"

"Captain." Lin stepped forward. Her voice was calm but firm. "I don't think this is the best approach—"

"Maybe not," said Mal. "But I'll enjoy myself in the meantime."

"Who the hell *are* you people?" whispered Larsen. "Does Collier know you're here?"

"Don't bet on it," said Mal.

"I don't believe you—"

"No? You should. Because Seth Robinson is lying out there in the dark, dead as the black, and if you're hopin' he'll come to save you, you're sorely mistaken." He caught the confusion in her eyes. "Seth Robinson," he said, "was the name of the man left here to look after you." His grip began to tighten around Larsen's throat. She didn't know. She didn't gorram know. The man had been left to protect her and now he was dead and she didn't even know his *name*—

"Sir," said Zoë. "Let her go."

Something was hard-wired into Mal that compelled him to listen to Zoë. He released his hold, and pushed Larsen back into her seat. Lin stepped forward. She was holding up a wallet she'd pulled from her pocket—although her pistol was still ready in one hand.

"My name is Amy Lin," she said. "I'm here on behalf of Parliament and operating under their authority. I've a lot of questions about what's happening here on Abel, and you two," she nodded at the pair of them, "are going to give me some answers. So let's start talking. She glanced at Mal. "All right?"

"Parliament, huh?" said Mal quietly. "You never mentioned that."

"You never asked," said Lin.

When I got back to the buildings, everything was quiet. Captain Reynolds had gone off with his new friend, and Zoë had followed after her captain. I got the feeling that a lot of Zoë Washburne's life involved followin' around after her captain. I told myself good riddance to the pair of them, but I must not tell a lie: I was more than a mite disappointed not to find them still here. I think maybe I was hopin' that Captain Reynolds would have a change of heart if he saw me again (though havin' given Jayne Cobb the slip and run off I confess in hindsight that weren't the likeliest outcome). All I could think was that if I had the chance to come face-to-face with him, tell him what was what, then maybe he would see the error of his ways and come good. Let me come along, as he'd promised. A man shouldn't break his promises, I'd've reminded him of that too. Maybe Zoë would have a change of heart, put in a good word for me, like she had back at the house when I took out my pistol and showed her what I was made of. So when I found that place seemingly deserted... Oh, that was a low moment for me. Everyone gone, and me stuck here like a fool, with only Jayne Cobb to give me a ride home. I was sore about the whole business, and angry, and tried to find solace in the thought that now I wouldn't have to pay a single pretty piece to anyone. But I knew in my heart I would rather have spent the money and seen my justice done. Didn't seem likely to happen now.

I walked slowly down the roadway between the rows of the buildings, keepin' an eye out for any trouble that might be headin' my way, including keepin' an eye out for that darn nuisance Jayne Cobb. Be exactly my luck if he found me. Didn't think his temper would be the friendliest. The only consolation was that my poor head wasn't hurtin' so bad by now, which was a blessin' from the Good Lord himself, and went to show that Captain Reynolds shouldna been so quick to send me on my way with that big fella. I thought maybe if I had a good look round this place, I might find something that would tell me where to find where Miss Lin was taking the captain and Zoë. Maybe then I could walk back to the Mule, and get past Jayne Cobb (I'd done that once already) and find my own way over. I tried the doors and such like, but everything was locked up. I didn't want to shoot or smash my way in like last time, since that would advertise my presence at the place, and I was starting to realize that I had no darn idea whether anyone else had come back here after me and the Captain had gone our separate ways. I didn't think so, but who was to know?

I made my way back to the building where we'd taken refuge earlier that day, and slipped, quiet as a shadow, to the room where we had sheltered when the Collier gang arrived. The door was still standing open, the chairs and such like still lying all round. Splash of Jayne Cobb's blood on the floor. I went inside and took a look round. Nobody there. I poked around them big benches for a while, looking for a console, so's I could do some investigatin' of my own, but the place was bare. All the fittings might be there, but none of the fixtures. This place weren't up and running yet. As I drew nearer to the door, I heard a strange old sound echoin' down the corridor. My goodness, that gave me a scare. I am not one to take fright at such things—I ain't no believer in ghosts and spirits, they are ungodly notions, superstitious, and nobody who follows the teachings of the Good Book should have a moment's truck with such lies and foolery—but I would beg a kindly reader to consider my position at that precise moment. All alone, in the middle of nowhere, without friends nor family, and not long since the villains who murdered my daddy had been takin' a pot shot or two at myself. Not to mention that bump on the head addlin' my thinkin'. I was about ripe for pluckin' when it came to being spooked.

That moan came again, louder'n ever. I nearly dropped my gun right there and ran all the way back to Jayne Cobb. It was only the thought of that big fella's smirkin' face when I turned up that made me pull myself together. Suppose I should be grateful to him for that if nothing else.

"Get a grip, Annie Roberts," I told myself. "'Cause it's see this through right here and right now, or else go back tail between your legs and let Jayne Cobb say I told you so."

I daresay the thought of having Jayne Cobb say, "I told you so," has spurred on better folks than me, and it was more'n enough to get my tired legs movin'. I crept out into the corridor, my pistol all at the ready, and fairly tiptoed along. I could hear that moanin' comin' worse and worse, from one of the rooms not far away, and I could see a little yellow light poolin' out from in there too. As I got closer, I could hear someone talkin' away in a low voice—was there more'n one of 'em? That would be too much for me, all on my lonesome—I wasn't such a fool as to think I could overcome a few of 'em. But then I started to pick out words, and—Good Lord, a sorrier ramble I ain't never heard in all my born days. Whoever this was—and he sounded almost a boy—he weren't happy about how things were workin' out for him. He was havin' a good old cry, and when he weren't sobbin', he were snifflin', and when he weren't snifflin', he were complainin'.

"Ain't *fair*," he muttered. "I done everythin' asked o' me. Done more. Ain't many done more. It ain't *gorram* fair!"

Well, at least now I knew there was only one of 'em, and from the way he was goin' on, he weren't expecting any arrivals in the near future. I crept closer to the door. It was dark out in the corridor, and I was all in black clothes, and figured it wouldn't be easy to see me, particularly when I was not expected to be there at all.

"Ain't fair! I'm hurt! Hurt bad!"

I peered round and into the room—and I saw him. I saw who it was in there, sittin' on the floor and clutchin' his leg like it were givin' him pain.

Young Bill Fincher.

What a sorry sight that villain was, snifflin' away and rubbin' his grimy old shirtsleeve across his dirty dribblin' face and rubbin' his hand along his greasy breeches. I was so shocked to see him there, sittin' on the floor grousin' away to himself, that before I could stop myself, I had let out a gasp. And it was my bad luck, because that boy weren't the complete fool that you might think he was, of course, or else Frankie Collier woulda had no use for him. Fincher looked up, stared at me, and I stared back.

Would you believe it—I felt sorry for him. He weren't any older than me, and it was like I heard my daddy's voice speakin' to me, remindin' me of all the good fortune I'd had throughout my life, with money and two lovin' parents, and how some kids were born with less than nothin'.

"Hey," I said to him. "You need help?"

What a fool I was. I saw a gleam in his eye—greedy and mean—and he reached for his gun. That boy was truly junk. I scrambled to get my own pistol out, but he was quicker. For all his self-professed agony, he was up off the floor in a flash, and over to me, and knockin' that pistol out of my hand. I made a dive for it, but he grabbed me, pushin' me down to the floor, and he weren't gentle, I was down, and he was pointin' his pistol at me. So much for kindness.

Oh, the indignity of it. To have walked in here and come face to face with my chance to win that justice I so sorely wanted, and instead, like a darn fool, to fumble over my weapon, like the kid they were all sayin' I was, and miss my moment, and find myself sittin' on the floor with my sworn enemy standin' over me, lookin' as pleased as Mr Punch himself at his capture. That boy—oh, he was nothing but a heap of *fèi wù*, let me tell you. The preachers and the scriptures, they say have pity, I know— and I say that's all very well, but where was the pity for my poor daddy? Those that don't show pity haven't earned it, is what I say. Never have I hated a body as much as when I looked up at that *fei wu* boy and saw him grinnin' down at me the way he did, teeth bared like the animal he was.

"Well," said Young Bill Fincher, the man that shot my poor daddy dead in Main Street, stepped over his bleedin' body and walked away like he'd done nothin', "ain't I hit the gorram jackpot?"

11

" **W**hy not take a break, Simon?"

"Hmm?" Simon looked up from the console to see Inara standing beside him, holding a cup of jasmine tea. "A break?"

"You've been stuck at that console for ages."

"Yes, well, Emory Scarlett has been very persistent." Simon stretched back in his seat, joints cracking. Scarlett had been sending across material about Rising Sun throughout the afternoon and Simon had assiduously worked his way through every brochure, every presentation, every financial report, and every piece of documentation. He probably hadn't studied this hard since his final exams, when at least the material was familiar. This had been a crash course in business administration, minutes from Parliamentary committee meetings, and, of course, the intricacies of the science behind the R&D work that Rising Sun intended to carry out on Abel.

"Have you learned anything?" said Inara, handing him the cup.

"I've learned a lot." He sipped at the tea. He was hungry. How long had he been at this? He checked the time. Early evening. The lights in the Guild House were starting to come on; the room was filling gently with a warm amber light.

"Have you learned anything of use?"

"I think so… Scarlett was pretty clear when we met him that his priority was the drought here. So far as I can make out, he's trying to attract investors to work on solving that. Genetically modified crops are one big area of research, and there's several planned programs related to soil science…"

"None of it sounds terribly exciting."

"Unless you're living on a farming world in the middle of a drought."

Inara laughed. "That's fair," she conceded. "But all of this seems perfectly respectable. Responsible, even. Why would this lead to the death of Isaac Roberts?"

"That," admitted Simon, "I've not been able to establish. We know that Rising Sun have been buying up the land from failing farms, but there's nothing illegal about that."

"Although it's a little hard to stomach," said Inara.

"True," said Simon, "although you could argue that it's better than the land going to waste… Anyway, I can't find any financial irregularities in the purchases. But that's no real surprise, given that all my information comes from Scarlett…" He frowned and tried to put his thoughts in order. He was sure he was missing something, some link in the chain, but he could not put his finger on what that might be. He turned back to the console, sipping at his tea, and was soon immersed once again in his reading. And then, suddenly, everything went dead. The screen of the console went blank; the lights went out. The room was caught in the half-darkness of late afternoon.

"*Wà!*" said Inara, in a startled voice. She rose from her seat and went over to the window. There were no lights on outside either. The whole Guild House seemed to be affected.

"Power cut," said Simon. "I'm sure everything will be back on in a moment—"

Five or ten minutes later, they were still without power when there was a tap at the door. It was one of the companions-in-training, carrying a lamp.

"Ms Serra, Mr Amery—Ms Vitale sends her apologies. The power seems to be down across the whole city. We don't know when it will back. We have our own generator here at the Guild House, which should be working soon. In the meantime..." She held out the lamp, which Inara took.

"The console isn't working either," said Simon.

"Connections to the Cortex are down until the generator comes online," said the girl. "I really am most sorry about this, Mr Amery—"

"It's not your fault," said Inara. "We're happy to wait."

The girl nodded her thanks, and left. Simon tapped his fingers against the console.

"Don't worry," said Inara. "River will be fine."

"I know..." Worrying about River was his default state.

The lights came back on, and the console whined and restarted.

"That's better," said Inara. "Do you want to try to speak to her?"

Simon nodded, but before he got the chance, the console chimed.

"It's for you," he said, moving out of the way so that Inara could take his seat.

It was Madame de Cecille. "*My dear Ms Serra,*" she said. "*I hope I'm not disturbing you.*"

"Not at all."

"*I'd intended to call earlier to enquire about your health. You did look quite shaken.*"

"Getting away from the lights was all that was required, madame," Inara said. "I was quite myself again within the hour. It's extremely kind of you to take the time to ask."

"*I'm delighted to hear you're well. Although I'd heard already from a mutual acquaintance you'd been out and about today...*"

She was leaving the space open for Inara to describe their meeting with Scarlett. Inara simply smiled.

"*Which led me to assume that you were much better.*"

"As I say, madame, I was entirely myself again within the hour. Lucas has been looking after me."

"*He's such a nice young man, isn't he? Very handsome…*"

Simon flushed.

"He certainly has his charms," Inara said, wickedly.

"*How did he get on with Emory Scarlett?*"

"I would say they had a great deal in common."

"*Good,*" said Madame. "*I know Scarlett was keen to make a good impression.*"

Inara made an encouraging noise. She had an inkling that Madame liked to be the one with privileged information.

"*Although truth be told I find him something of a cold fish. He doesn't think much of Abel, does he?*"

"These young men are often blind to all that's best about the Rim," said Inara. "But was there something in particular that you wanted, Madame?"

"*I think it might be wise if you joined us for dinner this evening,*" said Madame.

Simon shook his head, and Inara had some sympathy. Simon wasn't in his element, acting this part, and the more he had to, the more likely he would slip up and make a mistake. "That's most kind, Madame, but—"

"*I confess,*" she said, as if Inara had not spoken, "*I'm somewhat concerned about your safety there at the Guild House.*"

"Our safety?"

"*Did the power go down there?*"

"Yes, but they have a private generator—"

"*I don't want to give you any cause for concern—and certainly not give you the impression that Abel is some kind of lawless backwater,*" *but there's been some strife recently in the city, and it seems there may be further trouble tonight."*

"Trouble?"

"Tempers rising, a few people with too much time on their hands having too much to drink—"

"How alarming. It's not," Inara said with a straight face, "the kind of thing we're accustomed to back in the Core." Which was true. The surveillance nets would recognize the faces of troublemakers; access to most areas was strictly governed by having the right codes, and one's presence in the wrong area was marked against you.

Madame de Cecille was looking very comfortable. *"I don't want you to get the wrong impression of our world."*

No, she wouldn't want Lucas Amery—or, rather, his money—to be scared away.

"I gather a man was shot dead recently on Main Street," said Inara.

"Where did you hear that?"

"I... believe Lucas heard it mentioned at your party."

"A very tragic incident," said Madame. *"Another young man, worse for drink, deciding to take out his frustrations on someone trying to help him."*

"Has he been arrested yet?"

"I'm not entirely sure. If he hasn't, Sheriff Peters will surely be making an arrest soon. He's a good man—a trifle slow-moving—"

"That's good," said Inara. "I'd hate to think that kind of thing was usual on Abel."

"It isn't—"

"Like tonight's trouble."

"Exactly. You'll come, won't you?"

"I believe we'll be perfectly comfortable here, madame, but thank you for your kind offer."

The other woman looked put out, as if she wasn't used to being denied one of her wishes. *"It's very easy for me to send transport over to the Guild House for you—"*

"Thank you," said Inara firmly. "But no. We're settled here."

A few more pleasantries were exchanged, and then the call ended. Simon whistled softly. "She was persistent. I wonder how much we should read into that."

"She might simply mean what she says," said Inara. "As far as she's concerned, you're an important potential investor. I imagine the de Cecilles have spent a great deal on security around their house. There's probably nowhere safer in the city right now." Inara bit her lower lip. "Still, if what Vitale said earlier is true, the Guild House might not be entirely safe…"

Inara watched a shadow fall across Simon's face. He sat at the console and tried a couple of times to put a call through to the Roberts house, but it was no use. He got up and walked over to the window, looking out across the street.

"You're worried about River, aren't you?"

"When am I not?" He began to pace the room, rubbing and twisting his hands.

"I don't think Madame was lying when she told us that it might not be safe to move around the city—"

"I don't like to think of her alone."

"She's not alone, Simon."

"So that's one teenage girl and a preacher—"

"Simon," said Inara, sternly. "You know as well as I do that Book is not simply a preacher. River is safe in his care."

"I know… but…" He went back to the window and stood staring out for a while. "I'm going back to the Roberts house, Inara. It's okay if you want to stay here. But River's my responsibility. If there is going to be trouble here tonight, I can't leave…"

At some point, Inara thought, that was exactly what Simon

would have to do. He couldn't stand indefinitely between River and the rest of the 'verse. But he wouldn't be Simon if he didn't try.

Inara reached for her wrap. "Come on. We'd better go if we're going."

"Inara—"

"Stop quarrelling. The later we leave it, the more dangerous it will get. So grab your coat and get moving."

He shot her a look of intense gratitude, and pulled on his coat.

The concierge stopped them in the front of the house. "Not to alarm you, but it might be wise to stay indoors tonight."

"We've heard what's going on," said Inara. "We have a friend staying in town, and we're concerned about their safety."

Simon, she saw, was already out of the door.

A big hovercar was standing outside.

"Mr Amery?"

"Who's asking?" said Simon.

"Compliments of Monseigneur and Madame de Cecille. They'd like you join them for dinner this evening."

"I'm afraid that we're—"

"I don't believe," said the man, "they intended this to be a request."

Amy Lin's politer methods might not bring the immediate gratification that came from the application of violence against an unlikeable body, thought Mal, but he had to admit they were getting results. Townsend and Larsen, one eye all the time on Mal and Zoë, were telling her everything they knew.

"You've got to understand," said Townsend, "we're technicians, okay?"

"Sure," said Lin. No, thought Mal, she didn't believe him either.

"We're not experts about what's going on here." Townsend glanced at Larsen, who shrugged and nodded. "We think we have an idea. But…"

"We want to make sure we'll be okay."

"Corporate whistle-blowers are protected under Alliance law," said Lin.

"Yeah, well, Isaac Roberts was protected under Abel law," said Larsen. "And look where that got him."

"You're well informed," noted Mal, "about current affairs here on Abel. For a coupla technicians out here in the sticks."

"We're not stupid," said Larsen.

"That remains to be seen," said Mal.

"All right," said Lin. "Let's cut the repartee. I want to know what's going on here."

"You've heard about the up-levelling program," said Townsend.

"Yes," said Lin.

"You understand what it's about?"

"I'm here on behalf of Parliament," said Lin. "You can assume I know their business."

Stuck in the craw, but Mal approved of this tone of Lin's. It was certainly doing the job of scarifying these two.

"The plan for Abel was always to increase its agricultural capacity," said Townsend. "Make it the breadbasket for this system and beyond. In the long term, that would mean plenty of work, plenty of jobs—"

"But in the short term the small farms and their owners were in the way," said Mal. "We know all about that. We know about the cheatin' and usin' the Collier gang to scare people away from their land—"

Larsen laughed. "You think *that's* what all this is about? That's nothing—small beans! You're not thinking big enough!"

"Gettin' a mite too pleased with yourself, Ms Larsen," said Mal.

"The problem," said Townsend, "was things weren't moving quickly enough. So… the decision was made to speed up the process. To make the land, well… not fit for purpose."

A chill was starting to go down Mal's spine. "You folks been poisonin' the land?" he said? "Pollutin' it?"

"Again," said Larsen, "your horizons are too limited."

"Lady," said Mal, "you got to understand I ain't a nice man, and I ain't above hittin' a woman—"

"Nobody will be hitting anybody," said Lin. "Am I supposed to be thinking that this drought is manmade?"

Again, that look between them. "Yes," said Townsend.

"*Lǎo tiān yé*," said Zoë. "*Why?* Why would anyone do such a thing?"

But Mal could see it. Could see all the workin' that had gone on in whichever evil mind had thought up this one. A mind that couldn't move quickly enough to make worlds like Abel completely redone, didn't care what damage was done in the meantime. Drought, poverty, people ruined, hopes and dreams smashed. But none of that mattered, did it, if there some great plan, some great scheme to remake these Rim worlds in the image of the Core. They'd claim, wouldn't they, that in time everyone would feel some benefit, but the truth was that there were people back in the Core— and some here, too, on Abel; there'd be willin' partners in this, no doubt—who would be makin' a killin' from this…

"I'll be damned," said Mal, wonderingly. "You think you've heard more or less every gorram evil thing can be done in the 'verse and then you get hit with a scheme like this, and…" He looked at Townsend and Larsen. "Were you part of this, the two of you? You musta been part of all this."

The two of them were shaking their heads wildly.

"You'll forgive me," said Mal, "if I find that mighty hard to believe." He looked at Lin. "Did *you* know?"

Her face was stony. "I did not."

"Well, Miss Lin," said Mal. "This is your Alliance. Hope you like it."

"This ain't my Alliance," said Lin, rather too quickly. Yes, she was shaken too. And so she might be. How often did they need tellin', folks like this—the Alliance, they meddled. They did folk harm.

"You sure?" said Mal.

"I was sent here specifically to find out what was going on and to stop it," said Lin. "And I'm going to stop it."

"But you will help us?" said Townsend. "We don't want to be left with the blame for this. This wasn't us!"

"You weren't exactly hinderin'," said Mal.

"Have you seen those guys?" said Larsen. "The guys with the guns? They shot some bigshot lawyer dead in broad daylight. They can do what they like! You think we were able to tell them 'no'?"

"We're technicians, nothing more," said Townsend. "We're here to set up the systems, make sure the site is connected to the Cortex, fix the *lights*!"

"And you both happened to find yourselves reading some top-secret files giving away the game of what's goin' on here. *Gŏu shĭ!*" said Mal. "You must think I was born yesterday!" He turned to Lin. "Can I get on with killin' these two now? We came out here to see some justice done and *rén ci de fó zŭ* I'm about ready now to do it—"

"Captain Reynolds," said Lin, rising to her feet. "A word in private."

Mal, reluctantly, followed her out of the room, leaving Zoë to keep an eye on their new friends. "What's your problem, Miss Lin?"

"Right now, my problem is you," she said.

"Well, that ain't friendly—"

"I need these people on side," said Lin, "and, ideally, unafraid."

"They should be afraid," said Mal. "Afraid of spending the rest of their lives in some godforsaken Alliance lock-up—"

"That's not going to happen," said Lin.

"*What?*"

"These two aren't going to jail. I need them to testify. Listen, Reynolds—I don't care about these two. Maybe they're in deeper than they say, maybe they aren't. But it's not them I want. I want whoever's behind them. Whoever came up with this idea, whoever signed it off, and whoever's diverting funds towards bankrolling the whole business. These two—they're nothing, other than my way into that. I want them taken back to the Core and ready to give evidence, not scared so much they won't say another word. *Dŏng ma?*"

"You really think you'll get someone to carry the can for this? Someone high up? They'll have packed up and covered their tracks already. You're foolin' yourself if you think you'll get anyone up high to pay for this—"

"It's worth a try." She sighed. "Captain, aren't you sick of seeing people get away with this kind of thing? Hollowin' out people's livelihoods? Walkin' away without consequence? I don't know what will happen after this, but I'd like to try to see someone pay the price for what's been done here. So I don't mind if those two never face prosecution. Because they're too easy."

Certainly, Mal was to think later, she made a persuasive case. To see the real powers-that-were out in the 'verse brought to justice for once? That was most definitely a temptin' proposition. But Mal wasn't much of one for faith in anythin', and the rule of law and the bend of history toward justice were only a couple of things he'd lost hope in over the years. On balance, he thought later, he would most likely have fought his corner a little longer. But the fact was, he didn't get the chance. Because from outside, there came bright lights and the sound of hovercars descendin' from the heavens, and a voice callin' out:

"You folks inside. This is Frank Collier speakin'. And I'm here to say that you folks need to start thinkin' about surrenderin'."

Ryan's people were out and about. Wash and Kaylee had passed a dozen or so of them, further up the street, banners out, chanting their slogans. Fair pay and conditions, all of it perfectly shiny, but Wash wanted to keep his distance just in case. He followed Kaylee dutifully down the street. Wash loved Kaylee like she was a little sister, and he wished all good things for her, even in her pursuit of Doctor Simon Tam (who Wash didn't *dislike*, not as *such*, but thought that Kaylee could do so much *better*). However, there were limits even to Wash's legendary patience and good-humor, and being dragged across a dark city in the middle of a power cut with sirens blaring and people shouting, and a general sense that someone somewhere was going to throw a punch and then the whole place would blow up like a particularly explodey kind of explosive—that, *that*, was definitely reaching Wash's limits.

They had put a little distance between them and the demo when they came to a crossroads. Now here was a problem, and looked like it might be a serious problem. A bonfire had been started in the middle of the road, around which a dozen or so people were gathered. Every so often, someone threw something on the fire, and if it bore a Rising Sun logo, that got particularly loud cheers. An awful lot of booze was being passed round.

"*Āiya*," muttered Wash. "I hope your friend Ryan knows what he's started."

"These ain't his people," said Kaylee.

Maybe not, thought Wash, but their action had given these people the excuse.

"Kaylee?"

"Yes, Wash, what is it?"

"I'm thinking maybe being outside right now isn't the best idea?"

"It'll be fine."

"I'm not sure it will, Kaylee."

"All we have to do is go down this street, turn left, go half-a-mile along the main road, then left again, then right, then—"

"Kaylee," said Wash. "We're not gonna get past these guys. They're not letting anyone past." He looked back up the street. The demonstrators were getting closer and closer. When they met these fellas here, it wasn't going to be pretty... "Kaylee, we need to get inside, under cover, something. Quickly."

"Maybe there's another way back to the rendezvous—"

"You know how they build towns and cities so the parts that are prone to riots only have one or two exits? Means someone can come and seal them off easily?"

"I... didn't know that, Wash, no," said Kaylee. She frowned.

"Well, they do. And I'm gonna hazard a guess we're on the wrong side of that."

"But we have to get back to the others!"

"I mean, we actually *don't*—"

"But I'm worried about River!" (By which, Wash knew, she chiefly meant Simon.) "And Shepherd Book, of course."

"Kaylee, the idea of me and you running to rescue Shepherd Book of all people is perhaps the most ridiculous idea either of us has come up with. He's the one that should be running to the rescue of us."

"But River—"

"Is with the Shepherd, and Simon knows she is, and Simon—I hope—will have the good sense to stay indoors and sit this one out, and only poke his pretty little head up tomorrow morning when this is all over." As Wash himself was extremely keen to do. "Kaylee," he said, urgently. "Those fellas over there are looking our way, and I don't think they like what they see."

"Can't be me."

"Can't be me either."

"Do you have any shirts in single colors?"

"Why would I own any shirts in single colors?"

"So that you don't stand out like a beacon in the middle of a riot?"

"I'd like to be very clear at this point," said Wash, "that I was not the one that insisted we came outside this evening."

"You gonna hold that against me forever?"

"I hope I get the chance to hold this against you forever," said Wash. Throughout this exchange, they had been moving steadily along up the street, watching, intently, a group of six or seven *pretty impressively muscled* guys moving steadily towards them. "Kaylee," said Wash. "Did you ever think that you would miss having Jayne around?"

"Nope," said Kaylee. "But I do now."

"When do you think we ought to start running for our lives and yelling, 'Help'?" said Wash. "Or do you think that's too undignified?"

It turned out to be about five seconds later, and really very undignified. They sprinted up the street, their pursuers gaining rapidly. They came out onto a main road, dodging across, through traffic, and running along the other side, past closed shops. Nowhere open now to dive into.

"Gotta stop," gasped Wash, to Kaylee's back, a couple of feet ahead. "Outta breath…" He pulled up, doubling over and sucking in air. Kaylee pulled up and came back to join him. "We shook 'em off?"

"I think so," said Kaylee. "Too busy along here…"

Wash was still getting his breath back when a hovercar pulled up alongside them.

"Kaylee Frye and Hoban Washburne?"

"Yes," said Wash. "I mean, 'No'. I mean, Are you from Ryan Hunter?"

"Fella," said the driver, "quit talkin' and get in."

"Wash," whispered Kaylee, in an anxious, "I don't think this is our lift…"

"I ain't keen," said the driver, "on bein' out here longer than I have to, so I'd be obliged if you did me the favor of getting' in."

"Why?" said Wash, feebly.

"Mayor wants to see you."

"Oh," said Wash, faintly. "In that case…"

About fifteen minutes later, they were being marched through a very busy City Hall upstairs to a big office, where Mayor McQuinn, surrounded by aides and people shouting and banks of consoles telling her important things, looked up from the melee at the pair of them, and said, "You know, many of my present troubles seem to arise from the moment that gorram scruffy bag of bolts that you call your ship landed on Abel."

Wash, watching Kaylee turn purple, braced himself for impact.

"Ma'am," said Kaylee. "Missus Mayor—*whatever* you're calling yourself. I understand that you are having a difficult time this evening, but nobody—nobody—says a word against *Serenity*. In fact, I am *done* with all this *niú shi*, and I ask—no, I *demand*—a full apology for everything that has been said since I arrived on this gorram world not only about my capabilities as an engineer but against that beautiful ship herself."

Everyone in the room had gone silent, and was staring at Kaylee. After a moment, the mayor asked her staff to leave. When the room was clear, she turned to Kaylee.

"Okay," said McQuinn. "I take it back. I apologize unreservedly. And not only that—I'll ask the port authorities to write off the fine when all this business is done, and if they don't, I'll cover it from my own pocket. How's that for an apology?"

"I think," said Kaylee, "that's probably quite fair."

"Can we get down to business?" said Wash. "By which I mean, could you tell us why you've spirited us away here tonight? I mean, don't get me wrong, it was all very timely and everything, but... *Why?*"

"I have been tryna to speak to someone from your crew ever since you arrived. I knew Annie Roberts brought you here. I tried to speak to Ms Serra at the party, but she was whisked away by some smarmy businessman from the Core—"

Wash suppressed a smile at this description of Simon, and gently laid a hand upon Kaylee's arm to prevent her leaping to his defense.

"I told Annie Roberts this business was in hand. As if I haven't got enough to worry about with the city in the state it is right now—"

"You coulda left us alone," said Kaylee. "Let us get on with things."

"You're makin' a mess of things is what you're doin'."

"Not keen on us bringin' Isaac Roberts' killer to justice, huh?"

"What?" McQuinn fell back in her seat. "Miss Frye, I don't know what impression you've picked up or where, but me and Isaac Roberts were friends. Sure, he was on the wrong side during the war, but you can't hold that against a fella forever, and not when he's on the side of the angels now. Him and me knew there was somethin' goin' on here, funds from the Core assistin' all kinds of malfeasance. And when he was shot dead..."

If Wash wasn't mistaken, tears had sprung to her eyes.

"When he was shot dead, I sent for someone from the Core to come and deal with them killers, and next thing I know Annie Roberts has it in her head to bring you lot in, with no clue as to how tense things are around here, and now the whole city's on a knife edge and me and Sheriff Peters ain't sure we got enough people to keep things calm... Hell, I should deputize the *pair* of you!"

"Oh," said Kaylee. "I guess… I apologize too?"

"Well, so you should, the whole sorry lot of you should be apologizin'. And now Annie Roberts is nowhere to be found—"

"We know where she is," said Wash. "Well, we don't know where she is, not right this second, but we know who she's with."

"Your Captain Reynolds, presumably, and chasin' up and down the backcountry tryna find Young Bill Fincher."

There was a knock at the door and one of her aides looked in. "Ma'am," she said. "Someone here to speak to you."

"One more minute," said McQuinn. She looked at Kaylee and Wash. "*Gŏu shĭ*," she said, "if this city isn't on fire within a couple of hours, it'll be luck and hope holdin' the place together. You and your crew—you've been nothing more than a fatal distraction."

Kaylee and Wash looked guiltily at each other. And then: "You know," said Kaylee. "I think we might be able to help with that."

"Help? What, you two? We gonna blind 'em with this fella's shirt?"

"There's no need for everyone to keep on being be rude about my shirt," said Wash. "I *like* my shirt—"

"No," said Kaylee. "Not us. But how do you feel about speakin' to the people who've been causin' all this disruption? I mean, the ones that decided to pull the plug on the power and the lights and Cortex and so on."

"Um, Kaylee," said Wash, "I'm not sure that the mayor can negotiate with the people who are more or less holding a gun to her head?"

"They're not the ones holdin' the gun, Wash. They're… leaning on the off switch for a while."

"That's maybe splitting *hairs* slightly?"

"Mr Washburne," said the mayor. "How about you let me decide for myself?"

"Oh," said Wash. "Yeah. Of course." He mimed zipping his lips. "I'll shut up now, shall I?"

"If you could, for a moment or two," said McQuinn. Her eyes narrowed as she looked at Kaylee. "Your friend here's right though. Why should I talk to these fellas? Look at the trouble they're causin' this city. A place that's as much mine these days—mine and my constituency—as it is theirs. Why should I trust 'em?"

The door opened again. "Ma'am," said the aide. "Got someone here wants to speak to you urgent."

"One more minute!"

The door closed. Kaylee, taking a deep breath, said, "Cuts both ways, you know. Them fellas, they think you're sellin' 'em out."

"Sellin' 'em out?"

"Say you're in bed with Rising Sun, tryna bring in private contractors, cut their wages. Jobs for the farmers and not for them—"

McQuinn was shaking her head. "It ain't like that—"

"No? Well, you need to start making that clear, Missus Mayor, because as far as the city workers are concerned, the signals you're sending out are quite the opposite."

McQuinn ran her hand through her hair. Sat in thought for a moment or two. Wash glanced at Kaylee, who gave him a tentative smile back. Simon Tam, thought Wash, you are an idiot.

"You know these people, do you?" said McQuinn, at last. "Friends of yours?"

"Wouldn't say they were *friends*," said Kaylee. "But they might be willin' to listen to me. Why? You willin' to talk to them? Make a deal?"

"Miss Frye," said the mayor, with sigh. "I'd make a deal with Old Nick himself, if he could stop this city burnin' tonight—"

The door swung open. A young man strode in, looking for all the world as if he owned the place. He had a smart suit, a corporate badge, slicked-back hair, and Wash instinctively hated him.

"McQuinn?" said the man. "What's going on in here?"

Kaylee turned to the mayor, eyes flashing. "See?" she said. "See what I mean?"

12

"*Come out, Captain Reynolds. Come and talk to me—man to man.*"

Mal, crossing to the window, looked outside. Three hovercars were lined up, with a half-dozen fellas, all armed, silhouettes against the darkening sky.

"*Zāo gāo*," muttered Mal. "Zoë, what you thinkin'?"

"Thinkin' it's a bad idea, sir."

Mal tended to agree, and more—might be the worst idea in a day full of terrible ideas.

"*Simply want to talk, Reynolds. Nothin' more. Word of honor.*"

Honor. This from a fella who'd sent someone to kill Isaac Roberts in cold blood.

"*Want to see if we can come to an agreement. Man to man. Browncoat to Browncoat. Or are you workin' for the Alliance now?*"

"Don't fall for it, sir—"

Far too late for that, though Mal. He wanted to look this fella in the face. Tell him what was happenin' here on Abel; the kinds of folks that he was workin' for. Man to man. Browncoat to Browncoat.

"All right, Collier!" he yelled back. "I'll trust your word as a Browncoat. But you'd better believe my folks are here lookin' out for me."

"*Come round to the front. It'll be me and my second. Bring your own fella if you want.*"

"No," said Mal. "I'll come down there. But first I want to see those friends of yours get in those cars and pull back."

There was a pause, then, "*All right,*" Collier called back. Mal watched him exchange a few words with his crew, and then most of them climbed into the hovercars. They lifted and pulled back. "*That good?*" said Collier.

"That's good," said Mal. "I'm ready to talk." He turned to the two women. "Zoë, you're with me. Lin, you cover us from up here." He glanced at the two technicians. "You'll be all right?"

"I can handle these two," Lin replied.

Mal was sure she could. With a nod to Zoë to follow, he left the rec room and went downstairs. Before going out of the back of the building, he checked in with Lin, who confirmed that Collier's men were still holding back as agreed.

"All right. We're going out."

He went out the back door, Zoë behind, into the dusk. Two men were waiting, nine or ten feet away. Mal moved slowly forward, risking a glance over his shoulder and up at the rec room. The lights were down, but he could just about make out a dark shape by the window. Lin was covering them.

"Collier," he said, and raised his hand in greeting.

One of the two men moved forward. "Pleasure to meet you at last. Captain Reynolds, ain't it?"

"That's right. My reputation precedes me, huh?"

"Word gets round real quick on Abel," said Collier.

They eyed each other. Not much that was striking 'bout him, Mal thought; another ordinary fella caught up in the war, tryna find a way to live afterward. Takin' on whatever job came up. One thing Mal didn't miss though. Eyes hard as nails. There'd been some real bloodshed, hadn't there, at the Battle of Sturges.

"I'm hopin'," said Mal, "between us we can find some common ground, work out our differences—"

"Our differences?" said Collier. "Seems to me they're plain enough. You're interferin' in business ain't got much to do with you."

"Asked to intervene. Young lady name of Annie Roberts. Heard of her?"

"Oh," said Collier, "I think everyone on Abel knows Miss Roberts. Amazin' how much trouble one little girl can cause. She can talk too, can't she? Talk the bark off a tree."

A prickle went down Mal's spine. "You've met her?"

"Met her?" Collier laughed. "Captain, I *got* her. I don't know whether you were meant to be lookin' out for her, but fact is she's been wanderin' round out here in the wild, all on her lonesome, and as luck would have it, she wandered straight into the open arms of Bill Fincher. Ain't that a grand joke? You need to take better care of your employers. Or else they ain't gonna be in much of a position to pay."

"*Āiya*," muttered Zoë. Mal agreed with the sentiment. Quickly, he said, "Now, listen, you and I both know that she's only a kid—"

Collier was shaking his head. "Nuh-huh. You listen to me—and listen good. I got the Roberts girl, and I've a mind to keep her. Unless…"

"Unless what?"

"'Less I hear news from Yell City that you and your crew have left Abel."

Tricky proposition, thought Mal, since they were some way from laying their hands on the money to get back *Serenity*. "Not sure I'm ready to make such a deal—"

"Oh, I think you are—or you should be. So, you go on back to Yell City, now, and when you're good and gone, I'll see Miss Roberts safely home—"

Mal moved forward. The man standing behind Collier raised his gun. Zoë did likewise.

"It's all right," said Mal. "Ain't makin' a move. But—you gotta hear me out, Collier. These people you're workin' for—whoever they are—they don't mean well for Abel. They don't mean well for anyone livin' here. You, your friends and family, your kin and everyone else on this good world of yours. They mean to bring you down on your knees, take what's yours and sell it back to you. I seen what's goin' on here, and I got people willin' to tell the truth. You're a man who fought for the future of your home, and I know if you hear me out, you'll be willin' to fight again—"

Collier wasn't laughing now. "Fight *again*? What's that? You think the war's still goin' on?"

"Kind of war, yes. A war between those who want to live and let live, and those who wish to meddle—"

"Then you're a *xī niú* fool," said Collier. "War's done. Over. We lost. Men like you and me—the sooner we face up to that the better. Ain't no place for them ideals of ours no more, Reynolds. Lost cause, and I ain't willin' to be a loser my whole life. I'm gonna make somethin' out of this new 'verse. I fought long and hard, and I've earned somethin' for me and mine—"

"Ain't goin' to earn it from the people you're workin' for now," said Mal, shaking his head. "They're the worst the Alliance has to offer, and they're harmin' your world, right now—"

Collier laughed out loud. "The *worst* of the Alliance? You hear yourself? We used to say they were all as bad as each other. Who's payin' you now? Annie Roberts? You know why Abel went Alliance in the end? Her father's doin'! We mighta least stayed neutral if it hadn't been for him! Him and his Core wife, talkin' fancy to their wealthy friends, sellin' us out—"

What? The world tilted. Mal didn't know; hadn't known...

"And you take his daughter's money? Call yourself a

Browncoat, Reynolds? You're like the rest of us—tryna get by in the 'verse, takin' money from whoever will pay. You ain't better'n me. And if I ain't a Browncoat no longer—neither are you."

"Sir," said Zoë, quietly. "He's hopin' to get a rise from you. Don't give him that particular pleasure."

"No," said Mal, softly. "I won't…" But he had much to think on, after this exchange. "I want the girl back, Collier."

"She'll go back, once you and your crew are gone. Listen now. You and whoever else is here tonight with you—we'll let you leave. No shootin', no killin'. You head on back right now to the city, and when I hear tell your ship has left Abel, I'll send Miss Annie Roberts home without a hair on her head harmed. But one hint of trouble… Well, you better believe me—that girl won't see her home again. You hear?"

"I hear," said Mal. "But we ain't goin' nowhere till you show me Annie Roberts. Show me she's safe and well, and then maybe we'll talk about what happens next." Backing away, he and Zoë retreated back indoors. Lin was waiting for them in the rec room. Townsend and Larsen were sitting on the couches, hands now in restraints, silent and watchful.

"What did he say?" asked Lin. "Did you appeal to his better nature?"

"Not sure he has one," said Zoë.

"Did you know?" said Mal.

"Know what?" said Lin.

"That Isaac Roberts sided with the Alliance in the War?"

Lin frowned. "Did you *not* know?"

"I did not," said Mal.

"Does it *matter*?" said Lin. "Roberts isn't the one pointing guns at us—"

"Not now, no—"

"He wasn't the one selling out his world to these people."

Lin nodded at their captives. "He died trying to stop it. Captain, they're poisoning this place! Wrecking lives. You know right from wrong, Reynolds. And Collier—he's in the wrong."

"He ain't a bad man," said Mal.

"You sure about that, sir?" said Zoë.

Might he have gone this way, Mal wondered, had turned out differently? Had there been no Zoë, and no *Serenity*? There'd been moments, he knew, when he'd looked so hard at the black that there hadn't been anythin' past it. But he'd dug in; dug deep. Found his way through, and kept on findin' it.

"No," said Mal, "he ain't bad. He's just a lost cause."

That was what it was, Mal thought; Collier and his people— they'd lost their way. Forgotten what had sent them off to war in the first place. Love for home and the way things were done at home. Wantin' to be left alone to get on with the business of livin'. That was how Mal tried to lead his life. But this fella? He was out for himself now, out to make what he could out of the trouble his world was in. And that wasn't right. That wasn't what they'd fought for. Even when you lost, you tried to remember what it was you'd fought for.

"Sir," said Zoë. "What are we gonna do?"

"What are we gonna do?" Mal looked out of the window. The cars were coming back. "We don't do anythin' until I've seen Annie Roberts standin' out there, safe and sound. And then… then it'll be time to put this fella and his whole crew out of their misery."

The journey from the Guild House to the de Cecille residence hardly took them through the less salubrious parts of the city, but even so, Inara could hear the distant sounds of trouble across town. Sirens wailing; hovercars throbbing. Their car swung round a corner giving them a view across the city, and

Inara saw flickering patches of light here and there, red and orange—something set on fire, she guessed. She sighed, and glanced at Simon. He was hunched forwards, chewing at his thumbnail. Worrying about River, she imagined. She looked out again. Some of the houses they were passing were cloaked in darkness, but the majority, like the Guild House, had their own sources of power.

Suddenly, Simon gasped. "Oh!" he said. "Oh! I see…"

"Simon?"

He turned to her, eyes shining. "Inara," he said. "I know what's going on—"

She jerked her head towards the driver. "Well, keep it to yourself for the moment."

"Yes, of course…" He smiled. "Don't worry," he said. "Everything's clear now."

The welcome at the de Cecilles was considerably less impressive this time. Their hovercar went almost furtively to a side entrance. Inara and Simon were all but ordered out and bundled into the house.

"They're lacking in courtesy this evening," Simon said cheerfully. "What do you think we did to offend?"

"Be careful…" Inara murmured.

"It's all right, Inara," he said. "We'll be fine."

Inara wasn't so sure. They were led into a large sitting room, where both the Monseigneur and Madame were waiting for them. Madame was sitting in one corner, almost in shadows. Monseigneur was standing, arms folded, watching as they came in.

"Good evening," Simon said, in a clear voice, crossing the room towards them. Was he taking the offensive? Inara frowned. What was going on here? "Forgive me if we didn't make ourselves clear, but we did not intend to come here this evening. Perhaps you can explain—"

"I think the explanations should be coming from you, Mr Amery," said Monseigneur. "If that is indeed your name."

"It's the one you can use," said Simon.

"As for you," Monseigneur glanced at Inara, "you seem to be who you claim to be—"

"Thank you," said Inara.

"But I'm not entirely sure who *he* is." He looked at Simon. "I'll find out eventually, when I have better access to the Cortex. In the meantime, I think you should remain here, until the sheriff's office can investigate. You're surely aware that deception is a crime across the Alliance."

"I like my privacy," said Simon. "And that's not a crime. But if we're talking about crimes—what about abduction? We were quite clear that we didn't want to come here this evening—"

"You're accusing me of a crime?"

"Oh yes," said Simon. "In fact, abduction might be the least of it."

"You're not in a position to talk to me like this, young man," said the Monseigneur.

"Actually," said Simon, "I think I am."

Āiya, thought Inara. What did he think he was doing? But Simon was quite relaxed.

"I'd advise you," said Madame, from her corner, "not to try our patience, Mr Amery. You're in a very vulnerable position—"

"You know Emory Scarlett is using you, don't you?" said Simon.

"Simon," whispered Inara. "Be careful…"

"Using us?" Monseigneur laughed. "We're in business together—"

"Mm," said Simon. "Well, it's been my observation over the years—"

Monseigneur laughed out loud. "How old are you, son? Twenty-four? Twenty-five? What do you know about life? Made some easy money in the Core? That ain't living!"

"You'd be astonished," said Simon, quietly, "at exactly how much I know about living—and dying. And it's been my observation, over my few but quite *intense* years, that in any partnership, one party is junior, and the other senior. Monseigneur," he said, "ask yourself honestly—which one do you think you are?"

The Monseigneur was beginning to look uneasy. "I think you should explain yourself—"

"Oh, I'm happy to," said Simon. "You know I met Scarlett, don't you? We had drinks. He didn't enjoy it much, and in retrospect the food probably wasn't up to much, but I always think that company makes all the difference. And I didn't like him. Didn't like his manner, didn't like his attitude, didn't like his casual distaste for Abel. You should hear what he says about you all, behind your backs."

"That won't work with me, son," said Monseigneur.

"No? All right then. After we had drinks, he gave me all this *reading* to do. And one of the most irritating things about me— or so I've been told—is that I always, *always* do the reading."

"I'm sure you're very bright, son—"

"Extremely bright," said Simon.

"Top three," Inara murmured.

"And very good at making connections." He turned to Inara. "Do you remember what she said? 'The world set into reverse...'"

It took Inara a moment, and then she remembered River's message. Of course, River. He always paid attention to River, even when nobody else did.

"Whatever Scarlett's promised you," said Simon. "It's going to come at a terrible cost—"

Madame leaned forwards from her dark corner. "Emory Scarlett is going to improve life for everyone on Abel."

"I don't think he will," said Simon. "In fact, he's already making life worse. You do realize this drought is very convenient for Rising Sun?"

Monseigneur laughed. "Next you'll be saying they're causing it!"

Simon didn't reply. He simply looked at the other man and waited for him to get there himself.

"Oh, this is nonsense!" said Monseigneur. "A conspiracy theory!"

"I can run you through the science if you like," said Simon.

"He can," put in Inara. "In more detail than you'll find bearable."

"Or I can put it in simple terms," said Simon. "You know they're causing the drought, don't you? Not enough water. Small-scale farming becomes impossible. The homesteaders foreclose. The banks—and whoever owns the banks—snap up the land. Doesn't that sound familiar?"

"Edward," said Madame. "This is ridiculous."

"I only wish it was," said Simon. "Look, let me use the Cortex. I'll show you…"

"No," said Madame, quickly.

"Oh, why not, Annette?" said de Cecille. "If the boy wants to make a fool of himself." He gestured Simon towards the desk. "Go on. Talk me through this fairy tale."

Simon, accessing the files that Scarlett had sent him, said, "Like I say, I thought it was only the drought. A piece of luck— from Rising Sun's perspective—that they were using for their own benefit. And, you know, I don't really believe in conspiracy theories, but the important thing is not to be *locked* into a certain way of thinking. So I pushed myself and I thought, 'but it's so convenient…' What if they *were* behind it? How would they do that? And then it came to me… It was something larger than that. Something they were willing to kill for."

He brought up some visuals. A green world, fertile and abundant.

"That's Abel," said Monseigneur de Cecille. "You think you're showing me something I don't know?"

"Wait," said Simon. "Watch. This is what's been happening over the last couple of years..."

The colors began to alter. The green began to give way to brown patches.

"And my projections for the next three years..."

The brown was dominant now; the green patches receding. Territory under siege.

"And how Abel will be in ten years."

Inara gasped. Abel had become a dead world, barren. "What happens?"

"Abel was terraformed before it was settled," said Simon. "Somebody has started setting that process in reverse... I don't know," he said, as they watched the brown and black world spin in front of them, "whether the intention is to stop the process when they have enough land. As far as I can tell from what I've read, the process *is* reversible. But of course, it's experimental. And it does have so many applications, doesn't it? Not least the military ones. Imagine if those Independents decided to rise up again. Insisted on their freedom. A process like this? You'd soon persuade them to stand down. So I wonder—*will* they stop this? Or is Abel going to be proof of concept?" Simon bit his lip. "They might not have decided yet."

"Nonsense," said Madame, but Inara could see that the Monseigneur was looking very uneasy.

"It's up to you whether or not you believe me," said Simon. "I *know* it's happening. The science of it is true. Perhaps you knew already. Perhaps you don't care. Perhaps you think it's worth it. In the long run, I mean—"

"No!" said Monseigneur, and Inara thought, we have him...

"You have no reason to trust me," said Simon. "Although you might want to consider some of the reasons why someone investigating this might use a false identity. All I'm asking is for you to stop for a moment, and consider what you really know about Emory Scarlett. Think about whether what he's offering really is for the benefit of the people of this world." The Monseigneur was playing the visuals back and forth: from green to brown to dead and back again, over and over. Simon glanced at Inara: *How was that?* She nodded her approval. She couldn't quite believe his chutzpah at suggesting that he was some kind of Alliance investigator—but that seemed to have caught de Cecille's attention.

"Edward," said Madame. "Stop looking at that."

"What?"

"Stop it. Come with me. I want to speak to in private to you for a moment."

With difficulty, the Monseigneur pulled himself away from the console, and followed his wife out of the room. Inara turned to Simon. "How did you *know*? Was it what River said?" She watched Simon take in a very deep breath. "You did know, didn't you? That wasn't a guess?"

"I… I mean… I did read through everything Scarlett gave us," said Simon. "And, of course, it's always a good idea to pay attention to River, and try to work out what's she's trying to tell you… So I put all that together, but mostly?" He was blushing, ever so slightly. "Yes, it was a guess. But I think it was a good guess?"

"*Āiya,*" said Inara. "Remind me never to play you at poker." She leaned over and kissed him quickly on the cheek.

Simon went bright red. "Also," he added, with a little more self-satisfaction than was good for him, "I am pretty much genius level."

"Oh, Simon," she said, shaking her head, "sometimes you really are your own worst enemy."

"Oh. Yes. Sorry—"

"What's your plan now?"

"*My* plan?" Simon blinked. "I... I guess... We find out what he already knew. The Monseigneur. I think... I think this has come as a shock."

"I think you're right."

"But I'm pretty sure he believes me. I think maybe... we persuade him over to our side?" Simon frowned. "Either that, or he's in it up to his neck. And if that's the case, then..."

"Go on..."

"We probably don't see out the night."

"Even though for all he knows you're an Alliance investigator?"

"Someone has already paid to have a lawyer shot, Inara. Might make me even more of a target." He frowned. "And it seemed like such a good idea when I said it..."

Inara stood up and went over to the desk.

"What are you doing, Inara?"

"Their uplink is still working," she said.

"I don't think anyone's around to spring us out of here," said Simon. "Unless Mal has gone against form and finished the job early—"

"No," said Inara, "but at least we can let people know what's been going on. Before they... well, do whatever it is that they're planning right now."

"You know, Inara," said Simon, "I don't really want to die for this world."

"Nor do I," said Inara, bending over the console. "But that's what might happen..."

She was only partway through the message when the door opened. The man who had driven them over came in, holding a pistol.

"Step away from the console, please, Ms Serra," he said. "Sit down—both of you. Hands in front, where I can see them."

"Allow me to introduce Emory Scarlett," said McQuinn. "He's with—"

"I can see who he's with," said Kaylee, in a disapproving tone. "Ma'am, you said you'd do a deal with the Devil himself if it helped you keep the city safe tonight. But *āiya*! You gotta draw a line somewhere!"

"Excuse me?" said Scarlett. "McQuinn, who the hell are these people?"

"They're… friends," said McQuinn. "At least, they mean well. I think."

"They don't mean well if they're keeping you holed up in here while the city's on fire," said Scarlett.

"They think they have a solution to that," said McQuinn.

"Yes?" Scarlett eyed Kaylee and Wash like he was looking at the trashcan. Wash *really* hated him. "Better than anything I have on offer?"

"Maybe," said McQuinn, in a mild voice. "They think I should talk to the strikers. The leadership, I mean."

"That's… a bad idea," said Scarlett.

"I'm wondering about that," said McQuinn.

"Wondering if I let that particular genie out of its bottle I might not be able to persuade it back in again."

"Exactly," said Scarlett. "You don't deal with terrorists."

"Terrorists?" said McQuinn. "I wouldn't go that far."

"Well," said Scarlett, backtracking. "People who are using force to get themselves heard."

"Long past time these folks were heard," put in Kaylee. "Long past time someone took their opinions into account."

"Huh," said McQuinn again. One of her aides came in, asking for a private word. "Give me a minute, folks," she said, getting up. "Let me deal with this." She left the room, Scarlett close behind.

"Have to say, Kaylee," said Wash, when McQuinn was gone,

"your turn to radical politics is something of a curveball."

"There's nothin' *radical* about what I'm sayin'," said Kaylee. "It's *common sense*. These folks need to work together."

Wash thought about saying something about how common sense was sometimes the most radical course of action when everyone else was behaving like a fool, but decided that was a discussion for another day. "Do you think," said Wash, "that Ryan and his people are going to want to get involved? He didn't think much of the mayor when we talked to him. I mean, it wasn't personal, but I don't see him having much interest in standing alongside the sheriff's people. Wouldn't he rather see them go down?"

Kaylee's eyes widened. "I hadn't thought of that."

"All that I'm saying is that politics is *weird*, there are people you think should be friends or allies that turn out to have all these complicated grudges against each other, and you can't predict..."

"I guess we won't know until we ask," said Kaylee.

Wash sighed. He loved Kaylee, he really did, and her freshness— almost innocence—about how the world worked was one of the nicest things about her. But people had a tendency to be jaded, and not so much innocent as mired in the muck. Wash didn't want to see her disappointed. He didn't want to see her *hurt*.

"What's troublin' ya, Wash?"

"I think asking Ryan to stand his people alongside the mayor and the sheriff might be like asking Mal to stand alongside someone who fought for the Alliance."

"Maybe it's time people put those things behind them," said Kaylee. "Or, maybe... things ain't always so clear cut as we'd like. But what's clear as day to me is that the people who want to cause trouble are most likely those as paid to have Annie Roberts' daddy killed—and that tells you somethin' about the kind of folks they are. Kind of folks want to tear down rather than build up. You'll see. Ryan will come good."

The craziest thing about this whole crazy idea, Wash thought, was that Kaylee pretty much persuaded him with that speech. "Okay," he conceded. "I guess it's worth a try."

McQuinn, having finished her call, came back to them, Scarlett following.

"All right. That's a whole district on the west of the city that the sheriff's men have more or less abandoned," she said. "So I think me and the sheriff and these friends of yours need to be having a little chat. I got Sheriff Peters ready here on the comm—"

"Mary," said Scarlett, urgently. "This is a bad idea."

"Maybe," she said. "What you got instead?"

"You know what Rising Sun can offer. We can mobilize nearly a hundred people within the hour. Arm them and put them on the streets alongside Peters' men."

"Funny, ain't it," said Kaylee. "How he can rustle up his own private little army, just like that. Almost like he's been preparin' for this—"

From the comm, came Ned Peters voice. "*Ain't that the gorram truth.*"

McQuinn raised her hand. "That's enough." She turned to Scarlett. "Tell you what, Emory. I'd like to know more about what you can do for me and Ned right now. But I want it in writing. I think you should go into that office next door," she jerked her thumb, "and you write down for me where these fellas are and how they'll arm themselves, and you put it all in a spreadsheet and tell me the cost, and I'll look that over right away and give you a decision within the hour. How does that sound?"

Scarlett, looking from the mayor to Kaylee and back again, said, "You want me to do you a spreadsheet?"

"Don't hold back," said McQuinn. "Do the whole business plan, if you like. Like I say, office next door's free." She stood up. "Or, if you prefer, you can do it from your ship. I got a car can take you to the space port. Might be tricky gettin' through tonight, mind you. City's in a hell of a state." She spoke into the comm. "What you reckon, Ned? Got anyone there you can spare to guarantee a safe run from City Hall to the port?"

"*Couldn't guarantee it, ma'am.*"

"Nope," said McQuinn. "Didn't think you could."

Scarlett, backing towards the door, said, "This is your last chance, McQuinn. To save your city."

"You know what?" said McQuinn. "I'm not sure you're right about that. But why don't you set yourself to proving me wrong? Give it your best shot."

Scarlett opened his mouth to say something, then decided against. He reached the door. "Close that after you, will you?" said McQuinn.

"Is he going to cause trouble?" said Wash, once the door was shut. "I mean—what's stopping him getting those men on the streets anyway?"

"He can try," said McQuinn. "But he's going to have a hell of a job getting the Cortex in that office to work for him." She winked, broadly. "Power's down. But more'n than that—there ain't a penny more comin' from City Hall, and he knows it. So how's he goin' to pay those fellas he's recruited? They're going to want a word in the morning. No, Mr Scarlett will be on his way to the docks in the next ten minutes, I'd say. And good riddance." She turned to Kaylee. "Which leaves me in need of some new allies. So. These associates of yours. Care to put us in touch?"

"I'll try," said Kaylee. "But I got my own condition first."

Lǎo tiān yé, thought Wash. Parliament ought to be approaching Miss Kaylee Frye. Appointing her as ambassador to somewhere or other.

"We got friends I'm worried about. Sheriff Peters, can you send a couple of your fellas over there, make sure' they're safe? They're stayin' at Isaac Roberts' house—"

"*Holy Christ and a Christmas cracker!*" cried the sheriff. "*You think my fellas ain't got enough on their plate right now—*"

"Ned," said McQuinn. "Do it."

"*Jesus, Mary and the gorram donkey,*" he said, shaking his head—but he gave the order to Kaylee's evident satisfaction. She got to work trying to find Ryan Hunter.

He was not an easy man to pin down. Kaylee couldn't reach him on the wave code she'd used earlier. They gave her another one to try, but no luck, and she was passed from pillar to post. Both the mayor and the sheriff were starting to make impatient noises. Wash, slipping out, checked on the office next door. No sign of Scarlett. Off to cause trouble? Wash had a feeling not. In fact, he'd bet the shirt on this back—this lovely shirt, that nobody appreciated—that McQuinn was right and Emory Scarlett was halfway to the docks by now. Good luck to him getting there. When he went back into McQuinn's office, he saw the mayor, tapping her fingers against her desk, trying to damp her frustration. *Āiya*, thought Wash. She really must be desperate.

"*Kaylee!*" said Ryan, when he appeared on screen. "*Where the hell are you? The fella I sent to meet you—told me you weren't at the rendezvous.*"

"We were… kinda waylaid," said Kaylee.

"*You safe? You and the little fella?*"

"*Zāo gāo,*" muttered Wash. "I'm right here…"

"We're fine," said Kaylee. "I've got… I've got a couple people here want to speak to you." She glanced at McQuinn, who nodded.

"*Oh yeah? Who's that?*"

"It's Mayor McQuinn," said Kaylee. "She wants to make a deal with you. And I want you to make a deal with her."

There was a pause, during which Wash thought that perhaps the comm channel had disappeared, or perhaps Ryan had simply disconnected. But, after a few more moments, he said. "*You want what?*"

"I want you," said Kaylee, "to put your money where your mouth is." She nodded at Peters, on the screen, and turned to McQuinn. "Well? What you two gonna offer?"

McQuinn leaned into view. "Mr Hunter. Pleased to make your acquaintance."

"*Huh,*" said Ryan. "*You know what? I'm sitting here listening to this city blowin' up and I'm thinkin' we can do that crap another day. You want the power back on, yeah?*"

"That would be a start," said McQuinn. "What do you want?"

"*You know what we want. We been askin' for ages now.*"

"I've not been in office ages," she said.

"*No, but you're the same as the rest, aren't you?*"

"Try me," said McQuinn.

"*All right. I'll try. I want our jobs guaranteed. Our pay. Our way of life. I want the people who put you in office to stop undercuttin' us. I know they got a right to work, same as the rest of us, but not at our expense. I want Rising Sun out of this town. I want a four-day week and funded childcare and you can throw in a decent pension scheme too.*"

Ryan was almost smiling. "*Are you not goin' to tell me to stop?*"

"Why should I tell you to stop?" said McQuinn. "I know what you folks think of me. I know you think I ain't on your side. That I'm here to push the interests of those folks from the country that put me in office—"

"*What you done to give us any different impression?*"

"What you done to give me the chance to show you who I am?"

"*We all know you're workin' with Rising Sun—*"

"Fella," she said. "I ain't sayin' that weren't a mistake. But you got to understand the fix I been in. Earlier this year the city was on the brink. Friend of mine shot dead on Main Street, tryna fix the whole sorry mess unfolding here. I got rich city families leanin' on me to find quick solutions, pointin' me in the direction of Rising Sun—"

"*You ran for office, ma'am.*"

"Don't I know it. And it ain't as easy sittin' in this chair as you fellas might like to paint it."

"*Ain't no reason to sell this world off—*"

"You got no need to worry on that score. I sent the Rising Sun fella packin' and now I guess we all have to live with the consequences."

"It's true," put in Kaylee. "Hoo boy! She had him on the hop. You'da loved it, Ryan!"

"You got grievances, Mr Hunter?" said McQuinn. "You ain't the only one. You fellas don't know anythin' about me and the people put me in office. You ain't seen the grief on the face of folks watchin' their land dry up and knowin' everythin' they've worked for has been for nothin'. Knowin' they've got nowhere to go but a place where they're not wanted, and where there ain't enough work to keep their folks fed. I ain't sayin' it been easy on you neither, but I *am* sayin' we'll get nowhere if we're at each other's throats."

Wash, glancing at Kaylee, saw her nodding.

"You give me the space, sir," said McQuinn, "and do me the courtesy of treatin' me like your friend and not your enemy, and we'll build up a city works for us all, a city to make us proud. But please! Will you gorram put the gorram power back on before whoever's tryna burn this gorram place to the gorram ground gets their damn way!"

"*Mary,*" said Peters. "*You sure about this?*"

"*Wŏ de mā,*" said McQuinn. "They ain't askin' for the gorram moon."

"*There's folks in this city,*" said Peters, "*powerful folks—won't be happy—*"

"Well, I ain't happy with the way they been interferin'," said McQuinn. "And I'm the gorram mayor. Mr Hunter," she said. "You send a list here to me at this office, and when everything in Yell City is up and running again, you come and pay me a visit, and we'll thrash out how we do all this. *Dŏng ma?*"

Ryan's expression was priceless. "*I didn't think it was goin' to be this easy.*"

"It won't be," she said. "But these next few days, if we play them right—them that's been rulin' this world, holdin' all the cards—they're gonna be the weakest they've ever been. This is our chance—your folks and mine. We get to set up Abel the way we want it. You in?"

Ryan didn't answer straight away.

"Ryan?" said Kaylee. "You heard the mayor. What's your answer?"

"*You think I'm going to say no, don't you?*" said Ryan.

"I don't know what you're going to say," said Kaylee. "I hope you're gonna say 'yes.'"

"*You any idea how long it takes to make a decision like this?*"

"Nope," said Kaylee.

"*Resolutions, proposers, seconders, discussions, amendments—*"

"That sounds like it could take a while," said Kaylee. "I reckon you have... coupla minutes?"

"*Question of trust, Kaylee. I'm givin' away only card we've had in years. For what guarantee? McQuinn's word?*"

"My word too," said Kaylee, though how she was going to make McQuinn and Peters to come good Wash wasn't sure. Maybe through sheer force of personality. "Ryan, listen. Maybe you don't trust these folks—but what about the others? Those boys runnin' through town right now, tryna wreck the place. Paid for by folks who'll throw the lot of you in jail the minute they get the chance?"

"*All right,*" said Ryan. "*I'll take this back to my people. Tell 'em we need—*"

"Ryan!"

"*Kaylee,*" he said. "*I ain't their captain or their manager or anythin' like that. We make a decision together. I'll tell 'em what I think and why I think it, and they'll choose what they want to do.*"

"*I got a request,*" said Peters. "*If you fellas are willing.*"

"*Try me,*" said Ryan.

"*Got some specially big trouble out in Westerly district right now. Not enough fellas to keep the peace. You got some folks might lend a hand?*"

"That's a big ask," said Kaylee. "Puttin' themselves on the line."

"*Kaylee,*" said Ryan. "*There's one incontrovertible and undeniable fact about me and my folks.*"

"Oh yeah?" said Kaylee. "What's that?"

"*Always there first.*" He looked at Peters and shook his head. "*Sheriff—we're already there. Been out there holdin' that line for hours.*"

13

A sorrier girl you have never seen than me right there at the wrong end of Young Bill Fincher's gun, but even so that weren't the sorriest I was by the time this whole episode came to an end. Fincher at last came to the end of his crowin' and so on, and—still ever so pleased with himself—he hobbled over to the console, and started yappin' away to another of his shady crew, he fairly couldn't spit the words out, he was so pleased with himself, like a mean little cat tormentin' some poor creature.

"Tell the boss I got her!" he cried. "I got the Roberts girl! You make sure he knows who got her. Tracked her down and caught her myself!"

I snorted at that: the boy couldn't help himself. Had to tell a tall tale. I said he was junk. But the next thing I knew, I could hear a hovercar comin' in our direction. Fincher, still limping, but smirkin' away with his pistol pointin' at me, said; "Get a move on, Miss Annie. They're here to bring us to Frankie Collier." He marched me out the building to wait for his crew, and all the while he was sayin', "That'll teach 'em to leave me here. They ain't reckoned on Bill Fincher."

Now I saw what had happened. When we'd landed here, and

shot at the crew, he'd been hurt, and they'd taken their chance to dump him like the dead weight he was. No wonder he'd been sittin' there grousin' away to himself. And then I, like a darn fool, had presented myself like a lamb to the slaughter, giving that boy a way to ingratiate himself with his crew again. "You're a gosh-darn fool," I said to him, as the car drew closer. "Think handin' me over will get you back in Frankie Collier's good graces? He's dumped you once and he'll dump you again."

For that I earned a whack across the face. Tasted blood.

"You keep a civil tongue in your head, Miss Annie," he said. "Or I'll *teach* you how to keep one."

What Young Bill Fincher knew about bein' civil I can't say, but my head had already had enough that night, so I kept quiet after that. But I'd got to him—I saw that. When the car landed, Fincher insisted on bein' the one to sit next to me, and through the journey kept on mutterin' things like, "I was the one caught her. They'd all be done without me…"

At last, I saw pale lights on the horizon, comin' closer by the minute, and the car slowed and began to descend. When we was down, I saw we'd come to a big bunch of buildings. There was lights on inside the one nearest to us, but my attention was drawn to the gaggle of fellas standin' around some cars, one of whom I thought from the look of him might be Frankie Collier. That piece of junk Bill Fincher ordered me out, and in the direction of that fella, and when I drew near, Collier said, "Well, well—Annie Roberts. What a pleasure to meet you at last."

"It's Miss Roberts to you, fella," said I. "And there ain't no pleasure for me meetin' the men shot my daddy dead."

Collier laughed. "You'll have to work hard to pin that one on me, Annie—*Miss Roberts*, I should say. Whole of Yell City saw Young Bill here leavin' your father's office."

"Yes, Mr Collier, sir," said Fincher, "it were me, and me what brought this girl here too." And I thought, you fool, he'll let you hang for everythin' that's happened here, and you'll do it without even knowin' you been stitched up. I caught Collier's eye, and he saw that I knew, and he smiled. Lord above, that man was *cold*. He turned away from me, and walked toward the buildin', and he called out, "Reynolds! Got your girl here. You want a word with her?"

Well, he didn't get no answer to that question, because that's when Captain Reynolds and his crew came out, guns blazin'. I do not know what exactly the plan was, and havin' had the misfortune to observe Captain Reynolds and his crew at first-hand prior to this occasion, I am prepared to say that there might not have been a plan. On the other hand, that woman, Amy Lin, was with them, as I learned later when I heard a full account of what transpired that night, and she struck me as havin' more than her share of good sense, so perhaps they did know what they was doin'.

It was chaos. Shots bein' fired, and weapons bein' drawn, everyone divin' here and there and all over the place. But I had my eye on one fella, and one fella alone, he wasn't gettin' away from me this time. Young Bill Fincher. When the shootin' started, he fell to his knees and started crawlin' away like the coward he was, lookin' for somewhere to hide. So I chased after him, kicking him hard in the stomach. I wrenched his pistol from his hand, and I said, "Vengeance is mine, saith the Lord." And I emptied what power there was in that pistol into that boy, until I was sure that justice had been done. All around me, the shootin' continued. And then I felt hands upon me, grabbin' me, and a voice in my ear.

"You little *jiàn huò*," whispered Collier. "Couldn't wait to do that, could you? Well, *mei mei*, let's see how brave you are now." He pushed me in front of him, like a shield, and put his pistol to my temple, and he yelled, "Reynolds! I got the Roberts girl! You stop now or I'll blow out her brains!"

Everythin' went dead quiet. I looked round—there was a lot

of dead fellas lyin' on the ground, but the captain and Zoë and the Lin woman was all still standin', weapons out. Maybe three or four of Collier's gang still left, movin' back towards us.

"You see how she's fixed, Reynolds? I'll kill her if y'all don't put down your guns."

There was a moment or two of hesitation, then, ever so slowly, I saw the captain and Zoë and Lin start to lower their guns.

"Don't!" I cried. "I got what I came here for! You get away from here, Captain!"

"*Zāo gāo*, Annie!" Captain Reynolds called back. "Can you not keep quiet for a second?"

I shut my mouth—and then I heard it. I heard the sound of an engine, comin' our way. And I knew from the way Collier's grip on me tightened that he wasn't expectin' anyone. And he surely wasn't expectin' what came thunderin' through. It was the Mule, and hangin' out from the driving seat was Jayne Cobb, and I swear I ain't seen an uglier and more welcome sight in my entire life. He was shootin' and yee-hawin' and havin' a whale of a time, and, good Lord, it set the fox among the pigeons so far as Collier's men were concerned. They started dashin' this way and that, but Jayne Cobb was firin' at 'em, and next the captain and the others had their guns back and they were firin' at 'em, and I took my chance. I elbowed Collier hard, in the gut, and he fell back, winded, and I made a run for it.

"Annie! Annie, *no!*" I heard Zoë yell, and then I felt a hot pain—fierce, it was, like the tongue of the Devil himself, licking at my side—and I was down on the ground. I heard Collier scream out in pain behind me, and I thought, He got you, you villain; the captain got you... and after that, things were suddenly very quiet and dark.

"Annie?" I heard a voice callin' my name, and for a moment, I thought: Daddy? But when I opened my eyes, it was Captain

Reynolds I saw. You might not believe this, but I ain't never been so glad to see anyone as I was to see that particular fella right at that moment. Because I knew that even though I was hurt—hurt bad—there was nothing in the 'verse would stop Captain Malcolm Reynolds from gettin' me where I needed to be, if my life was goin' to be saved.

O captain my captain, I thought—and, thinking back now, I suspect that I might have said those words out loud, because next thing I saw was tears in Captain Reynolds' eyes, and he said, "Gonna save you, Annie Roberts. You hang in there, *mei mei*, because I am gonna get you all the help that you need. You hear me? *Gǒu shǐ*, Annie, are you gorram listenin'?"

"Captain," I whispered. "You best mind your manners when you're talkin' to me or you better not say one more word..."

I was feelin' faint by then; faint, and like the whole world was fadin' away into black, so I didn't say no more after that—but he kept on talkin', and I kept on listenin', and I thought how nice his voice was, and how I might like to keep on hearin' it a while yet, so I kept on listenin', and I tried not to fade into that black...

"Poor gorram kid," said Jayne, shaking his head.

"Changed your tune," said Zoë.

"Huh." He shrugged. "She got guts, I guess. Though she's a pain in the gorram butt. Had me running halfway round this *niú shi* piece of crap world." He frowned. "Think she'll pull through?"

"I dunno," said Zoë. "I guess if they can find Simon in time."

"Another mercy dash... Doc'll love that, bein' the hero, and all."

Once the shooting was over, and it was clear that Annie was hurt, they'd wasted no time getting her into Lin's hovercar, to head back to the city. Lin was driving; Mal was riding with Annie. Zoë and Jayne watched the car lift off, and then Zoë, leading him back into the building, explained about the two captives and how they had to escort them back to the city so that Lin could take them into protective custody. Jayne, limping along beside her, shook his head when Zoë told him what they'd learned about the drought.

They entered the rec room, where Townsend and Larsen, hands bound, were sitting in the dark and waiting. Zoë threw on the lights.

"Bad news," she said. "Your friends didn't make it."

"Worse news," said Jayne. "We did." He lumbered over to them, to take a closer look. "Was that really the plan up here? Turn this world into some gorram dust bowl?"

"Looks that way," said Zoë.

"*Tā mā de*," he said. "Ain't right. And what about these two? Up to their gorram necks in no doubt."

"Now hold on," said Townsend.

"Aw, shut your gorram mouth," said Jayne. "Zoë?"

"They say they no inkling as to what was going on."

"Ain't right," said Jayne again, and fell silent, staring at their prisoners. After a moment or two, he said, "We could see justice done here right now, Zoë. *Dǒng ma?*"

Zoë eyed Townsend and Larsen, who were huddled together. "You mean to say—"

"We could say they jumped us. Tried to get away. Ain't nobody would know any different."

"I guess *we* would," said Zoë. And Mal would know. Of course Mal would know. But would he mind?

"Set a light to the place after, if you're worryin' they could tell from the bodies."

Zoë fell to thinking for a while. Hard to stomach, when you thought about it for a while, what these folks had been doin' here on Abel. Forcin' people off their land and their living was bad enough. But to meddle with what had made this world livable in the first place? Folks like her and Mal—they were the ones that people said were misbehavin'. Had officers and lawmen sent after them. And what, really, did they do? Broke a few rules here and there. Some smugglin'. All right, yes, and some shootin', but generally only when they were shot at first. And all the time, folks like these, comin' from the Core to these Rim worlds, with designs for them and their people.

Larsen, watching Zoë carefully, said, "Why are you looking at me like that?"

"Thinkin'," said Zoë.

"Thinking about what?"

"Thinkin' about what makes a body do the things you've done."

Larsen flushed red. "I told you. It wasn't our idea."

"Didn't stop you helpin' though. Did you never think maybe of not helpin'?"

"It's my *job*—"

"And they call us the naughty ones," said Jayne. "Whaddya say, Zoë? Shall we do the necessary?"

The two technicians looked at each other, as if suddenly understanding the danger that they were in. Jayne moved menacingly toward them. Zoë leaned back against the nearest table and watched.

"You can't do this!" said Townsend.

"I can do whatever the hell I gorram like," said Jayne. "Ain't nobody out here to stop me, hey? Ain't nobody out here you can call for help."

"You?" said Townsend, turning to Zoë. "You're going to let him do this?"

Zoë shrugged.

"Let him *murder* us?"

"So you care about murder now," said Jayne. "What you done, it weren't right. It weren't right at all."

"You can't let him do this!" cried Larsen, and appealed to Zoë. "Please, stop him. I've got kids—"

"Plenty here on Abel with kids," said Jayne. "You think about that?"

"Please!" she cried.

Jayne aimed, and fired—above their heads. Some of the ceiling came raining down on them. "You must think I'm a gorram fool," he said. "Think I'd do time for you two pieces of crap?" He spat on the floor at their feet. "You ain't worth it. You ain't worth my time."

Zoë stood up. "You done?"

"Uh-huh," said Jayne. "Shall we get 'em back to the city? Wouldn't mind the doc takin' a look at this leg of mine, when he's finished with the girl."

"Guess that's the next job," said Zoë. She walked over to the seats, gesturing with her gun for the pair of them to stand up. Townsend was furious.

"Was that supposed to be *funny*? Was that your idea of a *joke*?"

Zoë hauled him out of his seat. "I ain't laughin'," she said. "Word of advice. You keep quiet from now on. Save your talkin' for the sheriff or the lawyers or whoever it is comes askin' questions about what happened here. But I don't want to hear another word from either of you."

They were both of them quite biddable after that. Let Jayne lead 'em outside (Zoë followin' to make sure nothin' stupid was tried). Got into the back of the Mule and didn't make a single complaint. Zoë and Jayne stood for a moment looking back at the buildings.

"I dunno, Zoë," said Jayne. "Feels like there ain't been no real justice done here."

"Amy Lin thinks when those two get to talkin', she'll get some folks for what's been goin' on."

"Huh. Believe that when I see it."

"Got Bill Fincher," said Zoë. "And the rest of that gang."

"Still, it ain't like the people who were really behind this have been hurt, is it? I don't see any of them fancy Blue Sun business fellas lyin' dead out here tonight." Jayne rubbed at his leg. "Different time or place, coulda been me in a gang like that. You take the jobs come along, don't always ask questions..."

Zoë, thinking of all those Browncoats, got what he meant. Agreed. Sympathized, maybe. "You know," she said, "strikes me there's only one thing folks like that understand."

"Yeah? What's that?"

"Well, it ain't harmin' their people. Collier and his crew, dead. These two—if we killed 'em, you think those folks would care. No, they don't care about their people."

"No. What they really don't like—is harmin' their property."

Took Jayne a moment, but he caught her drift. "Now you're talkin', sweet lady."

"Uh-huh."

Didn't take long to see it done. Started off slow, as these things were wont to do, but soon got traction. You'd see this for miles, thought Zoë. And if you had any sense, you'd take heed.

They stood side-by-side for a while, companionably, watching their fire take hold. Jayne had collected up some Blue Sun signs and every so often he threw one into the flames. When the ceiling on the nearest building started to crack, he guffawed.

"Look at that," he said, happily. "Pretty as a picture." He glanced at his partner in crime. "What'll you tell Mal?"

"Reckon I'll tell him what I always tell him," said Zoë. "Accidents happen."

The moment the lights went down, Book knew they were in trouble. He'd figured already that something was most likely coming. River had been on edge since the middle of the day, prowling the house like a wild cat in a cage. Poor Maisie had been most unsettled by this, so Book sent her home, with his blessing, saying he and the little girl could surely shift for themselves for a few hours. Besides, Book wasn't sure he could guarantee her safety. If there was trouble in Yell City tonight, then someone would come take a look at the Roberts house, because that's where the evidence was.

Before Maisie left, he'd asked her to leave out a couple of flashlights, and he turned one of these on, low, and went in search of River. She wasn't in the kitchen, the study, or any of the reception rooms, so he went upstairs. Maybe she'd decided to try to sleep. The whole house was very quiet. Outside, sirens were blaring. He stood at one of the upstairs windows, in the dark, looking out, thinking about how busy the night was going to be. Suddenly, from downstairs, he heard a scream—a terrible, high-pitched scream that pierced his heart. He ran down the stairs, calling out River's name, and found her in the hallway, curled up around herself. He knelt beside her.

"River, honey, what is it?"

"Hurt! So hurt!"

"Where are you hurt? What's happened?"

The girl's face screwed up—pain? What had she done? "Show me. Show me where you're hurtin', River."

"*No!*"

"River, I can help—but you've got to tell me where you're hurtin'—"

"Not *me!*"

Ah, that wasn't pain on her face—at least, not pain that she was experiencing directly. That was more... frustration, the deep frustration that this poor girl seemed to feel most of the time, that she could not make what was plain to her clear to anyone else.

"Who's hurt, River? Can you say? Is it Simon?"

"Simon..."

"Is it Mal? Any of the others? Who is it?"

But River was disappearing into herself, wrapping her arms

around her body, as if to try to make herself as small as possible. Book had seen this before, and he wasn't sure now that he would get anything from her that he could make sense of. He'd spent enough time now with this girl not to dismiss what she said out of hand, but there were other matters pressing on his mind right now.

"River," said Book, clearly and calmly. "I need you to listen to me, and listen good. I don't think we're gonna be safe here much longer. I think people have their eye on this house and they're comin' here. You and I may have to get away. River—" He took her hand, pressing it between both of his. "River, look at me now."

From whatever place she was inhabiting, or vision she was seeing, River seemed to pull herself back, to him, at this place, here and now. "Shepherd...?"

"River, I think we need to leave this place. Think you can do that?"

Suddenly, she came into focus. "Have you something I can aim at someone?"

Gracious Lord in Heaven, thought Book, the hairs going up on the back of his neck, this girl... Whoever had taken her, they'd made a weapon of her—and now Book was thinking he might have to use her. Oh Lord, our Father, who sees all—forgive me this as You have forgiven so much already...

"Found a coupla pistols," he said. "Think they're Miss Annie's. Reckon you can manage one?"

She pulled a face at him, as if to say: are you joking?

"Good," he said. She followed him into the study, where the pistols he'd chosen were waiting, and she tried them both, picking the one she preferred. Then she followed him along the dark hallway to the front door. He listened for a while, waiting until he was sure it was quiet outside, and then carefully opened the door a crack.

"They're here…" River whispered.

Lights flared. Book, blinded momentarily, raised his hand to shield his eyes. River came past him at speed, like a creature released from its chains. He caught a glimpse of her dark figure, lit up against the blaze. A voice cried out:

"This is the police. Put down your weapon!"

Book saw her body tense.

"Put down your weapon."

She tensed further—

"River…" he breathed, hoping she could hear. She was like some weapon of mass destruction, he thought; once unleashed, unstoppable.

"River," he begged her, praying that somehow, after all the time they had spent together, peacefully, playin' chess and talkin' and listenin', that he had earned a little trust. *"Please…"*

She stood on the step, pistol out, body taut and ready. The sheriff's men, Book saw, were taking aim in their turn. There was a terrible moment of silence—and then River lowered her pistol, turned, and went back inside. "Guns," she said, handing hers to Book. "No touching guns."

The Shepherd, taking a shaky breath, disabled the weapon, and threw it out onto the step for the sheriff's men could see. "Nothin' for you to fear from us, fellas," he called out. He heard a few orders being given, and then a couple of them came up the step.

"We got word from the mayor's office," said one. "That this place might need some protection." He peered over Book's shoulder. "Looks like you've got that under control."

Book wasn't so sure. Still, no need to bring this fella into that business. "You got stable comms there, officer?" he said. "Only we've been trying to reach this girl's brother, and we ain't been having much success."

"Whole city network's been out," said the officer. "We got our emergency channels open—more or less."

"Reckon I could make a call?"

"I ain't so sure about that…"

"You were sent by the mayor, yes? Keep a special eye on this house and everyone in it?" said Book.

"Well, yeah—"

"I'm just sayin'," said Book, hoping that this one didn't come back to bite him, "that you might not want to get on the wrong side of the mayor."

The officer sighed and shook his head. "I can't tell no more what'll get me into trouble and what won't."

"It'll give that girl in there some peace of mind," said Book, "and that's good and right in itself." That swung it. The officer didn't look keen to be facing River again. Book put a call through to the Guild House. It took a little while, and the image, when it came up, was not as clear as he might like, and the sound fairly sketchy too.

"Name's Shepherd Book," he said. "I won't keep you, but I'm trying to reach Inara Serra and her friend. Concerned for their safety, given all that's happening."

The woman he was speaking to looked concerned in much the same way. "*They were here until late afternoon,*" he said. "*And then they took it into their heads to go out. My understanding is that the de Cecilles sent a car for them.*"

"The de Cecilles?" The woman who had visited the previous day, with the invitation for Annie. "You think that's where I'll find Ms Serra and Mr Avery?"

"*That's where they were heading, Shepherd. I can't promise you they got there.*"

Book thanked the woman for her help, and ended the call. He heard movement behind him and turned to see River.

"Reverse," she said. "They put everything into reverse." Tears were rolling down her cheeks. "We need Simon," she said. "We need to find Simon."

"I'm going to find him, River. Don't worry. I'm sure he's fine."

She shook her head. "Not him. *Her*. She's coming. She's hurt! We need to find Simon!"

Book looked at the officers on the step. Could he prevail upon their good natures to take him out? Maybe take a trip over these de Cecilles, whoever they might be, and enquire as to whether or not Simon and Inara were there, or had been there?

"River, I'm not sure it's wise for us to go out—"

"No, no!" The girl was shaking her head. "We have to stay here! We have to wait for her… But we have to find Simon!"

One more call wouldn't hurt, surely? He glanced out of the room to make sure that the sheriff's men were otherwise engaged, and set to work. Wealthy folks like the de Cecilles did not customarily make their private lines easily available, but it was trivial for a man with Book's know-how (and access to an official channel) to find his way around such security.

Madame de Cecille, when her image appeared, looked extremely annoyed. He was going to have to mind his manners rather more on this occasion. Still, looking like a preacher went a long way, even when you'd hacked your way into this conversation.

"*Who is this? How did you get this number?*"

"Madame," he said. "Name's Shepherd Book. We met at the Roberts house—"

"*Book? Oh, yes, I remember.*"

"My apologies for disturbing your evening."

She looked mightily unhappy at this interruption. "*What do you want?*"

"I'm tryna find some friends of mine. Inara Serra and Lucas Amery. They left the Guild House in a hovercar that you sent for them, and I'm tryna learn whether they made it through all this trouble—"

"*No,*" she said. "*They're not here. Please—I'm trying to keep this line clear.*"

The call ended, unceremoniously.

"—to your house," said Book, to a blank screen. "Well. Not the best manners I've seen on show, even from someone as a rich as she must be."

"He's there," said River, without absolute certainly. And since Book, some time back, had made the decision to believe everything that this girl said, even if it sometimes took a while to work out the meaning, he didn't doubt that she was right, nor that Simon was in more than a peck of trouble. Besides, not only did he have River's word for it, he also was fairly sure he'd heard Inara in the background, calling out his name.

"*Shepherd!*"

14

Longest hour comes right before the dawn, or so the sayin' goes, and when you're chasin' away from the risin' sun back toward the black, those hours become even longer. Ages, it felt to Mal Reynolds, sitting in the back of Amy Lin's hovercar, holding Annie Roberts' hand and talking to her, trying to keep her with him. Sometimes her eyes drifted shut, and he would squeeze that one good hand and say, "Now Miss Annie. You ain't fallin' asleep on me, are you? You got to keep an eye on. Ain't knowin' what kind of mischief I might get up to, without you keepin' your eye on me."

Miss Annie would smile, and look at him, and say, "You mind yourself, Captain, when you're around me…"

But she was slippin' away, and for all her ornery nature and the gorram trouble she'd caused him these past coupla days, Mal was thinkin' she was a kindred spirit. Knew her own mind. Didn't take so well to orders. Tough little pony, kept on trottin' when thoroughbreds failed. But even those ponies came to the end of their strength. Mal knew that feelin'. Been there himself, not so long ago, when *Serenity*'s compression coil blew, and he'd been left alone to fix the ship, then shot by folks he'd thought had come to save him. He'd had to dig deep then till his crew came back. If they could do that for him, he could do that for this girl. But she was fadin' away; a little pony on falterin' steps.

Desperately, Mal said, "You like horses, Miss Annie?"

The girl's face lit up. "Oh… love 'em! *Love* 'em, Cap'n Reynolds… You know horses…?"

And there it was, the thing that was goin' to save her. Malcolm Reynolds, tellin' her tales of the ranch on Shadow where he'd been born, and hauled up to manhood by his mother and three dozen or so hands. Weren't the people she wanted to hear about; it was the horses—each one that he'd known and ridden and seen come and go, and the foals comin', and the sadness he felt when a horse he loved was sold and he had to say goodbye, and the joy of ridin' free, wind in your hair… On and on Mal talked, and Annie Roberts held on for grim life, as the 'car sped over Abel in search of the doctor.

Somethin' had gone wrong in town, that much was plain from even before they reached the city limits. More than half the lights out, no reachin' Shepherd Book on the Cortex, and sirens blarin' away in the distance. Sheriff's men out across the major roads, slowin' 'em down, and only Amy Lin's passcodes opened the way for them. They surely came in handy sometimes, thought Mal, those Alliance verification codes, remembering the time that Shepherd Book had been and got himself shot, and the doors suddenly opened after he held up his identification. Big questions there, of course, but not ones Mal thought likely would ever be answered.

"Hold on there, Annie," he said. "We're nearly there."

At the Roberts house, there were a couple of lawmen standing guard, who let them through when Mal, carrying Annie in his arms, started hollerin' for Shepherd Book.

"Shepherd!" he cried. "Where are you when I need you, preacher?"

Book came out of the study. "*Wŏ de mā!*" he said, when he saw who Mal was carrying, stepping quickly out of the way so Mal could carry her into the study and lay her down on the big sofa. "She shot?"

"One of the Collier gang done it."

"She get her man?"

"Oh yes," said Mal.

"Good girl," murmured Book.

"Where's the doc?"

"Ain't here, Mal," said the Shepherd. "Been tryna find him myself. Spoke to the Guild House and the last they heard he and Inara went off in a car sent by some wealthy folks name of de Cecille. Mal, they're important folk here on Abel—"

"The Monseigneur and Madame," said Lin. "Very important."

"Ma'am," said Book, turning to her with a nod of greeting. "We ain't been formally introduced, but from the look of Mal, you're on our side."

"More or less," said Lin.

"I'd say less than more," said Mal. "But you help me save this girl's life, Miss Lin, I'll forgive a multitude of sins. You know this fella de Cecille?"

"Not personally," said Lin. "But I've had my eye on him. This where your doctor's likely to be?"

"That's my best guess," said Book.

"We know where they live?" asked Mal.

Book reached into his pocket, pulling out a cream-colored card and handing it over to Mal. "Madame visited yesterday," he said. "Left this for Annie."

"Well, look at that," said Mal. "We got an invitation and everything. Let's go pay 'em a visit." He nodded at Lin. "You ready, Miss Lin? Those authorizations do seem to come in mighty handy."

"They certainly have their uses," she said, and went to get the hovercar ready.

Mal turned to Book. "You'll look after her?"

"I'll do my best, Mal. Can't make any promises. Hurry back."

"You bet," said Mal.

"*Captain!*"

Annie, calling for him. Mal went over to where she lay, and took the hand she was offerin' him. "What is it, *mei mei*?"

"Don't want you to go..."

"I know, *mei mei*. Has to be done, you know that. Or else you won't be here soon to tell me when to mind my tongue and my manners. And I ain't havin' that."

"I want to hear about the horses..."

"I'll tell you more about 'em when I'm back with the doc."

"I'm here, Miss Annie," said Book, gently taking her hand from me. "You know me—Shepherd Book. You talk to me now, tell me the tales Mal's been tellin' you."

"Horses," said River, suddenly, from the foot of the couch, her voice a monotone. "Large hoofed herbivorous quadruped. Present on almost every settled world. Domesticated on Earth-That-Was in prehistoric times, and used for multiple purposes such as carrying or pulling loads, riding, racing—"

Gǒu shǐ, thought Mal, if the blood loss don't finish poor Annie, this might...

But River, it turned out, was only warming to her theme. She slid onto the couch next to Annie, put her arm around her shoulder, and leaned her head against the other girl's. Her voice became soft and warm, like she was sharing a secret. "And when you get up on the back of 'em, it's almost the freest you can ever be. You ride off into that horizon, and you let yourself go, and like lookin' out across the black of space, seein' all the stars, and knowin' that you can't ever be stopped, that no power in the 'verse can stop you..."

Quietly, Mal slipped away. Annie was in safe hands. But now they needed to find the doc, and bring him back, quick as they might. Outside, the hovercar was waitin', shifting off as soon as Mal leapt inside.

"Ready?" he said to Lin.

"Ready," she said, and hit the gas. They were off on their mission, fighting their way through the city. To Mal's eyes, things seemed a little calmer than earlier. Folks out protecting their businesses; a few lights back on here and there. Mal Reynolds, who no longer believed in any god, never mind a merciful one, nevertheless hoped that maybe Shepherd Book's imaginary friend might take a moment out of His busy day to look kindly upon Annie Roberts—or, failin' that, River talkin' away, girl to girl, might make all the difference.

When the de Cecilles came back into the room, the Monseigneur, confronted with the sight of Simon and Inara held at gunpoint, said, with considerable alarm, "Casey? What's going on?"

Casey gestured at the console with his pistol. "Caught them poking around your desk."

"I don't need to poke around his desk," said Simon. He was leaning back comfortably in his seat now, projecting confidence. "I already have all the information that I need for my investigations. I was trying to let my people know that I was safe. Monseigneur," he said. "This is your last warning. You brought me and Inara here under duress, and now you're keeping us against our will. The evidence I've collected shows that some serious crimes are being committed on Abel—crimes against life that would see people extradited to courts in Londinium." Simon thought that was probably true. He was betting that Monseigneur didn't know the legal technicalities either. "Do you want to add extra charges to the list?"

The other man was wavering, Simon could see. He pressed on. "I think you should let me get in touch with my people. Start earning some mitigation. You might even," he said, "consider making a statement to me, now."

Madame stepped forwards, quickly. "This is preposterous," she said. "We know exactly who you are. Associates of Malcolm Reynolds. Came here at the request of Annie Roberts. You're not an investigator!" she said to Simon. "You're a member of some ragtag crew of small-time crooks—"

"Another cover identity," said Simon smoothly. It was amazing, really, how easy this was all coming to him. His friends, back on Osiris, would never have credited that the quiet, contained, polite, and studious Simon Tam had this in him. But then he'd always had nerves of steel, hadn't he? You couldn't be a surgeon without nerves of steel. You couldn't break your sister out of that place, and get halfway across the Rim, without nerves of steel. "Certainly meant that Reynolds was happy to bring me here. Or do you think a Browncoat would willingly carry an Alliance investigator halfway across the Rim?"

For a moment, Madame was lost for words.

"Annette," said Monseigneur. "Maybe we should consider this—"

"No," she said. And: *Oh*, thought Simon, with sudden realization. It isn't him. It's her… Watching the Monseigneur, he saw the same understanding start to cross his face.

"Annette," said de Cecille. "What did you know about all this?"

"What do you mean?" she said.

"About what he's shown us. The de-terraforming. Did you know about that?"

"It wasn't going to happen," she said. "It was a test. Scarlett assured me of that. A test on land that people had already lost—"

"Land lost *because* of the tests," put in Simon. "This

drought was artificial, sir. Deliberately caused."

Monseigneur was looking at his wife in horror. "*Rén ci de fó zǔ,* Annette! How *could* you?"

"Someone had to do something for this world," she shot back. "There's dozens of places out here on the Rim, clamoring for Alliance support. You think we're *special?* Abel isn't special! You and me—for all the fancy titles we've got, the money we've got—we're not special. These folks from the Core—Scarlett and this fellow here—they *laugh* at us behind our backs. They think we're a joke. Provincial. But their money—that's real. I'm happy to take that. Give this world of us whatever advantage it can get—"

"They were willing to *destroy* it!" said Monseigneur. "Destroy it all! This beautiful place!"

Madame smoothed down the front of her blouse and took a deep breath. "I'm going now, Edward," she said. "Scarlett's offered to take me with him back to the Core."

"You think you can live off his charity?" said her husband.

"You think I haven't got off-world investments?"

"Oh, *lǎo tiān yé…*"

Simon almost felt sorry for the Monseigneur. What crimes had he committed? Wined and dined investors. Turned a blind eye, perhaps, to the speed with which Rising Sun had been acquiring land? Simon doubted he'd been involved in having Roberts shot. Emory Scarlett—he wouldn't have risked getting his hands dirty. Just made a suggestion, perhaps, that this lawyer would be better out of the way. Madame, Simon suspected, was the one who had seen to those arrangements.

She was moving away from them, towards the door. "I'm sorry it's come to this," she said. "I'm sorry that you can't see the vision behind what we were trying to do. Perhaps you will one day. But I won't be here."

She turned to leave—but her way was blocked. Casey, pistol

in hand, was in front of the door. "Madame," he said, real hate in his eyes. "You're not going anywhere."

They might have stopped her, too, if there hadn't suddenly been a hammering at the front door, and a hue and a cry, and Casey took his eye off for her. She made a grab for his pistol and Casey pushed back. Monseigneur ran across the room to help him, and then, suddenly, a shot was fired.

Everything went still for a moment. Then Monseigneur stumbled back, clutching his stomach. Blood was flowering across his white shirt.

"*Rén ci de fó zŭ*," murmured Simon, diving to help. "Inara, pass me something—a cushion, anything…" From the corner of his eye, he saw Madame, holding the pistol, moving towards the door.

"Edward," said. "You shouldn't have got in my way."

The door swung open, and Mal Reynolds came bursting into the room. "Doc!" he cried. "What in the name of all that's holy have you been doin' hidin' out here?"

"I'm *trying*," said Simon, "to save someone's *life*!" Dimly, he was aware of Madame pushing past Mal, getting away, but there was only so much he could do… "Not to mention, you know, exposing a massive criminal conspiracy that's currently being perpetrated against both the people and the ecosystem of this planet. *That's* all." He grabbed the cushion Inara was holding out, and turned his attention back to his patient, pressing it against the wound. So much blood… "*Gŏu shĭ*, will someone call for an ambulance?" He turned to Casey. "You! I'm a doctor! *Move!*"

Casey snapped into action.

"Huh?" said Mal. "What's been going on?"

"Mal…" said Inara, a warning note clear in her voice.

"What?" said Mal. "I'm in a hurry here, Inara—"

"It's completely true," said Inara. "Simon's been… He's been amazing, actually."

At least someone appreciated his efforts, thought Simon. But he was losing his patient, he could see... There was only so much he could do here... *Could* an ambulance get through? The city was in chaos... Monseigneur, shuddering with pain, looked up at him in terror. "You're a doctor, son?" he whispered. "That true?"

"Yes," Simon said back, his voice gentle. He wiped at the sweat beading upon the other man's brow. "You hold on. We're getting help..."

"Well," said Mal, from behind. "That's... very good, doc. But now I, er... I need you to come with me."

"Mal!" cried Simon. "Are you actually *unable* to see what I'm doing right now?"

"I can see fine," said Mal. "And I need you to be doin' exactly that, only to someone else." He grabbed at Simon's shoulder. "Come *on*, doc! Man's as good as gone! You know so! And Annie Roberts needs you!"

Annie...?

"Mal, I can't leave this man—"

"Annie's shot, doc. Hurt bad. You stay here, you're killin' her. Tough decision to make, I know, so I'm makin' it for you—"

Suddenly, the Monseigneur gasped, hideously, and died. "*Zāo gāo!*" Simon cried, falling backwards. He looked down at his hands, smeared with blood, and punched his right fist into his left palm. If there was one thing Simon hated more than anything in this 'verse, it was failing a patient. "I could *kill* you, Mal Reynolds!"

"You ain't the first to say that, son," said Mal, pulling him up and bundling him out through the door. "Sure as sure you won't be the last."

Wash and Kaylee, safely ensconced in an office on the upper floor of City Hall, watched as the lights sprang back on all around town. A huge cheer went up from the mayor's staff. Only a matter of time now, surely, Wash thought, with the power back on, before the mayor and the sheriff and Hunter's people got things back under control. And then, Kaylee, standing by the window, cried out, "Wash! Look!"

"What is it, Kaylee?"

"Come see!"

He went to join her. Kaylee pointed out across the skyline. The faintest pale pink line was visible upon the horizon. "Sun's risin'," she said. "Dawn's comin'!"

When I woke, Captain Malcolm Reynolds was sittin' in the chair at my bedside, snorin'. Good Lord in heaven above, it amazes me I hadn't woken sooner given the noise that fella was makin'. Enough to lift the roof and send it out into the black.

"Captain Reynolds," I muttered. "Will you cease that racket?" My voice came out weak, and dry from thirst, and I doubted anyone would hear, but a familiar face came into view. Shepherd Book. I was glad to see the preacher then. He'd brought a glass of water with him, and helped me sit. Sweet Father who looks over us all, but that water was good to taste— clean and cold and pure as a spring morning here on Abel when the times was good and we was all happier people, gathered in fellowship and not in strife.

"Well, Annie," said the Shepherd, as he helped me to sit up comfortably. "From what I hear you've caused more than a mite of trouble over the past day."

"Hope so," I said.

"I think none of us would have it any other way."

"Got my man, Shepherd," said I.

"I know, Annie," he said, and laid his hand upon my head.

"I know. I hope now you'll be able to let go of the anger and the sorrow, and let peace dwell in your heart."

And I thought that perhaps I might.

Beside us, Captain Reynolds snored on.

"Can we shut him up?" said I. "That is the most appalling noise."

The Shepherd leaned over and jabbed at him. "Mal." No change. "Mal!"

The captain jumped. "Whassat? Where're they? Who now?"

"Noise like that you'd wake the dead, Captain Reynolds," said I to him. "And you'd be lucky if they didn't drag you off after them."

He sat up properly and smiled at me. His hair was all mussed up and his shirt open at the neck and—heavens above, so dirty. I'd a feelin' he'd been sittin' here the whole time, watchin' me. "You need a wash," said I. "And a shave."

"And I'll be happy to go and get them," said he. "Now I know that you're back to your old cantankerous self." He stood up. "I'll send in the doctor, shall I?"

"Please do," I said, grandly, since I was both mistress of this house and his employer. The doctor came in, checked me over, and told me how it had been touch and go, but he'd got here pretty much in time, and with some rest and common sense I should be fine. I was a little sneaky, questioning him while he was concentrating, and it didn't take me long to find out that the only reason my life had been saved—apart from the skill of that good doctor, which should not be underestimated—was that Malcolm Reynolds, with the help of Amy Lin, had dashed all the way back from the countryside, through Yell City and a whole deal of trouble, to get me back home and find the doctor for me.

I think I had known already, even though my memories of everything that had happened was hazy after I shot Young Bill Fincher, because I could recall the captain's voice, talking to me, about horses. That voice blended into a girl's for a while, until Captain Reynolds voice came back. Yes, indeed—not content with dashing round Abel, he'd come and sat with me after the doctor had finished, and sat talking to me till he'd fallen asleep himself. No wonder he looked so grubby.

I was feelin' much better, though very tired, and so I lay there and asked all the questions that I had. Captain Reynolds, and Ms Serra—Inara—sat with me and answered everything they could. Turned out we'd missed a busy night in Yell City, and even now the sheriff and the mayor was busy cleanin' up the mess. Sheriff Peters was mighty relieved to hear that the Collier gang wouldn't be troublin' him no more. And I learned now who was behind my daddy's death, who done the hirin' of Frankie Collier who in turn sent young Bill Fincher to do the deed. Fella from the Core name of Emory Scarlett—and Madame de Cecille herself. Scarlett was gone during the mess of the night, but Madame was arrested at the space docks. She'd gone lookin' for Scarlett, and seemed he'd left her in the lurch. No sign of him, Captain Reynolds said, and Amy Lin had been lookin'. He seemed to have disappeared into the blue.

After hearin' the news, I was very tired and more'n ready to go back to rest again. Ms Serra leaned over and kissed my brow— Oh, her scent was so sweet! That woman was a godsend!—and told me to sleep well. Captain Reynolds, foldin' his arms, looked down at me, and cleared his throat, and said, in a gruff voice, "You're a gorram menace, girl. And I hope you don't ever change the way you are."

"I have no intention of that," I said. "I like myself 'xactly the way I am."

They left me then to get my sleep, but, right as my eyes were closin', I saw a figure at the door. The girl, River Tam. Standin' there, all hunched over, watchin' me. That girl had something else about her. She lifted her head, and I saw her eyes were sparklin'. She smiled, and blew me a kiss.

"Black is white and white is black," she said. "Reverse is reversed, and everything's sweet at the Rim and the Core."

No, I didn't have a clue what that meant. But since it felt as much a blessing as anything the Shepherd or Inara had bestowed upon me, I had no trouble sleepin' soundly afterwards, at peace with the world and all about me for the first time since my beloved daddy died.

Early in the morning, the Mule arrived back at the Roberts house. Mal, standing on the step with Amy Lin, watched Zoë order the two prisoners out from the back. "Where do you want these two?" she said to Lin.

"I'll put 'em in the car," said Lin, and took them into her custody. Zoë, walkin' up to Mal, said, "How is she?"

"Doc saved her life."

"He's good at that."

"Most likely saved the whole gorram planet at the same time, curse him," said Mal.

"He did what now?" said Zoë, but got no further information. Wash, who had arrived back at the house with Kaylee an hour or two earlier, was already pushing past Mal. "I'll tell you the full story," he said. "*Later*." He pulled her inside after him.

"Gotta go," said Zoë to Mal, feigning regret.

Jayne came hobblin' up.

"Leg's killin' me, Mal."

"Long as it's the only thing killin' you." He clapped Jayne on the back as the big man limped up the step, and said, "Doc's in the kitchen. Get yourself seen to."

"Huh," said Jayne, and went on his way.

Lin came back. "Guess I'll be on my way now, Captain Reynolds," she said. "More or less got what I came for. More than I was expecting, if I'm honest." She nodded at him. "I'm grateful for your help."

"Huh," said Mal. He looked beyond her, at her hovercar, and the two figures within. "You think you'll see some justice done? Someone punished for what was happenin' here?"

"I hope so."

"You're more trustin' than me," said Mal. "I see where this will go. All tied up in red tape, in some committee or other. Everyone a little blame so nobody carryin' the can. And they'll move on to the next world, and do somethin' different there but equally as bad."

"I can but try," said Lin, she offered her hand.

"'Spose I can't fault you for that," said Mal, taking her hand to shake it.

"Feel like I should be paying you something for your troubles," said Lin.

"You'll forgive me, Miss Lin, but I wouldn't take Alliance money if it were the only thing would keep *Serenity* afloat."

"Still," said Lin. "Check your account."

And then she was gone.

Back in the house, Mal found his crew gathered in kitchen. Jayne was patched up and hooverin' up breakfast, lookin' cheerful. "That woman paid up, Mal?"

"Nope," lied Mal, because what was going to happen to that money was not the business of any man hadn't fought in the war. "Seems she's seen fit to put something our way."

"No? I was expectin' a cut, Mal! Took a shot to the leg here, in case you're forgettin'. Saved the day, you might recall, when you and Zoë and Amy Lin was being beaten by the Collier gang—"

"Ain't nobody goin' unpaid," said Mal. "Annie Roberts has seen us right. Tripled her fee."

"Oh," said Jayne. "Guess that's all right then." And he turned back to his breakfast.

Mal went to find Zoë, out in the garden with Wash.

"You and me, Zoë," he said. "We still got a job to do."

Zoë jumped up. "With you, sir."

"A job?" said Wash, frowning. "Not a shooty weapons-firey kinda job, I hope?"

"No, husband," said Zoë.

"But a soldiery matter-of-honory kind of job, yes?"

"Correct," said Mal.

"I'll, er… leave you to it," said Wash.

Mal was thankful for his tact in the matter, since there weren't no pleasure in this particular task, to his mind. First stop was the bank, to take out what Lin had put in a mere hour, which was an hour too long to be in possession of Alliance money, as far as Mal Reynolds was concerned. Next stop was a small house in one of them poor districts not far from the space docks. Area was subdued today, Mal thought, like a man waking up after a night's heavy drinkin', regrettin' the decisions of the day before. Someone was pulling down Blue Sun adverts. Someone else was sweeping up broken glass.

The house Mal was visiting was well kept but by no means well appointed. The woman who opened the door looked older than the picture in the wallet he was carrying, and he could see from her red eyes and black clothes that she'd heard the news.

"Missus Collier, ma'am," said Mal. "I am so very sorry for your loss."

He held out the wallet. She took it, and looked him over, not missing his brown coat. "Who are you?" she said. "How'd you come by Frankie's wallet?"

"Just the one given the task, ma'am," he said. "Best we don't deal in names."

She opened the wallet and her eyes widened. Well they might, given the amount Amy Lin had put his way. "Where's this come from?"

"Browncoats look after their own, ma'am."

"Browncoats," she said, her voice bitter. "I curse the day my Frankie ever went off to that losers' war." She looked at Mal with loathing in her eyes. "You can go now," she said. But she put the wallet in her pocket. No surprise there. Four kids there'd been, in those pictures of Collier's, and the oldest surely not more than twelve.

Mal went back to the Mule, where Zoë was waiting. As they made their way back to the ship, she said, "Keep thinkin', sir."

"What's on your mind, Zoë?"

"What Collier said. 'Bout the war being over."

"War ain't over," said Mal. "It'll never be over. Not as long as I'm still livin' and breathin'. Not as long as anyone like that woman back there is still livin' and breathin'—and grievin'." *There but for the grace of God*, Mal might have said, once upon a time, about Frankie Collier. But the truth of the 'verse was that there wasn't no God—nor was there much in the way of grace.

House was awful empty and lonesome after Captain Reynolds and his crew left Abel and went on their way to heaven only knows where. I missed 'em all something dreadful, even that big lump Jayne Cobb, although that fella woulda eaten me outta house and home if he'd stayed much longer. But there was plenty to be gettin' on with, what with all the clearin' up to be done around the City, and the doorbell didn't stop ringin' for a while. Only person I had any real time for was Mayor McQuinn, who had risen considerably in my estimation as a result of that time, and particularly as I came to understand that she had been the one approached folks back in the Core to send out someone to investigate Rising Sun and find out who was behind my daddy's death. She and Daddy were friends, that was clear, and she missed him sorely too and was glad to see justice done. Wished she mighta told me what she was up to, but I understand why not. Security and safety and suchlike. Still, coulda saved us all a deal of bother.

I suppose if you've taken the trouble to read this far, you'd like to be hearin' how things turned out for other folks I have mentioned in this tale. First of all, let's say that Sheriff Peters announced that he would be takin' retirement come the spring, and while I think we are all fond of the man, it was plain he'd run his course as chief of policin' in Yell City. Coupla younger fellows behind him ready to take on the task, full of ideas and energy. Jacky Colson, you'll surely be glad to hear, was approached by another lawyer in the city, offerin' to take on his case *pro bono*, but it never reached trial. Whole business settled out of court, for a tidy sum, I'll bet, although that was not disclosed, and Colson got his farm back. I heard there was more'n few cases like that settled round about the time and a fair amount of land passed back into previous ownership. Funny, ain't it, what can be done when folks have a mind? I hear some of the money came from Monseigneur de Cecille's estate. Rest of that family had some work to do, cleaning up that tarnished family name. I believe it will be said of them one day that if ever someone is in dire straits in Yell City, they need only approach the de Cecilles, and they will find the means to help. Takin' on my daddy's mantle, in a way. As for Madame, the less said the better. May justice be done in this world and the next, to her and everyone she aided and abetted.

All that was left was for me to find somethin' to do with my time—and my money. Mayor McQuinn came to me and said she wanted to see the statue put up, and although at first I was minded to say 'no', not bein' much of a one for fuss and ceremony, I decided in the end that the statue weren't for me. It was for Daddy, and everyone whom he had helped in his good short life. I would say most of the city came out the day we cut the ribbon round his statue—and there you'll find it, on Main Street, should you ever pass that way, and they caught his look, I think, which was kindly, and with a twinkle in the eye. There was some fuss, as there often is, about what to write underneath, but I had my way and kept it plain and truthful.

Isaac Roberts
Good Man
Fine Citizen
Beloved Father

After the statue went up, I knew I was done with Yell City. It was all that talk of horses than done it, you see. Made me realize what I wanted most. So I tracked down Young Ted Doughty, and made him an offer, and we went and bought back Great-aunt Brenna's land and set to breedin' horses. He didn't have a bean, of course, but I put Young Ted's name on the deeds, nonetheless. Let the house in the city to Ryan Hunter and his folks. They're usin' it for all kinds of community purposes. Maybe one day they'll start a revolution from there. I don't care as long as they pay the rent which, I will say here, I believe to be more than fair and most likely below market rate. Turnin' into my daddy, ain't I?

Sometimes, out here on the ranch, when night falls and the sky is the deepest, inkiest black you could ever hope to see, and the stars are all a-twinklin' and a-sparklin', I'll go out, lie on my back and look up at the heavens, and I'll wonder where he is right now— my captain—and I'll pray that he and those he loves, his crew, are keepin' well, and findin' themselves safe. Ain't more you can hope for in this 'verse, is there, and a deal worse that you can get.

ACKNOWLEDGEMENTS

Huge thanks to all at Titan for their help with this project, particularly Cat Camacho for commissioning, and Daniel Carpenter for concluding! Amy H. Sturgis provided inspirational input, for which I am very grateful. Thank you to my agent, Max Edwards, a true mensch who looks after me so well. And my love and thanks as ever to Matthew and Verity.

ABOUT THE AUTHOR

Una McCormack is a *New York Times* and *USA Today* bestselling science fiction writer who specialises in TV tie-in fiction. She has written novels and audio dramas based on numerous TV shows such as *Star Trek*, *Doctor Who*, *Blake's 7*, and *Firefly*. A former lecturer in creative writing, she has academic interests in women's science fiction and transformative works ('fanfiction'), and is on the editorial board of Gold SF, an imprint of Goldsmith's Press which publishes intersectional feminist science fiction.

For more fantastic fiction, author events,
exclusive excerpts, competitions, limited editions and more

VISIT OUR WEBSITE
titanbooks.com

LIKE US ON FACEBOOK
facebook.com/titanbooks

FOLLOW US ON TWITTER AND INSTAGRAM
@TitanBooks

EMAIL US
readerfeedback@titanemail.com